"Who is it?" The man's voice coming from behind the hotel door was groggy with sleep.

"Louisa. Louisa Wentworth," the woman whispered softly. The door opened and she slipped in. She felt the man's presence rather than saw it. The room was pitch-black. She heard the key turn in the lock.

"Won't you light the lamp?" she asked.

"No."

She could not exactly trace the sound of his voice. He seemed to be all around her.

"What do you want?" he inquired.

His voice was so cold that for an instant she thought she had committed some dreadful mistake. How did she know what he wanted? She had no guarantee that the information she gave him would promise her freedom—or anything else. She reached into her bodice, fingering the derringer.

His hand clutched her wrist.

"How many times do I have to tell you, you don't need that," he said. His fingers tightened around her wrist until she could no longer maintain her grip on the small weapon. Her fingers yielded. He took the gun from her.

"Why won't you turn on the light?" She tried to keep the pleading note out of her voice.

"Because, ma'am, I'm stark naked, and I don't think it's fitting for a lady to see me this way."

The Tucson
TEMPTRESS

by Chet Cunningham

A Dell/Banbury Book

Published by
Banbury Books, Inc.
37 West Avenue
Wayne, Pennsylvania 19087

Dell ® TM 681510, Dell Publishing Co., Inc.
ISBN: 0-440-09140-3
Printed in the United States of America
First printing—June 1981

Chapter 1

The tall man in the dust-grey Stetson squinted into the fierce glare of the noonday sun and watched the two riders work their way slowly down the dusty trail. Skirting a patch of fat barrel cacti, they headed down through the red, flowering cholla. The man in the Stetson hung back, giving his roan a chance to breathe. No use crowding them. That would only increase his risk of being seen. After all these miles of careful tracking, he didn't care to scare those two rabbits into sudden flight.

Far down on the barren desert slopes, Brad Spear could see a faint track cutting across the land. He had been here before. The white ribbon was the San Diego to Tucson stage road. Spear lifted his Stetson just enough to rub a finger across his brow, scraping some of the two-days' dust off his forehead. For two days solid he'd been tracking this pair by horse, and he was dead sick of it. Wasn't right for a couple of strangers in the desert to push so hard, especially when one of them was a woman. As Spear shifted in his saddle, he suddenly realized he'd developed a pretty keen admiration for that woman over the past couple of days. The dust was bad. The heat was bad. But she'd kept right on riding like there was no tomorrow.

Spear sighed, touched his heel to the roan and turned her down into a shallow arroyo, going at an easy walk. The riders were just on the other side of that rust-colored ridge and Spear knew he'd have to lay back a ways here so as not to show himself. As far as he knew, they hadn't spotted him once, though he'd picked up their trail just outside of Denver.

Mr. Pinkerton had given him a dandy goose chase this time, Spear thought, testing the taste of the Arizona dust with the tip of his dry tongue. The pair of them up ahead had perfected the art of zigzag. First, they'd gone by train from Denver to Salt Lake City. Then they'd picked up a stage heading south and rode it to the end of the line. There they'd bought horses and kept going. Naturally, a Pinkerton man couldn't ride in the same stage with the suspects. Fellow passengers always got to know each other much too well. So Spear had bought the roan in Salt Lake City and trailed them like a dutiful dog following in the wake of his master. And this was his reward: another bunch of goddamn miles leading who knew how far into the sizzling countryside. At least the chollas were in bloom. Pretty, too.

Spear angled the roan across the arroyo and started up the far side, taking his time. The trouble with a job like this—apart from the bad pay, grim accommodations and pesky saddle sores—was the lack of a real, rewarding roundup at the end. This was one of those cryptic see-what's-going-on assignments in which Allan Pinkerton seemed to take special delight. The honeymoon couple ahead had stolen a packet of jewels worth well over one hundred thousand dollars. No debate about that. Question was, what had they done with it? And the only way to answer a question like that was to put a well-qualified detective on their trail and make him ride till his tail was black-and-blue. A detective like Brad Spear.

"Come on, Lil," urged Spear, as the roan took a stumble. "One little ridge and I'll promise you a road somewhere." The good thing about animals was that they didn't remind you later of promises you hadn't kept.

Spear stopped the roan as soon as he could see over the top of the ridge and peered downhill toward the stage road. He leaned forward on the pommel, biding his time. There was nothing else to do. The landscape below was dotted with yucca, cholla and barrel cactus, but there was no cover for a horse and rider to hide behind. If he followed the gully he was in, it would just take him along parallel with the stage road, which was pointless. So Lil had a break, and Brad Spear had a chance to rub his fingers through his beard and wonder when he'd get a chance to trim it again. His beard was dark brown—same as the color of his full head of hair—with a few streaks of red mixed in. And after a few days of neglect, Spear knew, that smoothly cut, half-inch layer of beard began to look like Grandpa's briar patch. Riding into town with a briar patch for whiskers was no way for a man to make a good impression.

Spear lifted a pair of binoculars to his eyes and had a look at the goings on. It was plain the two riders were going to wait for the stage, and as he watched, he saw a puff of brown dust moving its way down the road. The riders noticed at about the same time and dismounted. The woman lifted her canteen, uncapped it and poured a hefty cupful of water down her neck.

There was much to admire in that neck, and Spear's deep grey eyes burrowed just a bit deeper into the eyepiece of his binoculars. As the woman tilted her head back to take a long drink, Spear took special note of the way her white throat rippled with the pleasure of gulping long and deep. And then his binoculars kind of went their own way, drifting down to the triangular expanse of smooth flesh where her blouse was parted, to where the dampened shirt clung like dripping seaweed to the gentle curves of her breasts.

So this was Louisa Wentworth. Though he'd shared many a mile and many forms of transportation with her, always keeping his distance, Spear had never, up to now, fully appreciated her assets. Now he appreciated. She had long, dark hair and soft brown eyes that were wide set, almost pleading. The pert nose, miraculously only slightly reddened from the Arizona sun, should have been worn by an insolent twelve-year-old instead of a buxom twenty-six-year-old. But her mouth showed her years. Sensuous, well-formed, those lips betrayed knowledge, possibly criminal intent and certainly female experience.

But she was no criminal, at least not to anyone's knowledge. Which was a lot more than could be said for her traveling companion. Spear swung the glasses to the left and took note. Horace G. Klonner was thirty-five, an ex-gambler who had worked his way up by his bootstraps to talented jewel thief. He was just six feet tall, slender, a fine dresser who sported a shapeless, clerkish mustache. Klonner often carried a cane that Spear knew well by sight: it came loaded with a one-shot .45 and was fired from the handle. The file in Chicago had revealed no shoot-outs in the two times he had been arrested for jewel theft. Both times were in the East, and there had been no convictions.

Back East, it took a certain suave bravery to pull off a jewel heist. Out West, it took a gun. So far, Spear was convinced of the man's suaveness. His ability to shoot was as yet untested.

Led by a team of six, the Tucson stage pulled closer, now visible through its enshrouding cloak of dust. Klonner raised his hand, flagging the stage, and the horses pulled up, snorting and pawing at the dry, white road. Spear watched through the glasses as Klonner talked to the driver. Throughout their conversation, Spear noted, the man riding shotgun was doing his job. A pair of suspicious barrels never wavered.

Louisa Wentworth was doing her job, too. Never had a female looked so in distress. Spear could see from her pitiful hand gestures and the limp in her step that she was feigning the limits of exhaustion. The driver, Spear noticed, was swept away by waves of compassion, though he seemed more attentive to her body than her grand performance. Spear chuckled as the two tied their horses to the back of the stage and climbed aboard. Never had a woman's way been put to better use.

As the whip cracked and the stage moved toward Tucson, Spear took a quick check of his position. Behind were the Owl Head Buttes. The stage road to Tucson, according to his map, took a long loop around Coyote Bluff. No one had bothered to cut a stage road up and over the bluff, but a man on horseback could cut across and save himself eight miles. Spear would be halfway through his second whiskey by the time the coach and six pulled in.

"Fresh hay, Lil," Spear said aloud, as he touched his heel to the roan and turned her toward the bluff. "Just keep that in mind, old girl. Fresh hay, fresh oats and a roof over your sweet little fly-bitten head."

Lil's head nodded as she made her way up the steepening slope and, if Brad wasn't mistaken, her pace picked up just a bit. Nine times out of ten, when it came to creature comforts, a man and a horse had pretty much the same pipe dream.

Numerous trails had been cut by other riders across the steep bluff, and Spear could take his choice. But clear trails didn't necessarily guarantee security. This was Apache country. Mostly, there were Chiricahuas around, but now and then a few Mimbrenos drifted over from New Mexico. Spear had never encountered any real trouble in dealing with Indians. It helped to look like you could defend yourself. But it also helped to avoid stupid risks in unfriendly Indian territory.

About a mile farther along the trail, Spear found himself wondering whether this short cut was a stupid risk. Halfway up the trail, coming along a rocky ledge, Spear saw three Apaches mounted on horses. There was no war paint in sight, he noted with relief. Hunters. Each had a bow and three arrows in his right hand, a hackamore in the left. The pintos picked their way easily along the treacherous ridge with only a light tug at the hackamore now and then to remind them of their riders' presence.

The lead brave, a foot shorter than Spear on his small pony, gave no quarter as they approached. Spear understood. It would be a sign of weakness for the brave to move out of the way and let the white man pass. On the other hand, there were practical difficulties. The trail was barely wide enough for two men to stand shoulder to shoulder. If the Indians refused to give him room, Spear would be taking Lil along the outer edge of a hundred-foot drop. It was no way to trail break a temperamental roan.

Spear fumbled in his leather vest and his heartbeat evened out a bit when his fingers touched the smooth, round sides of his last cigar. As the distance between him and the Indians shortened, Spear held up his hand and offered the cigar. The lead brave, suddenly tense and ready, put his hand to his waist, touching the handle of his long dagger. Spear halted his horse. He held up the cigar for all three of the hunters to see, then gave it to the lead brave.

The Indian hesitated, eyeing him, still fingering the hilt of his dagger. The brave evidently had seen cigars before and his eyes glistened in anticipation. Then his expression clouded. He jerked the knife from his waist. Spear's hand moved toward his gun.

Then he stared. The knife was held out to him, handle first, motionless in the air. An enormous quantity of perspiration, all acquired in the past two seconds, had collected around Spear's hat brim. His hand trembled visibly as he accepted the knife in exchange for the cigar. Some voice deep down inside accused him of being a coward, fool and jittery old lady even as some cooler, calmer voice informed him that he was just about the bravest white man to cross this bluff alone. Not only had he kept his nerve, but he'd also won himself the better part of an Indian trade.

The knife was a good one. The cigar, God forgive him, was a stale stogy. And some squaw's tepee was going to stink like hell tonight.

Trade accomplished, Spear pulled the roan to one side as the three braves passed him. They had ceased to acknowledge his presence and none of them looked back as they proceeded down the trail.

He wondered whether they were Chiricahua. The Apaches were fractioned into dozens of small bands. Each took its name from a river, a canyon or string of mountains. This trio of hunters might have come from any of the bands.

Spear had another look at the knife, thinking that some marking on the handle or blade might give a clue as to where the Indians had picked it up. He turned it thoughtfully in his hand and, as he did so, his rein hand tightened. The roan stopped, turning her head in curiosity, as if to find out why her rider had halted again so suddenly. But Spear wasn't thinking about the roan anymore. He wasn't thinking about the trail to Tucson or the pair of thieves he'd been assigned to track down. Out in the middle of the Arizona desert, high on the bluffs above Tucson, the tall Pinkerton was staring hard at a rocklike, glittering crystal embedded in the handle of an Apache hunter's knife.

Spear held up the knife and turned the handle so the crystal caught the sun. Splinters and fragments of light went shooting in every direction. The gem sparkled and glittered, radiating a white light more piercing than any reflection from a mirror.

There were only two ways a crystal of this caliber might have come to be in the handle of an Apache's knife. Spear was fairly convinced that no white man had bartered the gem with an Indian, so that was out. The alternate conclusion was obvious. Somehow, probably quite casually, the brave he'd just met had been handed this trinket, and he'd promptly incorporated it into the handle of an extra dagger. The marks around the handle confirmed this observation. Where the stone was embedded, the handiwork was crude. The Indian had carved out the butt of the handle, implanted the gem, then worked it into place with some softened lead.

On the other hand, Spear cautioned himself, it could be glass. Could be. There was an easy way to find out and, when he arrived in Tucson, he'd have a gem cutter examine it. If it wasn't glass, then it was a diamond. A diamond of the size and quality that no Indian in Arizona Territory ever picked up along the trail. Ever.

Spear tucked the knife in his saddlebags, showing considerably more care than he would have with his first-born son. There was a slight possibility that these Apaches had come across the jewel thieves' cache and that Horace G. Klonner was now short a few diamonds. But that conclusion didn't quite make sense. Spear figured he was carrying about twenty thousand dollars' worth of stone in his saddlebags. And it wasn't the kind of stone that Klonner and Wentworth had lifted in their heist. According to the Pinkerton office, they'd taken finished jewels—small gems already set into rings, necklaces and other jewelry. This one was rough, unfinished, and big. If it turned out to be a fat piece of glass, it might have come from anywhere. But if that chunk was diamond, it came straight from the mine, and the tale of its travels was probably as long as the Book of Exodus.

There were still a few hours of sunlight remaining when Spear broke the top of the bluff and got a lookout's view of Tucson. He was well ahead of the stage. He angled the roan down the track directly toward the stage road and urged her into a canter. Once he reached the road, no more spurring was necessary. She loped on toward Tucson as if she could see the promise of a stall up ahead, and Spear's heels hardly touched her flanks over the last two miles of road.

Spear slowed down about a half mile outside of town, letting the roan cool as they made their way toward home. There was another reason to approach this town at an even pace. Tucson had a reputation. With the parceling of states and territories and law forces, Tucson had turned into an out-of-the-way harbor for thieves, outlaws, cutthroats, high riders, high graders and every description of man looking for a quick dollar. One additional benefit of such a community was enough fancy ladies to take care of every scruffy male who staggered into town. Some folks called it hell, plain and simple, all warmed over and spread out to dry in the sun. A lot of blood had been spilled in Tucson streets, but it wasn't enough to hold down the dust. And every man who made a noise riding into town was likely to be tested, whether he asked for it or not.

Spear came in at a walk and rode directly to the Tucson Livery. The liveryman, a dour old fellow who called himself Cranby, had to be roused from the kind of dormancy that gets bears through the winter. But once in motion, Cranby managed to find a stall for Lil and get out a can of oats which cost about two bits more than it should have. Spear didn't care. The roan had served him well, and as soon as the saddle came off her wet back, he rubbed her down. She got the oats, some fresh hay and, after awhile, all the water she could drink. Then Spear looped his saddlebags over his shoulder and walked down a partly finished boardwalk two blocks to the stage depot.

The depot was right across from the Commercial Hotel and, from its front porch, a man could see the full extent of Ft. Lowell Road. The hardware store on one side and the general store on the other weren't attracting much business, and Spear was generally satisfied by the way people neglected his existence. He found a straight-backed wooden chair on the porch of the depot, tipped it back and waited.

His hat was pulled down low over his eyes but, after awhile, the last rays of the sun started to find their way under the low brim. Spear could see everything that went on along the street and boardwalk, but that didn't exactly make for excitement. He feigned sleep. Pretty soon, he wasn't feigning anymore.

The sound of the rushing stage woke him. In an

instant he was on his feet, the high-backed chair smashed against the porch, with his six feet one inch crouched into a four-foot target and his special-made .45 halfway out of the holster. It took him a full two seconds to realize that bad nerves combined with a bad dream had shocked him out of a sound sleep into a position of ridiculous readiness.

Cooling down, he looked around to see whether anyone had noticed. No one had. He straightened, slid the .45 into its holster and pushed back his hat. Nasty jitters, all right.

The team of six clattered to a stop in front of the stage office, harness jangling, twenty-four big hooves stirring up a swelling cloud of dust. Just about the time the sweating driver pulled the stage to a halt, the gawkers and drifters began to ease out of the Commercial Hotel saloon. The stage came only once a week to Tucson. There was always news, sometimes mail, and usually a good chance that half a dozen untried fancy ladies might be aboard.

The driver yelled howdy to the depot manager, tied the twelve reins and climbed down from his seat. Taking his time, he strode around to the left side of the rig and gave a wink to the men at the Commercial. Then, like a merchant displaying a new case of goods, he opened the door.

A low whistle like the west wind seemed to make its way through the crowd of onlookers. Louisa Wentworth had done some prettying up inside the carriage and her long, dark hair glistened in the fading sunlight. She still wore the men's trousers she'd had on the trail, but the way she made the back end of them move looked like something new. She smiled at the men, and Spear suddenly realized that a cosmetic coat of lipstick, applied to the kind of lips that deserved it, could make a woman into a weapon of power and passion.

Funny things were happening around Spear's midriff, and something eerily close to jealousy crept into his heart as he watched the men ogle Miss Wentworth. After all, she'd been his and his alone for the past six hundred miles, and the presence of these two-bit ogling roughnecks was intruding on his private dream. When Louisa smiled, they nodded at her like a bunch of polite schoolboys who had misbehaved.

Klonner handed the saddlebags to the driver and said a few words. The driver nodded, took the bags and escorted Miss Wentworth toward the Commercial Hotel, while Klonner went around behind the stage, unhitched the pair of horses and led them toward the Tucson Livery.

It didn't take Spear long to get to the lounge of the Commercial Hotel, and he was already next in line by the time Louisa Wentworth finished signing her name to the hotel register. From there, it took only one clumsy, rude gesture to establish contact. Pretending to trip, Spear rammed up against her shoulder, a bit harder than he'd meant to, and she almost went down. Just in time, his big hand reached out, caught her elbow and rescued her.

"Mighty sorry, ma'am," he apologized, tipping his hat. "Guess I've been working with longhorns so long I act like one."

She smiled sweetly. "Are you sure that isn't pigs you've been working with?" she asked.

"Ah, hell," he smiled just as sweetly. "You talk to me like that, I'm gonna go out and shoot myself."

"Make sure your gun's loaded first," she replied, turning to go upstairs.

Shaking his head, Spear aimed toward the register to sign in. As he did so, he noticed two things, in quick succession, that he decided might improve his relationship with the elusive lady. She'd left a small, embroidered handkerchief alongside the register. And she'd signed her name as Linda Farnsworth.

"Oh, Miss Farnsworth!" he called. She didn't turn around. Spear had to grin. The lady might be cool as ice, but she didn't remember names very long. Even her own.

"Miss Farnsworth!" he shouted at the top of his voice. About six cowboys in the lobby turned around to look, which was just the effect he wanted. Jolted awake by his bellow, Louisa Wentworth, alias Linda Farnsworth, whirled around on the landing. She burned a bright red when she saw every man in the room staring at her.

"Sorry," said Spear. "For a minute there, I could've sworn you didn't know your own name."

"What is it?" she demanded, suppressed rage in her voice.

"I do believe this is yours," offered Spear, holding the embroidered handkerchief aloft in two fingers. "Unless one of these-here cowpunchers carries around his lady's silk kerchief flavored with . . . ," Spear sniffed delicately, ". . . ambergris."

Several of the cowpunchers guffawed noisily and the lady shot them a look that roasted them into quiet submission. Step by deliberate step, she descended the stairs, seized the handkerchief from his grasp and turned on her heel.

"Am I right?" demanded Spear.

"About what?"

"Ambergris."

She faced him again, her expression giving no encouragement.

"Yes. You are right. You are also an insolent boor."

"Yes, Miss Farnsworth. Of course, Miss Farnsworth."

Her face reddened. Her hands shook. But he'd won several points starting from the moment when she failed to recognize her name. And she knew it. Turning again, she made her way up the stairs. Spear, once again, admired the movement taking place in the men's trousers that she wore, as did every man in the room. She suffered under the humiliation, but their open gazes only made her move faster in retreat.

No longer smiling, Spear turned to the register again.

"I want a room," he told the clerk, glancing quickly at the register again. The alleged Linda Farnsworth was in 213.

"Something unlucky," continued Spear, "like three-thirteen."

Either very stupid or very blasé, the clerk feigned innocence.

"Sure," he replied, and fetched the key from the rack.

Spear took the key to room 313 in his hand, lifted his saddlebags and trudged up the stairs. At least six cowpunchers and a hotel clerk now knew that a private, personal god named Brad Spear was keeping quiet watch over Linda Farnsworth.

And if they all knew, so much the better.

One-half block from the stage depot, Henry Underwood stood at the window and scratched his groin.

"Butler!" he bellowed. Underwood crossed to his stand-up desk, picked up an orange and started to peel it, his pudgy fingers moving deftly over the skin, the pith and juices gathering under the grubby nails.

"Butler!" he shouted again, dropping the peel into the spittoon. What was keeping that man?

There was a sudden pounding on the stairs and a

young man burst into the room, panting hard, with his small bottle-eyeglasses askew.

"You don't want to work for me any longer?" asked Underwood softly, biting into the orange. The juice ran down the creases on either side of his jowls and he wiped the dribbles away with the back of his hand.

"Oh, yes, sir, I do. I'm sorry. I just . . ."

"You just don't bother to come the first time I call anymore, do you?" Underwood queried. He was still speaking softly, but now he wore a smile.

"Well, I saw the stage come in, sir, and I thought . . ."

"You thought you'd take a gander at what kind of womanflesh stepped out of it. Is that it, Butler?"

"Well, sir, yes, in fact. . . ." The assistant grinned sheepishly, obviously pleased to be sharing confidences of a personal nature with his employer.

"Well, *don't*!" roared Underwood. "You hear me, Butler?" Underwood felt his face redden in spite of himself. "If there's any woman to be looked after, I'll do the looking. Is that understood, Butler?"

"Yes, sir."

The secretary was about five and a half feet tall, slim as a rail, and when he cowered, as he was doing now, he seemed to curl up on himself like an inchworm that had just been knocked from its thread.

"Now then, *Mister* Butler," Underwood went on, regaining his composure, "please find out who that fine woman is who came in this evening dressed like a man."

"How . . . how . . ."

"Check the register, stupid," interrupted Underwood, anticipating the man's question, not even bothering to raise his voice. He spat the collection of orange seeds, which he'd reserved in the pouch of his cheek, into the spittoon, where they rattled around and splashed to rest. Extracting the uneaten pulp, which he disliked, from the gap between his tongue and back molars, Underwood let it fall into the spittoon along with the seeds. There was a plop as it fell into the sludge of tobacco juice that lined the bottom of the cuspidor. It might have been his imagination, but Underwood thought he saw a wrinkle of disgust flash across the brow of his assistant. The very idea that this man would choose to bear comment on his personal habits caused Underwood to redden again.

"And, Mr. Butler, will you please, if it isn't too much trouble, ascertain whether my new supply of oranges—which you claim to have ordered—is on this stage."

"Yes, Mr. Underwood."

"If it is not, Mr. Butler, I will be forced to conclude that you did not, in fact, order them . . ."

"But, sir, I did . . . !"

". . . Which oversight will, of course, cost you your job." Underwood smiled. "I'm sorry. Now go."

"Yes, sir."

The secretary turned and headed for the door, his highly polished, patent-leather shoes making a skittering noise that somehow always reminded Underwood of rats in an attic.

"And Mr. Butler," Underwood directed toward the departing backside. "I will be out of the office for the next half hour or so. I suggest that when you return, if you return, you sit at your desk and remain motionless."

The secretary turned and looked at Underwood questioningly.

"That's so you won't do anything wrong."

"Oh, yes, sir. I see, sir."

The assistant turned and fled out the door.

Idiot. Underwood turned to a large, maple-framed mirror that hung on the wall opposite his desk and tried desperately to find something to admire in his over-large features. The gilt-colored vest, with its sparkling watch chain and plethora of carmine trim, didn't do anything to hide the underlying bulk of the man. But it did lend a certain radiance to his presence, all that gilt, trim and sparkle plainly marking him as a man of substance. No, the sheer massiveness of his present structure was not what bothered him, nor was he particularly disturbed by the rhinoceroslike droop of his fleshy jowls. These were the sacrificial aspects of his life—sacrifices made by his surface on behalf of his great love of rich food, well prepared and delicately wolfed down. No, what bothered Henry Underwood was the top, the dome to this prepossessing structure. Emerging from a straggly fringe of grey hair, gleaming foolishly in the orange light of the evening, outshining both his vest and his watch chain, his bald head seemed like a ridiculous and unfitting end to the uppermost height of his body.

Grimly, with a certain stern dissatisfaction, he ran a comb through the limp, grey fringe, wishing once again for some kind of restorative miracle that could make him, if not youthfully tousled, at least slightly hirsute again. Reflected in the mirror, wearing an expression equally grim, portrayed in a full, white head of hair, was the painted portrait of his father. The great mountain man and Indian fighter, Franklin Underwood seemed to glower at his son, who glowered right back. Their eyes—one set belonging to the hardy old trapper, the other pair belonging to Tucson's most successful and unscrupulous businessman—met and held for just a second. And for that fraction of an instant, each seemed to find the other wanting.

Underwood turned away from the mirror and adjusted his vest. The room was cool, despite the long, hot hours just past. Its coolness was attributable to a system newly devised and fabricated for Underwood, which he was finding at least temporarily satisfactory. Faithful Butler kept filled a washtub that dripped continually over a cheesecloth in front of the window. A fan, connected with a direct gear and pulley drive, turned continually to force air into the room. The whole system was powered by a windmill on the building's roof and it all worked splendidly as long as the wind blew. When it didn't, the system stalled and Underwood sweltered. He hated heat. He hated summer. Thinking of it, he couldn't imagine what force or power of God or man had kept him in the stinkhole of Tucson for so many years.

Then his eyes met the portrait of Franklin Underwood. And, once again, he knew.

"Bastard," he muttered, heading for the door.

Underwood locked the office door and headed down a long corridor to his rendezvous. Suddenly he stopped. He thought he had heard a footstep, very light. Not the rat-scratch step of Butler, but something softer. He looked over the edge of the banister and, for just an instant, thought he caught the glimpse of a shadow.

"Hello?"

There was nothing. No movement, no reply.

Underwood shrugged and straightened. Probably just nerves. Wouldn't be the first time.

As he reached the last door at the end of the hallway, Underwood hesitated a moment, brushing back the thin strands of hair. Would she like him? he wondered. Would she be pleased? He moved his hips ever so slightly, practicing for what was to come, then smiled to himself. Yes, he was irresistible. His technique was perfect. And besides, she was well paid by Butler. This woman would not fail to be pleased.

Gently, Underwood opened the door and stepped inside.

"Good evening, darling."

"Hello, Henry."

The sultry voice enveloped him in its generous warmth. The woman who rose from the bed had light blonde, almost white hair and her body was slim. On a figure that was as firm and smooth as an athlete's, some architect of nature had placed a beautiful pair of breasts—long, full, gently sloped. Underwood appreciated the blonde as she moved toward him, lithe, naked and catlike, and he felt himself relaxing as she removed his vest, button by button.

He had no idea where this beautiful woman had come from, but he was delighted. Some things Butler did well. Finding the right kind of woman was one of them. Even before the woman had completely removed his clothes, Underwood found himself trembling in response to the touch of her fingers.

The fingers were long, tapered, cool. They reached into his trousers, stroked him, held him, found that he was ready. Her eyes never left his. They were shimmering blue eyes, fixed on him as though he held her in some kind of a trance. And when she closed her lids, Underwood let his gaze wander over her smooth, white skin, hungering for her as her shoulders worked, her breasts trembled and her fingers played with his desire.

Underwood took the woman by the shoulders and pressed her down on the bed. Her eyes were fixed on him again, unblinking, opened wide in an expression of innocent delight and pleasure. She spread her legs apart and suddenly she was all open to him, the dark forest of hair cloven to expose her pinkness. He could not wait. Underwood pressed toward her, pushing his face down between her breasts, licking her body hungrily.

Suddenly, there was a delicious, warm sensation around his waist and he felt her reaching around to hold him firmly. The eyes widened still more.

"Oh, Henry, please . . . ," she sighed.

Then he felt one arm release him, felt the touch of those tapered, feminine fingers guiding him, leading him down till his tip touched the hot, moist core of the sighing woman who stared up into his eyes. She blinked. Her tongue played along her lips. He felt himself being driven into the parted warmth, the grip of her arm around his waist insistently pushing him deeper and deeper into her body.

The blonde woman groaned. Her lips parted and Underwood felt her hot, panting breath rising around his face. And then she pushed him aside, rolled him off. His face was flushed. He was enraged at being separated from her delicious body in this sudden way. If she had laughed at that moment, he would have killed her.

But then he felt her touch again, felt the expert fingers playing with the tip of him as if to restore feeling to the flesh that was almost numbed by lust. She smiled. Her glistening blonde hair spread on the pillow framed her flushed delicate features. Her fingers sought their own pleasure. Her shoulders trembled as her free hand reached down and then Underwood felt his own pleasure, duplicating hers, the hands reaching, insisting. It seemed to give her such pleasure to play with him this way. He wouldn't allow it. The sensations were more than he could endure.

Struggling to his knees, Underwood pinned her hands to the bed. She writhed, her thighs spreading wide. Her eyes closed finally, and he was free to enjoy the vision of her twisting in his grasp, undulating upward to meet him. Underwood entered her. At his first thrust, the woman quivered. She raised her hips to meet him. Suddenly responding to the man who drove deeply into her body, the blonde quivered, clutched his head, pulled his lips down to hers. Her tongue shot into his mouth. Her body was wrenched by spasms as Underwood exploded inside her.

It was some time later when Underwood found himself resting comfortably on his side, the woman's hands clasped carefully around him as if to protect him.

"Who are you?" he asked.

"Lucille," she replied.

Underwood's smile widened into a grin of satisfaction. This new woman whom Butler had procured was a gem. Underwood figured he would have to forgive his secretary for the delayed oranges, for his gawking stupidity, for everything. This one gift made up for a world of incompetence.

"Henry, darling," she asked, "are you comfortable?"

"Sure am, Lucille. You're a right, fine whore."

It was nearly dark in the room. About time to go. Butler would be back with the oranges—if they'd been on that stage—and supper couldn't be too far away. But the heat of the woman was so comfortable. The gentle weight of her breasts, pressing at him, provided Underwood with such pure contentment that he dozed off again.

He didn't know which came first—the soft, almost imperceptible sound of the door opening or the response of the woman beside him as her arms instinctively tightened. Whatever had alarmed him, he was suddenly awake, alert and keenly aware that something was wrong, very wrong. Someone else was in the room.

Whoever it was had the tread of a jackal. Underwood was in danger; his spine prickled with the sensation of horror. But his back was toward the intruder. It was Lucille who saw him, Lucille who tightened her arms, whose eyes widened, whose face became a horrid, ugly mask of despair as her mouth opened and she screamed.

"Henry! It's an Injun . . ."

Lucille's shrill shriek was consumed by the unearthly howl of an attacking warrior, hungry for blood, thirsting for the kill. In the same instant, Lucille clutched at Underwood as she used his body to protect herself from the marauding Indian. The howl was appalling. Being trapped and clung to by the woman was worse. But with some strength, the strength of fear multiplied twofold by desperation, Underwood rolled, flinging himself over the blonde. His naked body fell to the floor with a thud that shook the room.

As he landed, Underwood caught a glimpse of the Indian brave, his face ghastly in a mask of war paint, his glistening dagger already descending to the spot where Underwood had been a moment before, where Lucille now lay, emitting an unearthly wail, her hands upraised as she futilely tried to ward off the onslaught of the Indian.

"Henry!" Lucille shrieked one last time.

Her voice turned into a meaningless gurgle as the Indian's blade caught her in the throat. She jerked once, blood spurting from her neck, then lay still.

Throwing aside the woman's corpse, the Indian leapt on the bed, blood dripping from the blade of his knife. Underwood heard his own voice, as from a distance, whining, "No . . . please . . . no." The Indian was smiling. Now they were alone in the room—alone, except for Lucille, who lay where the Indian had dropped her, blood draining from her neck.

Naked, defenseless, Underwood backed against the wall feeling a terrible weakness in his bladder. So this was to be his end. The son of an Indian fighter, cornered by an angry brave. Angry, for what reason? It might be any number of crimes. God knew, he had been no saint in his dealings with these savages. Yet he had given them may gifts.

"Wait!" cried Underwood. "Gold! I have gold! I will give you plenty gold!"

Talking to this brave as though he were a child gave Underwood renewed confidence. These Injuns were all children, after all. Weren't they? Just stupid, half-naked, savage children.

"Gold? You like? You want?"

For an instant, Henry Underwood actually believed he was having an effect. Then he saw the Indian's expression, mad with rage, working with hatred. And he recognized the face. Long ago, he had arranged a trade. A perfect deal. So perfect. . . .

The Indian raised his blade, hatred gleaming in his eyes. Underwood cowered, raised his hands to his face, edging along the wall.

"No, please, please . . ." His voice broke. He whined, shrill with despair and pleading. "No, no, please, I beg you . . ."

The Indian lunged forward, slashing with the knife. With a gesture that held more desperation than courage, Underwood brushed the knife stroke away, turned along the wall, crouched.

He could not look. He was going to die. It was too awful.

The Indian howled, triumph mingled with vengeance. His hand grabbed Underwood's fringe of hair, pulling at the scalp. Underwood felt the nausea in his throat. Now, at the hour of death, he was going to retch.

There was a sudden, sharp crack. Then another, and another. The Indian's howl broke loose in a scream. The hand, wrapped up in Underwood's hair, went limp. The knife clattered to the floor and the Indian fell over Underwood, his blood spilling on Underwood's bald head, running down his face.

"Oh, my God. Oh, my God," Underwood moaned, pushing the Indian aside.

"Get up, Henry. It's all over."

The calm, icy voice of Sheriff Pitkin broke through the haze of Underwood's mind as he climbed to his feet, using the wall for support. Pitkin shouldn't speak to him like that. No, he paid the sheriff too well. Such insolence wasn't to be tolerated. No, absolutely not.

Underwood brushed his hand across his face, pushing the stream of blood out of his eyes. Naked, helpless, he stood against the wall, the Indian's blood running off him, the dead brave at his feet.

Half smiling, Sheriff Pitkin stood at the door, reloading the empty chambers of his six-shooter.

"Poor . . . Lucille," Underwood managed. ,

"Yes. Poor Lucille." Pitkin's voice was still icy. An insolence not to be tolerated. He would pay for this later. Yes, he would pay.

"Now, get dressed, Henry," the sheriff continued. "You're a mess."

Fifty-five miles north and west of Tucson, at the confluence of San Pedro River and Aravaipa Creek, stood the small U.S. Army installation known as Ft. Grant. There wasn't much to it. The post consisted of four wooden structures housing officers, supplies and ammunition—in approximately that order of priority—and there was one barracks for enlisted men. The cavalry horses, without stables, had to graze outdoors and there were no barns for storage of hay or oats.

According to Army directives, Ft. Grant was set up specifically "for the mutual protection of the Indians, their containment on assigned lands and maintenance of the peace." What that boiled down to, in Army life, was making sure settlers didn't rile the Indians and the Indians didn't rouse themselves suddenly to any kind of sneak attack.

Lt. Royal E. Whitman had been given the thankless task of overseeing Ft. Grant, and he did the best he could. A serious-looking man of medium height, he wore a full beard and mustache. He had a parcel more concern for the enlisted man than was normal in an officer—witness the barracks—and he'd had the good sense to learn enough Apache to converse with the Indians. In circumstances such as he faced at present, that knowledge could prove useful.

His visitor was Chief Eskaminzin, head of the Apaches, a man to be treated with respect. Rising from his camp stool, Whitman offered his hand as the Indian strode into the room. Eskaminzin was thoroughly familiar with the gesture and he rewarded Whitman with a crushing handshake. The officer knew enough not to flinch, but he could feel his knucklebones rubbing together a lot closer than they were supposed to.

Escaping from the vise, Whitman produced a cigar and offered it, with numb fingers, to the chief. Eskaminzin accepted the gift and ran it back and forth under his nose, sniffing speculatively. He nipped off the end between his teeth and spat, hitting the corner, then waited patiently while Whitman lit a stinker match. When the end glowed red, the Indian sucked deeply to get the stogy in operation. A cloud of tobacco smoke settled around his head, through which the bulldog face peered patiently.

Whitman waited.

Eskaminzin led a small band, consisting of perhaps one hundred and sixty braves, squaws and children. The band lived only a short way from the fort, up along the Aravaipa Creek. The Aravaipa had a reputation for showing hostility toward white settlers. More than one white trapper, foolhardy enough to set out alone up the Aravaipa, had never returned. But Whitman considered the Aravaipa predictable. Left alone, they would mind their own business.

Eskaminzin's strong, thoughtful voice filled the room.

"We want peace. At your word, we will turn in our rifles. We will live without firearms. Only on the condition that you protect us. You must send soldiers to the camp to keep away our enemies."

Whitman studied the big Indian closely and felt something in his stomach plummet. This bulldog of a man was no fool. And he hadn't trekked ten miles down the creek just to barter a few pelts. Whitman had dealt with the man before and now he heard, quite clearly, what Chief Eskaminzin was saying.

The Indian expected trouble and not from other Indians, but from the white man. Eskaminzin didn't want to get caught out. If the white man was going to attack him, let there be white soldiers to protect him. Let them fight it out among themselves, kill each other and leave his tribe alone. It was the only way his tribe could hope to escape blame and inevitable massacre.

Lt. Whitman tugged at the collar of his blue shirt. He had come out here ready to protect settlers. He had come prepared, if necessary, to fight Indians. But he hadn't expected to be put into the position of protecting Indians from the white man.

Eskaminzin, appearing to be totally engrossed in the pleasure of his cigar, was clearly aware of every expression of the cavalry officer. Whitman had to choose his words carefully.

"Chief, I can't personally accept your surrender. I will have to write to my headquarters. I will make a request to do as you say. If my general gives permission, I will gladly protect your tribe in exchange for your arms."

Whitman was evading the decision, and knew it. The odd thing was, so did the Indian. Their eyes met and, for a moment, there was perfect understanding. Chief Eskaminzin smiled.

"We want peace," he declared. "We want to fish, plant corn and beans, and hunt on our land. Do you understand?"

"I understand," Whitman replied grimly.

Sometimes the simple strength of this other race—a race that Whitman could never understand—made him almost ashamed of the complexity of his own. If only he could stand here, like that smoke-ringed Indian, and promise that his people would obey him, that his soldiers would be guided by his absolute command. But he could not. There were orders. Countermands. Legislation. Settlers' rights. And, out in this part of the West, there were plenty of outright, unpredictable, greedy lunatics, ready and willing to use their guns for any kind of meaningless slaughter.

"Chief, I speak only for myself when I say I want peace. But there are other chiefs over me, and I can't promise for them."

"Some braves would turn in their bows and arrows to be left alone by the white man. I say no."

Eskaminzin looked closely at Whitman. Was there a veiled threat in his eyes?

"I say we need bows and arrows for hunting deer and rabbit," continued the chief. "Those are the only weapons we need. Send your bluecoats with guns to keep us safe."

Whitman had to look away.

"I can't do that, Chief. I can only promise you that I will send my dispatches today to the great chiefs. If they approve our agreement, then your people will be protected."

"When?" asked Eskaminzin.

Whitman shook his head.

Suddenly, Eskaminzin took the cigar out of his mouth and handed it to the officer. Not entirely sure of what the gesture meant, yet knowing that some bond had to be established, Whitman accepted the cigar. He puffed on it twice and handed it back. Then he took another cigar from his shirt pocket and presented it to the Apache, who slipped it into the pouch at his waist. Eskaminzin turned, and without a word or a nod, went out the door.

When the chief had gone, Whitman turned to his camp desk and wrote out an urgent dispatch. He signed his name, stamped the letter and sealed it. Calling in one of the adjutants, he handed the packet to him.

"See that this is put in the hands of Colonel Follansbee," he ordered. "And await an immediate reply."

The adjutant saluted and awaited his dismissal. Whitman sighed.

"You might as well take along a change of uniform, soldier. I believe you might have a hefty wait for that reply."

"Yes, sir!"

The adjutant saluted briskly and turned away.

When the soldier had gone, Whitman sat for a while at his desk, motionless. It was a golden opportunity. Here was a hostile tribe, long known for its irritability, offering a permanent settlement. All Eskaminzin wanted in return was protection. And here was Royal Whitman, commander of this outpost of civilization, sending away the chief empty-handed. No promises. No assistance. Sorry, Chief, but you'll just have to keep on collecting guns and fighting us off the best you can because, by God, we're just going to keep coming and coming, and there's nothing that a goddamn lieutenant or anyone else in this crazy country can do for you.

That's what Lt. Whitman had said to Chief Eskaminzin with his eyes. And the chief had responded without anger, without accusation—even with a touch of sympathy for this white soldier's position. Perhaps they both recognized the tragedy that was to come.

Yet it was so avoidable. And so goddamn stupid.

Whitman's fist crashed down on the camp desk and the fragile structure collapsed, scattering papers across the floor. An enlisted man, passing by, heard the racket and burst in the door, ready to protect his commander.

"Are you all right, sir?"

Struggling to recover his dignity, Whitman gestured toward the collapsed desk, the papers scattered across the floor.

"Clean it up, Perkins," he ordered. "And make it snappy."

Whitman strode out, leaving the baffled private, mouth agape, standing at full attention.

Chapter 2

From his room on the top floor of the Commercial Hotel, Spear could keep an eye on Ft. Lowell Road and keep an ear tuned to any distinctive rustlings in the room below. The floors and walls were thin. Miss Wentworth could be heard testing the bed, closing the curtains, turning the key in the door. After a short while she went out, and a few minutes later Spear heard the splash of water in the bath at the end of the second-floor hall.

Maintaining his post by the window, Spear was gratified to see Horace G. Klonner enter the Depot Hotel directly across the street. Brad smiled. The two partners apparently were going to pretend they didn't know each other. So much the better. It would give him ample opportunity to converse with the alleged Linda Farnsworth.

A movement of the curtains at the hotel across the street confirmed Spear's suspicion that Klonner had positioned himself carefully in a second-floor room to keep a hawk's-eye view of the proceedings. No harm in that.

Spear picked up his only change of fresh clothes and headed for the bathroom on the third floor. When the tub was filled with hot water, he climbed in, basking in the luxury of the steamy water that singed his skin. One layer at a time, the grime and grit of the trail worked its way out of his hide. He washed his beard and hair, cleaned his fingernails and finished the job with a quick back scrub. Then he dressed in his clean pair of pants and shirt, and headed back to his room.

An inspection in the wavy dresser mirror confirmed that his beard needed attention. With a quick application of barber's scissors, the scraggly bristles were cropped down to size again. Spear dabbed some bay rum and rose water on his cheeks and hands, and grinned.

"Call me a pig farmer *now,*" he remarked aloud.

Opening his saddlebags, he removed the dagger the Indian had given him and looked around the room. Other than the bed and dresser, the room was bare. There was a framed bit of embroidery on the wall, tilted crazily, reading "Home Sweet Home." It didn't rate as a hiding place either. But it might work as a sheath. Spear unhooked the handiwork from the wall, cut out the center piece of cloth, wrapped it around the blade of the knife and tucked it inside his shirt.

He always carried a vial of flour in his saddlebags, just enough to lend a light coat of dust to a bare floor. On his way out of the room, Spear gently spread some of the flour just outside his door, backing out as he did so. Then he turned the key in the lock and dropped the key in his pocket.

Hotel rooms were too easy to break into. Any door that could be opened with a master key might as well be no door at all.

One flight down, Spear made his way along the hall to Room 213 and knocked. There was a quick rustling, then silence.

So, the icy Miss Farnsworth had not expected visitors so soon. And was just a little edgy.

He knocked again, hard, feeling sure that a useless chunk of derringer was pointed at the oak door right now.

"Miss Farnsworth," he said, sounding very bored, "why don't you answer your door?"

"Who—who is it?" The quaver in her voice indicated she was coming down from some unnecessary height of alarm.

"Me. Brad Spear."

"Who?"

"Perhaps you don't remember." His voice was deliberately laced with boredom. "The cowpuncher you met in the lobby just now."

"Oh, you!" All alarm was gone, and Brad smiled to think that the derringer had been tucked into her tender bosom again. "Go away!"

"Well, sure, Miss Farnsworth, I wouldn't want to trouble you. But I thought you might just like to have some supper, having been on the road so long."

"I'm not dining tonight, thank you. Now, go away, mister, before I call the manager."

Brad Spear lowered his voice a notch. He put in a few grams of cynicism and just a touch of threat.

"No, I wouldn't do that if I were you, Miss Wentworth."

There was a brief silence, then the quick, hard whisper.

"Who are you?"

"Pardon me, but I'm getting sick of talking to this oak panel. It doesn't look like you, and it doesn't give me a very good impression of your manners. Now, I think if you'd just give me a foot or two of room, I could probably come in. As it is, I can't budge. And I certainly don't aim to go away."

He didn't have to wait long. The door opened a crack and the toylike barrel of a two-shot derringer poked out like a pair of vertically oriented, greedy eyes.

"Oh, for Christ's sake," grumbled Spear in exasperation. "Put that toy away."

She opened the door wide, backed off, holding the derringer in two unsteady hands, and allowed him to enter. Spear bowed slightly, smirked visibly, closed the door behind him and ostentatiously neglected to lock it.

"May I?" He indicated the only chair in the room.

She nodded. He sat, looked up at her and smiled. She didn't smile back.

"Why did you call me Miss Wentworth?" Her voice carried some hysteria.

"Sorry. Must've got you confused with someone else."

"You're lying."

Spear sighed.

"I called you Miss Wentworth because I'm not in the habit of calling women by their Christian names on first encounter. So I figured it would be kind of rude to call you Louisa."

The hands that held the derringer shook just a little more.

"Put that thing away!" shouted Spear.

She was so startled by his command that she actually jumped. She looked at him, glanced at the derringer in her hand and finally, as if it were some bauble that she didn't really want to hold, she laid it down on the dresser. Spear leaned back in his chair.

"Much better. Now we can talk."

"My name is Linda Farnsworth."

Spear sighed again.

"Okay, okay. Your name is Queen Victoria. I

don't care. That's not interesting. What's interesting, apart from your natural attributes, is the way you got involved with a man named Horace G. Klonner and the way he got you involved with the jewelry industry . . ."

"Who are you?" she demanded again.

"I'm Prince Albert." Spear was studying his fingernails very hard and thought he detected some trail grime where a true gentleman shouldn't have any. "Damn," he muttered. "It's so difficult to keep your nails clean when you have to keep after a couple of fleet-footed thieves, day and night, all the way from a godforsaken place like Denver to a stingy, fly-bit cattle dump like Tucson."

Louisa Wentworth backed away, staring at the man, her hands reaching out behind her, seeking the edge of the bed. As she found it she sank down, obviously thankful for the support. She wasn't taking this well.

"Careful, honey," counseled Spear. "You want to keep control of yourself very carefully during the next five minutes. And you want to keep smiling at me like I was just the cutest pig farmer you ever met. And the reason for all this play-acting is that your partner there, Horace Klonner, is sitting in the hotel room across the way fixing his sights on you."

She started to turn her head to look, but Spear's voice stopped her motion.

"No. Don't look."

She managed to control her expression.

"Now, smile."

She smiled.

"And I'll smile right back, see?"

Spear smiled at her.

"And now," he continued, "Mr. Klonner has just the right impression about our relationship."

Spear crossed his right leg over his left knee, folded his hands contentedly across his muscular stomach and looked up at the ceiling.

"Now, the way I figure, you weren't really too involved with this thing in the beginning. You just kind of went along for the ride and perhaps for the love of Mr. Klonner."

Spear thought he detected a slight nod, but he was concentrating so hard on a leafy-green patch of mold on the ceiling, shaped like a hovering cloud, that he couldn't be sure.

"That was at the beginning," Spear went on. "As it is now, you might be considered equal partners, at least in the eyes of the law. And that, unfortunately, would mean hanging together."

Spear dragged his eyes down and shook his head sadly, as if he'd just received news of a stock market crash that would ruin everyone else in the world but him.

"It's a poor situation for a young lady to be in."

"What do you want from me?"

Her voice was low and there was something about the movement of her hand that seemed to indicate she was thinking about the derringer again.

"Do me a favor. Don't pick up that toy until you hear my proposal."

Her hand stopped moving. "I'm waiting."

"Simply this. Tell me where the jewels are. Tell me what you're doing here. Then scram."

She considered it for a second. It was a woman's right, thought Spear: think of herself first.

"And Klonner?" she asked.

"Might not be so lucky." Her expression clouded with doubt. "Look here, Miss Wentworth." Spear's voice was cutting and cruel now. "He got you into a situation where your pretty little neck could end up

wearing a rope necklace. And for what? A bunch of
stones? I've caught up with you lovebirds. It won't be
long before the law does, too. Time's running out, Miss
Wentworth. There aren't many gentlemen who are going to make the polite exit arrangements that I've just
specified."

"Why are you doing it?" she questioned.

"I like pretty jewels," he replied. "Tell me where
they are and I'd be a very happy man. Happy enough
to share some of them."

Louisa Wentworth rose from the bed and Spear
was struck once again by the natural grace of this creature. Somewhere in her saddlebags she had found a
slim, silk dress that hugged her curves without distort-
ing them. Her white arms were bare to the shoulders,
and there was a light covering of down on her arms
that shimmered in the glow of the kerosene lamp. She
crossed the room, took a pale-colored shawl from the
hook on the back of the door, raised the ends in her
delicate hands and, with a quick spin, wrapped the
shawl around her shoulders.

Spear felt that disturbingly youthful sensation that
he always experienced in the presence of a grown
woman who knew her stuff. God had created these
beings for the pure torture of man, and there was no
way out. She lowered her head, the shimmering hair
falling about her shawl-covered arms. Then she looked
up slowly, with a wan smile, her brown eyes seeking
his.

"I don't know where the jewels are," she said.

"Of course you don't." Spear hated being manipu-
lated like this.

"You must believe me."

And now, the husky voice, the sultry look. She
wouldn't get away with it.

"I'm sorry. I must remind you, once again, of the rope."

She shrugged. Amazingly enough, the shrug was real. She meant it. She really didn't care. Or else—and this was entirely possible—she'd been trapped so long she didn't know what anything else felt like.

Spear felt some renewed admiration for this woman—an admiration that had nothing to do with her catlike figure.

"You came to Tucson for your health?"

She flinched at his sarcastic question, but she was also annoyed.

"No, of course not. Klonner has a plan. He knows where the jewels are from the last job. And he has a plan for another one. I've been promised my share."

"You believe him?" Spear cut in.

She made a gesture of annoyance. "That doesn't make any difference. I can't do anything else. Besides, it's supposed to be something big. He's talking about millions."

"Millions?" Spear's surprised tone was genuine. "In little old Tucson?"

"I wouldn't underestimate him, Mr. Spear."

"I shall endeavor not to, Miss Wentworth. I'm also trying very hard to believe you."

"Believe me or not, there's nothing I can do about it. I have no jewels. I'm at the man's mercy. I have to go along with him. And now that he's seen me with you . . ."

"Oh, don't fret about that. I'm just a cowpuncher come to call on Miss Farnsworth. And I believe I've overstayed my welcome."

Spear got up from his chair and strode toward the door. Louisa Wentworth stepped back, allowing him to pass.

"I should have shot you on sight," she declared

softly. The deep brown eyes bore a striking resemblance to those of a dead lynx.

"It wouldn't have helped," remarked Spear. "I've already left an envelope with the sheriff, to be opened in case of my death. The story of Klonner and Wentworth would leave an indelible impression on his mind."

It was a quick lie, but a good one.

"No, Miss Wentworth. For your own sake—and, of course, for mine—I think the best policy would be to repeat nothing of this discussion to your partner. For the moment, I expect I'll have to accept your highly questionable statement that you don't know what you're doing here. Still, I don't like the ring of it. If it occurs to me, I might ask again, sometime when I'm not busy. Think about it, Miss Wentworth. Freedom's a pretty word."

He opened the door.

"Mr. Spear, how did you know my name?" she asked quietly.

He grinned. "Intuition, ma'am. Just a man's intuition."

The cold glare of her eyes, reflecting the yellow light of the kerosene lamp, remained fixed in his mind for quite a while after he'd left the room. Truth was, he had to admit to himself, the sight of a rope around that fine neck would make him downright sick. And that was a dangerous thing to admit, even in the privacy of his own thoughts.

The burro had walked all day as though each step would be its last. It resisted every slope, slowing to a crawl on any incline, and plodded painfully even over level ground. A long-suffering animal, it resented its work with an indomitable will. But when the wind brought the scent of the Gila River to its nostrils, the burro moved along quickly. So quickly, in fact, that the slightly drunk little man on its back had to concentrate to stay on the animal. And the Indian girl that walked beside them had to jog now and then to keep up.

"God deliver me from this land," the dust-coated rider muttered. "Its horrors grow with every year and I have been away for quite a while."

The woman beside him looked into his face, not quite understanding his words. He spoke so strangely, this white man. He mumbled to himself, not praying to his God or talking to her, just making noises. Strange, she thought.

"Asha-yo-mo," he said to her, "take this damned animal and let it drink." The rider parted his straggling hair with his fingers and dismounted, a bottle in one hand. "The muddy water of the Gila for it, mescal for me."

A very strange man, she thought.

Asha-yo-mo led the burro to the slow-moving waters of the river. It was nearly dusk, the cool air of evening coming on. At least now they would stop. He would eat too little, swear into the darkness and then sleep. It had been the same for many nights. She left the burro, carrying the wicker baskets from its back, and returned to the man.

"Dufond," she spoke, pronouncing every letter of his name with almost painful clarity, "we stop here." The dirty, drunken man shrugged and sat down on a rock.

The Indian girl busied herself with their few possessions. Two bedrolls. Two spoons and a pan. Matches, bacon, dark, dried corn. And she set the rifle, bright and gleaming, beside him. He talked to it sometimes, she thought. Its spirit important to him for reasons she could only guess at. But though she rested it against him, the muzzle leaning on his thigh, he ignored her.

She remembered how he'd used the rifle. Killing them. Two men who owned the burro had taken her, made her their woman. The sort of Mexicans who often dragged Apaches along for sport. She had hated it. But until their lust grew dark with drink, she had survived well enough. They had been only difficult to be around. In the end, though, they were ugly. They had grown bored with her, were ready to discard the Indian girl. But they decided on a game first. A grim, drunken game. She thought back to being naked in the chill of the night for a long, painful time and then recalled the sound of the rifle, killing them.

Her hands tied up that way, she was afraid as he approached. But Dufond had neither killed nor used her. He'd cut her loose to drag the Mexicans' bodies into the night. And now, six days later, he drank their mescal and ignored her. Over and over he told Ashayo-mo with a smile that he had killed them for the burro, only for the burro.

"Dufond?" she asked, the name difficult for her.

"Damned animal," he croaked suddenly.

"Damned animal!" he shouted. "Blisters."

She shrugged. Your backside, my feet, she thought. He never let her ride.

"Is there food left?" Dufond asked, almost an accusation.

"Some," she replied.

During the hours that passed thereafter, he said nothing more that she could decipher. He drank a bit but ate nothing. She scrubbed the pan in the river, glad she wasn't forced to scour it only with desert sand. Then she replaced their few provisions in a burlap bag and put it in the baskets that the burro carried.

"Girl," he said. Having heard but not listened to

so much of his rumbling for so many hours, she didn't seem to notice him as he called her. "Girl!" Dufond shouted. She snapped around. "Sit here," he directed, gesturing beside him.

Asha-yo-mo walked through the cool air and squatted at his feet.

"How old are you, anyway?"

"Eighteen summers," she answered.

"Humph," Dufond grunted, "and still not pretty." He drank from the bottle again.

It was true, she knew. Asha-yo-mo was young and thin, strong from her hard life, but not pretty. The broad, dull features of her face were plain, her hair dark, but not shining. The girl looked down, apparently studying the stones at her feet.

"No matter," he shrugged. "I've had my fill of pretty girls."

She peered at him. He was drunk. She wanted very much to go back to her bedroll and sleep.

"I loved one once, you know. A pretty girl, I mean. Not far from here. Not so far." His eyes, red and squinting, searched the horizon. Asha-yo-mo wondered if it was true, wondered if such a bedraggled, filthy, desperate man had ever loved anything. She added sticks to the fire, ignoring him again as Dufond sat staring into the distance.

"Your medicine men, or priests, or whatever, do they take women?" His question came from a reverie she couldn't understand.

Asha-yo-mo nodded. She knew some white priests did not marry. She also knew that many of them took women just the same.

"I was a priest." She looked at him, surprised. "And a good one. I never took a woman. Until her beauty entered my life and sank my faith. Her loveliness betrayed my service to the Lord. I was a priest, before her, but then I wasn't." It seemed to have been a mysterious transformation to him, like magic, unexplained.

Perhaps the shame of losing his God made him this way, she thought.

"It was a curse, I think, from our most beneficent Lord, a gift of evil grace from the all-powerful son of a bitch. He sent me a married woman." Dufond laughed at the thought of a malevolent God playing dirty tricks on him. His cackle was high and piercing, a laugh that shattered the quiet sound of running water nearby. The burro snorted, pawing the dirt, then calmed.

Asha-yo-mo felt the cool, moist air of the river all around them. After days of traveling through the arid lands to the north, the farms and trees and rivers of the south were refreshing. Somehow the heat from their small fire felt different to her, its warmth spreading through the small campsite in a way it never did in the desert. She watched the light flicker on Dufond's sad, worn face, the uneven illumination giving him the look of an actor on a stage.

"I come, you know, from Mermosillo, the capital." Asha-yo-mo's eyes narrowed. "Ha! You doubt it?" He laughed again, this time with a chuckle burdened with self-pity. "It's true, though. I was a priest to the governor, Enrique Delgado. And lover to his wife." He drank again, sucking the last drops from the bottle. But even with his head tilted back unsteadily, his eyes searched her for a response.

The Indian girl had heard the story whispered among Mexicans and Americans as far north as Tucson. Heard of Delgado's fury and the tortured death his wife suffered at the man's hands. She'd heard the lover was a priest, but she had heard other stories about the beautiful young woman's death that seemed more likely. Could she now be hearing the truth? If

Dufond really was the lovely Josefina's lover and not just a drunken storyteller, it was dangerous just being with him.

"She was very beautiful, as they say?" she asked.

"Very."

The emptiness on his face told her he was telling the truth. This one little man had, like a paring knife, opened all of the province of Sonora to chaos. And he'd escaped, abandoned her and escaped.

"But, Dufond, you left her to die?"

Her simple question cut him to the quick. Even the bitter blur of mescal couldn't protect him from it. He had run away, a coward. Dufond's first instinct was to deny the thought, explain it away somehow. But he couldn't. The man wept, sobbing to himself, not for Josefina's suffering but for his own loss, for having left behind a woman he loved, wanted, needed.

"You must hate yourself very much," murmured Asha-yo-mo.

"Very." Dufond thought to himself that he'd become good at running away, very good at surviving and a master of self-loathing. This last his profession, as it were.

"My heart aches for yours," she whispered.

Dufond looked at the Indian girl. Through his stupor she seemed to waver before his eyes. Homely and young, an innocent. He wondered why she was there. Tried to recall how they met. But there was no memory whatever. Had he bought her? He shrugged.

"Drink no more, Dufond. Sleep."

He waved off the suggestion. She was annoying him.

Asha-yo-mo stood and lifted him by the arms. Stumbling, she led him to his bedroll and dropped him on it. Now he'd sleep, she thought. But, half-sitting, half-lying down, an ugly sound came from his belly, an angry noise of wrenching muscles and tortured juices. He vomited, the foul stuff spreading across his shirt and trousers.

Dufond rolled over on his side, spitting. A fog of despair swept over him. He was lost, he thought.

Asha-yo-mo turned away, tears welling in her eyes as she considered the little man with no woman. He was demanding, even cruel to her. But, like herself, he'd been cast off, discarded by the world that mattered. Perhaps, like Asha-yo-mo, Dufond deserved his wretched state, maybe the gods were punishing him, too. It was a simple bond. She knew him, knew him well, this man without a place or a woman. And in knowing him, she felt sympathy, the comradery of hopelessness.

The homely Apache girl walked to the river with Dufond's shirt and trousers. She rinsed them and returned to the man with a dripping rag, ready to clean him. She was tired. The heat of the day, the long walk through barren country and the late hour all conspired to exhaust her. Still, she knelt beside him, sponging his naked body, administering to him like a child.

Half-conscious, he moaned beneath his breath. Better in the morning, she thought. Better you were sick tonight.

As her hand ran gently down his chest she watched him breathe, slowly and steadily. She washed his side and noticed that he flinched under her touch. Then she lifted the blanket and cleaned his thighs. As rinsed as she could manage in the half-light of the camp, she sat back and studied him. Dirty, thin, drunken and confused, he might easily have been disgusting to her. But the runaway Apache girl smiled down on him. The white man was many things, she thought, but not weak. Like the stray camp dogs that follow the hunters, ownerless, he was sad, strange, frightening, but not weak.

Asha-yo-mo reached and touched his shoulder. He was warm and quiet, finally. The girl stroked him, running her hand comfortingly down his side, reaching his legs. He burbled, unconscious. The sight of him, ravaged by drink and hunger, worn by fear, but still smiling under her touch, sent a shiver down her spine. There was, she thought, nothing to stop her.

The girl reached for his manhood, a fallen flag, and touched it. Her fingers brushed his thighs and rested on his belly. He stirred but didn't awaken. And as she watched him move, lifting, her caress a balm to his skin, she saw Dufond grow harder. Asleep, she thought, he wants me.

He rose slowly, bobbing with her touch, and finally erect twitched in front of her. Dufond muttered something, a request racing through his dream.

She strained to understand his mumbling, but couldn't. It didn't matter, she thought. His dream was his own. Above him, she would enjoy her own illusion. Captivated by her control over him, thrilled by his unconscious response to her, Asha-yo-mo slipped her britches to the ground. Half-naked, she touched him again, his loins aching beneath her hands. She smiled, pleased with her toy, infatuated by her remarkable command of him. She had never owned a man before.

"Josefina," he spoke clearly and with a sad longing that stunned her. "Oh, Josefina."

Asha-yo-mo pulled back from him. With his eyes closed, I am beautiful, she thought. Then the plain, sad Indian girl shut her eyes and became the spectacular woman Dufond imagined. She saw herself a chief's wife, the most honored woman in her tribe. She stood and straddled him, looking down on his sweating face, simpler and less troubled in the moonlight. And gazed on his loins, huge and wanting, hers, all hers.

She held him in both hands, guiding him into her as she lowered her hips around his body. As Dufond slid into her, he gasped, some dream teasing him. But Asha-yo-mo ignored the white man. Locked in Josefina's arms he would not awake.

Then, moving slowly above him, the fantasy blurred. His dream surrounded her and then disappeared. The images of great men and beautiful women vanished from her mind, displaced by a yearning that overwhelmed her. She bent over him, her weight on the palms of her hands. The feeling of him, his sounds and the sweet pounding between her legs drove her on. Awkward above him, almost hovering, she felt herself reaching back, aching and struggling, searching for him. She rose and fell with a cadence she neither controlled nor recognized, her movements something that were simply happening to her.

And she saw him, rolling from side to side, then surging up and down toward her and away. Dufond smiled, his arms reaching out, and Asha-yo-mo succumbed to the wave of passion that engulfed her. She lifted herself, arching, and rode the feeling into the darkness. She twisted, rising and falling desperately for an eternity. But finally, as the sweet echoes of feeling burst slower in her, she felt him lift, grunting, pushing, exploding below her. His fists tightened, his joy a terrifying vision of anger, Dufond burst into her, his wide, blank eyes filled with hate.

Leaving the hotel, Spear noticed that the light in Klonner's room at the Depot Hotel had already gone out. He figured Klonner had two choices, to trail him or to have a heart-to-heart talk with Louisa. Assuming the man was a bully, which seemed a fair assumption,

he would undoubtedly take the first opportunity to corner Louisa and badger her into submission.

Spear winced. Hands, as well as rope, could make
a mess of that fine neck. Yet he felt a certain confidence that Miss Wentworth could take care of herself.

If she talked, Spear wasn't particularly worried.
Those two could run or they could try to gun him
down. Either way, Spear figured, he'd win.

The noise was already building up at the Antelope
Saloon and two poker players had been thrown outside
to settle their differences. As Spear watched, one of
them landed a punch that sent the other off the edge of
the boardwalk. The man in the dust got up howling,
and Spear saw the flash of a blade in his hand. So did
the onlookers. A bunch of men standing around the
door cheered. As the man with the knife tried to climb
up on the boardwalk, the tip of a boot met his chin
and sent him flying back in the dust. The impact left
him spread-eagled on his back, and he didn't stir again.
The knife spilled out of his limp fingers.

"How many aces you got now?" yelled one of the
men from the boardwalk. The others hollered with
laughter and pounded the man on the back. One by
one, hurling epithets and spittle toward the prone figure, the men turned and went back inside.

When the street was quiet again, Spear crossed
and looked down at the man lying in the dust. The
eyes of the man flickered, then opened. He took one
look at Spear and made a grab for him. Spear kicked
the hand away and stepped back.

"That's the way you got hurt in the first place,"
reminded Spear.

"Whatta you want?"

The sound of the voice made Spear realize this
man was very young, hardly more than a boy. He was
a thin kid, dressed in a plaid shirt, wearing leather

chaps that had once been fine. They weren't so fine anymore.

The kid looked around.

"Wha'd you do with my . . ."

"Your knife's over there," Spear pointed with the toe of his boot.

The kid grimaced as he reached for it.

"Sons of bitches," he grunted, struggling to his feet.

"You were lucky. Coming at that crowd with a knife, they could have killed you. Probably would have, if you weren't so young."

The kid bristled.

"I ain't young, mister. I'm twenty-six."

"Sure you are. And I'm the mayor of San Francisco. You live here?"

"Looks like. Don't it?"

"What's your name?"

"Frank Emory."

"Well, Frank, I don't know whether you're brave or just plain drunk and crazy, but it took something along those lines to go up against that crowd there."

"Thanks. Now I got some business to settle . . ."

He started toward the bar door again. Spear grabbed his arm. The kid whipped around, knife ready.

"Jesus," swore Spear. "You never learn."

"Look, mister, just leave me alone. I don't know who you are or what you want, but you better just keep out of my way."

"Sure," promised Spear. He turned to go. "Oh, say . . . ," he turned again. "You're not a jeweler by any chance, are you?"

"Who, me?" For the first time, the kid laughed. "That's a good one."

Spear shrugged. "Just thought I'd ask."

Emory laughed again. "Well, you got the wrong party, mister. I ain't got two dollars to my name."

"Hard up, huh?"

The kid looked away without answering and slipped his knife in the sheath at his belt.

"I want to work honest."

"That shouldn't be hard to do," replied Spear.

"Around here?" The kid laughed shortly. "It ain't so easy. Half the scum in that Antelope there are working for Mr. Underwood. And the other half's working for the men that are working for Mr. Underwood."

"Huh," grunted Spear appreciatively. "I gather Mr. Underwood is one fine man to work for."

For the first time in their conversation, Frank Emory registered outright respect. In fact, his respect was so complete, it bordered on awe at Spear's ignorance. A low whistle escaped the kid.

"Gee-up, mister. You are a stranger 'round here, ain't you?"

"Yep."

The kid laughed.

"Well, hang around. You'll hear about Mr. Underwood."

"Sure. Maybe you can introduce me to him."

Emory's face clouded. "Don't think I could do that," he replied. "Underwood and I don't get along so good."

"Seems like you don't get along with a lot of people."

"Yeah." It seemed, from Emory's expression, that Spear had made a depressingly accurate observation. "Yeah, maybe I get riled too easy—or something."

"Well, you haven't riled me, at least so far. In fact," continued Spear, squinting his eyes at the light in the saloon, "there might come a time I could offer you honest work."

"Doing what, for instance?" Emory was instantly suspicious.

"Just for starters, showing me the way to a man who knows a thing or two about precious gems."

"You got something you want to sell?"

"Now I know what gets you in trouble—too many questions."

Emory bowed his head and scuffled a foot in the dust.

"No," continued Spear. "Nothing to sell. A little appraisal matter."

The kid leveled his gaze again.

"Try Hal Quinn."

"Where's he live?"

"First house around the corner. He's got a blacksmith shop downstairs."

"The way I figure it," said Spear, "that's a dollar's worth of information."

Emory's eyes lit up, and there was a quick struggle to hold on to his pride.

"Keep it," he spoke finally.

"Didn't hear you," replied Spear, holding out the bill.

Emory couldn't hold back a grin.

"I didn't say anything," he responded, taking the dollar.

Spear turned to go, then paused for a second.

"This Quinn—does he work for Underwood?"

"If he did, I wouldn't have mentioned him."

"That's what I figured," nodded Spear.

When he turned the corner, the kid was still standing in the middle of Ft. Lowell Road, watching him.

Along the side street, there weren't any lights. But Spear didn't have any trouble finding the blacksmith shop. Apparently Quinn was working late, and the steady clanging of the hammer on the anvil stunned the night air with its angry, heavy clatter. He worked close to an open fire and, as Spear approached the wide-open shop door, Quinn gave a few pumps to the bellows, sending orange-red sparks flying in different directions. The hot fire lit up the features of his broadly lined face.

Returning to the anvil, Quinn stood to his full height, and a single word flashed across Spear's mind: grizzly. Bigger, broader, hairier and more barrel-chested than any man was meant to be, the enormous smith filled the shop as if he were the sole occupant of a private cave.

The little thumping at his door frame, which was Spear's excuse for a knock, made Quinn look up only a second from his work. The big smith grunted and waved for Spear to come in.

Spear stepped inside, but Quinn didn't seem to notice him any further after that first grunt of acknowledgment. Grizzly. There was that word again. Spear had been just a boy, back there in Oregon. Roaming around the woods when his daddy had said he shouldn't. Just one boy, facing a mad, mean old grizzly mama with her cubs about ten yards away. It was hot as blazes in the smithy's shop, but that memory brought some icicles to Spear's spine.

"Hal Quinn?" yelled Spear.

Quinn held back on the hammering, lifted the massive pair of tongs that was in his right hand and peered expertly at the foot-long barn door hinge that was clutched in the jaws of the mighty pincers.

"What's your business?" asked Quinn.

"I need an appraisal, Mr. Quinn."

"Who are you?"

That question again. Natural for people to ask. It was the tone they asked it in, the marked suspicion, that seemed kind of needless.

"Brad Spear."

"Come in today?"

"Yes."

The smith nodded, tucked the hinge in the fire, pumped a few times, pulled it out and commenced hammering again. At this pace, Spear thought, it might be several weeks before he got what he wanted.

"I'd like you to look at something, Mr. Quinn," Spear shouted over the hammering.

"I don't do appraisals no more," replied Quinn without changing his pace.

"That's not what I heard."

"Who'd you talk to, mister?"

"Frank Emory."

The hammering stopped. Quinn looked up. With one hand, he opened the tongs and released the hinge. It clattered into the wooden box on the floor, knocking metal against metal.

"Frank told you to come here?"

"That's right."

Quinn took off his leather apron, jerked his head toward the back of the shop and led the way to the door. Spear followed.

Opening the back door, Quinn led Spear into a small room furnished only with a table and pair of chairs. The big man crossed the room and turned up the wick in the coal oil lamp that guttered on the table. He closed the shutters from the inside.

"Shut the door," he directed.

Spear did so.

"What do you have?"

Spear reached into his shirt and drew out the

knife, wrapped in its sheath of embroidery. He handed it to the big smith, who carefully unwrapped the blade. Quinn set the piece of cloth aside, spread it flat and suddenly, without warning, burst out in a bellow of laughter.

The laughter seemed to shake the room and echo from the walls. Quinn's whole frame jiggled up and down as if those powerful muscles had been turned to jelly by merriment. His fists pounded the table, his big head wobbled from side to side and tears came to his eyes as he looked down at the embroidery.

"Home sweet home," he pronounced. "Home sweet home." He took a good, long look at Spear, trying to see out through the haze of tears. "I must say, young feller, you sure do a fine piece of needlework."

"Thanks," replied Spear, somewhat shaken by Quinn's temperament. He couldn't help wondering, if only for a moment, whether Tucson's resident blacksmith and appraiser might be ever so slightly unbalanced.

"Ah, never mind me," soothed Quinn, apparently noticing Spear's uneasiness. "Just don't often get a chuckle around here. Now then . . ."

He settled into a chair, pulled open a table drawer and extracted a small glass, which he fitted into one eye.

"Let's see the item."

"Right there in front of you," responded Spear, indicating the knife handle.

Quinn casually picked up the knife. Then he looked more closely. Then, just as Spear had done on the trail, he lifted the handle to the light until the glow of the lamp could be seen through the shimmering crystal on the hilt. He looked at Spear. He looked at the gem again. He squinted, peered through the eyepiece. Opening the table drawer once again, he took out a small mirror. He inverted the knife, touched the gem to the glass and made a sharp movement. There was a clean line across the face of the mirror.

Quinn handed the knife to Spear and nodded almost imperceptibly.

"That's what I thought," said Spear. "How much?"

"Hard to say until it's cut," replied Quinn. "If I had it to pay, I would give you twenty-seven thousand four hundred and fifty dollars for what's stuck in the end of that knife." Then he looked at Spear closely. "Assuming you could prove it was yours, and honestly come by."

"I got it from an Indian," explained Spear. "Fair trade for a cigar."

If the last bout of laughter had been a rumble, this round was an earthquake. It filled the room and burst its seams, sent trills, whirlpools and cyclones of sound whistling through the air. It reduced the bearish giant to a quivering mass of shattered amusement and made him clutch the table for support.

When he had recovered, when the tears had been wiped away and Spear's nerves had settled down, Hal Quinn apologized again.

"Think nothing of it." Spear waved his hand. "I'm pretty pleased myself."

Quinn got to his feet and Spear was astonished to discover how quickly all traces of amusement could be erased from the smith's visage.

"We don't have diamonds like this around here. I've looked at a potful of gems the past twenty years, but I never saw anything that came to a tenth of that size." He fixed his eyes on Spear, as if to make his warning clear. "If you're thinking of prospecting for some more of those, forget it."

"Prospecting isn't my game."

"It wouldn't be fitting for a humble smith to be asking what your game is, Mr. Spear. But I'll tell you this. Get that out of this town and fast, or you won't have it much longer."

"Oh? Why's that?"

Quinn came around the table and for a good, long second, Spear had to recall the way that mama grizzly's paw came slashing down toward his face, and he had to be reminded of that snarl that would never leave his memory so long as he lived.

Quinn wasn't snarling, though. In fact, he looked almost pitying.

"Mr. Spear, when you came in here, you mentioned the name of Frank Emory. He's young. He's still got an honest streak in him. But the truth is, Mr. Spear, there ain't more than half a dozen like him in this entire booming city of three thousand. You understand?"

"No."

Quinn looked annoyed. "How can I make it clearer?"

"Tell me about Mr. Underwood."

Quinn winced. He thought a minute, then shook his head.

"No, Mr. Spear. I won't tell you about Underwood."

"Why's that?"

"Mr. Spear . . ." Hal Quinn lowered his voice and there was something incredibly regretful welling up from the depth of his words. "I knew that man's father, Frank Underwood, when he was getting along in years. He helped to settle these parts, Mr. Spear. He helped make them civilized. A better man never lived. But if that man were alive today, Mr. Spear, he would take his own son off in the woods where no one could hear, put a gun to his head and shoot him."

The two men, by a kind of mutual agreement, let a long pause follow Hal Quinn's words, while they both seemed to think about that idea and paid their respects with silence. Finally, Quinn turned to the table and lowered the wick in the lamp.

"Any other questions, Mr. Spear?"

"Nope. I guess that's about it."

"Well, I've still got the other side of that barn hinge to finish tonight, so if you don't mind . . ."

"Of course," Spear nodded.

He turned and went out.

Brad Spear was correct in his assessment of Klonner's priorities. But even so, he would have been astonished to observe how soon after his departure from the Commercial Hotel Mr. Klonner arrived outside Room 213. When Louisa let him in, he didn't waste any time getting to the point.

"Who is he?"

Louisa shook her head in disgust.

"Cowpoke," she stated.

"Cowpoke? And you spent thirty minutes talking about longhorns?"

"I couldn't get rid of him," she complained.

"I've seen you cut a man down so fast he was on his knees before he knew what hit him."

"Listen, Horace," she began, "you drag me to this place. You dump me in a hotel room. You leave me to rot. And a nice, polite cowpuncher comes to the door, you expect me to tell him to jump down a well?"

"I didn't bring you here to improve your social life."

"I'd like to know just what in hell you *did* bring me here for."

She put some venom in her words, and she could tell, even as she turned away, that she had hurt him.

That was the thing that had always puzzled her about this white-faced, strutting man—how a word or two could cut him to the quick when gunfire, jail sentences and the threat of hanging failed to have any effect whatsoever on his temperament.

Yes, she could hurt him. And he kept after her. Those two characteristics forced her to a conclusion that she didn't like, had never liked, but was forced to accept. He loved her. This thieving, pleasure-thirsty individual actually cared about her. As far as she knew, he was the only man who ever had.

So that was his hold over her. It was her own need. For some reason, quite suddenly, that was clearer to her now than it had ever been. And she wondered why, so abruptly, she was looking at this man with clearer eyes. Surely her conversation with the other man—that Brad Spear—had something to do with it. He had threatened her. But he'd also given her an out, a zone of safety. And that was something she'd never had with Horace G. Klonner.

Lost in her own thoughts, Louisa didn't even hear him speaking to her until his voice roared in her ear.

"Listen to me!"

His hand struck her cheek, sending wild anger through her veins. Instinctively, she reached inside her bodice and pulled out the derringer. Fire, she told herself. Fire, and end this. You could finish him now.

But his soothing voice washed over the heat of her emotion.

"Now, Louisa, Louisa . . ."

He placed his hand over hers, forced her gently to lower the derringer. Then he came closer. Her cheek hurt. Tears of shame and anger welled up in her eyes.

"Louisa!"

He kissed her. His hand opened her fingers, lifted the derringer from her grasp and placed it on the table.

He kissed her cheek, her ear, and then his mouth moved to the base of her neck, to the ivory hollow where his lips sucked at her skin, so softly, gently warming her.

The shawl slipped to the floor and her hands held his head, pressing him against her. The sensations were so wonderful that she forgot everything, giving herself up to his grasp. How was it possible that a man who touched her this way did not love her? He must. He must.

The lantern was burning low and only a dim, warm light illuminated the room now. Louisa waited patiently as he stepped away from her and unbuttoned the front of her silk dress. She could not look at him. Her eyes were on the floor, where the shawl had fallen. But every touch of his fingers was like the touch of a helpless, lovable child on her skin. She did not have to think of him. She was totally wrapped in her own pleasure, at the feeling of nakedness that was like being completely released—released to enjoy her passion. Her bodice was open. He pulled down the thin straps from her shoulders, baring her breasts. Again, she reached out for his head, bringing him close to her until his lips were pressed to the smooth valley between her breasts. Her arms went around him, holding him totally, pressing her breasts to the side of his head as the nipples rose, sensitive in their own delight.

But now Klonner was anxious, searching. His hands pushed down over her buttocks, pushing at the cloth that clung to her hips, fingers clawing at the smooth flesh, so eager to spread her apart. Yes, she wanted it. She wanted to be parted, opened. She wanted him thrusting into her, opening her thighs, entering, penetrating. That was all she wanted. And his hands were anxious to please her, obliging her in their soothing motions as they found their way along her buttocks, around her hips. The deft, gentle fingers touched the hair, moved down and played at the wet, quivering, tiny point of her pleasure.

"Oh, Horace."

The oil lamp guttered and died. Louisa stepped back, lay on the bed, luxuriated in the feel of the coverlet against her back. The cool, evening air spread across her, just like his hands, washing across her warmth and seeking the private, damp cleft in her nakedness.

She felt the bed sag as he climbed up. Then the mattress evened out as he knelt between her thighs, pressing her legs apart. She opened her eyes and in the dimness she saw his face, the expression cold but the eyes hungering after her.

"Wait," Louisa sighed. For once, just for once, she wanted to join him in his pleasure, to lock her own rhythm with his.

It was not to be. She groaned in sharp surprise as he entered her suddenly. She wasn't ready. She couldn't be. He entered her so abruptly that it was more like violation than love. She was locked in his embrace, her legs forced to open, her body forced to accept as the pace quickened and his grip hardened into a man's clutch of desperation. She was not aroused. It was too sudden, too brutal. She could not accept him. Yet she must. Her taste, her touch, all her sensations were consumed by his insistence. His explosion rocked her. Her head jerked back on the pillow. He thrust and thrust again, like a colliding pendulum.

Then it was over. The muscles in his groin seemed to collapse. Her body sagged. Klonner released her and fell back, gasping.

He lay on top of her, limp and unresponsive. Her nakedness surrounded him. She held the helpless man.

But now it was different. Louisa didn't want him between her widespread thighs. Her legs were open, her
body was still offered to him, but the ache of her desire
had turned to anger.

She let him doze for a while, thinking of other
things.

"Why are we here, Horace?" She knew her words
would awaken him, and they did.

"Huh?"

"Why have we come to Tucson?"

He was lulled, vulnerable, completely sated with
pleasure. "Jewels, darling."

"Well, of course."

He raised his head, peered into her eyes, stroked
the hair away from her forehead.

"Diamonds!" There was gloating in his voice, an
enormous satisfaction. "More diamonds than you can
imagine."

She laughed. "That, again."

His body stiffened and, for a moment, she thought
he was going to slap her a second time. And she was
sure, if he did, she would kill him.

"One year ago," he spoke softly, bragging, tortur-
ing her with the insolent beauty of his greed, "a man
left South Africa with two million dollars' worth of diamonds in a carpetbag. He was never caught."

For just a moment, Louisa was frightened. There
it was again. Millions. Horace was either lying—or
completely overcome by his own illusions. Or perhaps
he could no longer distinguish between the truth and
his own fictions. And this was the man who held
her...

But she didn't dare laugh. She did not even dare
argue with him.

"Why would he come to Tucson?" she asked.

Klonner shook his head. "He's not in Tucson, of

course." She felt him laugh. "Who could be safe in Tucson with that much loot?"

Louisa pushed him aside. She pulled her legs up, crouched in a sitting position at the head of the bed. She couldn't stand it anymore. She couldn't.

"Then what the hell are we doing here?" Her voice was sharp, damaging.

There, she had hurt him badly. But this time she felt no sympathy, no remorse. The idea of jewels, diamonds, all those glistening gems, seemed ugly, dirty and useless. There was nothing here but a dried-up town full of crude, violent men, a flea-bag hotel, a man who took his pleasure and then gave her none.

"I asked you a question, Horace. Why did you bring me here? What do you want with me? Why the hell am I here?"

"Listen, Louisa . . ." His voice quivered with a kind of boyish excitement, as if he were starting out on some new, great adventure. "There are Indian tribes all around here. They're up in the hills, along the creeks, in places no one will go because every white man in the territory is afraid of those Indians. But there's one man up there . . . a man with diamonds . . ."

"Horace—how do you know?"

She could not keep the astonishment out of her voice, for somehow, without question, she was sure he did know. He had done it again: surprised her. To him, it was all fun, all a risk. She wondered whether she ever thought about the jewels anymore—or what they would really buy. He had not even cashed in on their last haul. No, now he played for the game, and the game alone.

"Louisa, darling, have I ever been wrong?"

"No, Horace, you've never been wrong . . . about jewels."

He was hard again, pressing against her thighs. But she was far away, lost her in own thoughts.

A man from South Africa, with two million dollars' worth of diamonds! Somewhere, among the hills and streams of this awful place, he sat with his jewels, protected by the Apaches. So this was what she had traveled here for. All she had to do was say a few words to the man who called himself Brad Spear, and she would have a ticket out, away from here. Only a few words . . . her ticket to freedom. . . .

Chapter 3

First, breakfast.

Then, new clothes.

Stretching his saddle-weary muscles on the first real bed he'd enjoyed in a week, Spear got his priorities in order. A light sleeper, with ears well-tuned to the telltale creak of bedsprings, Spear knew that Klonner and Wentworth had shared a night of bliss and torment. They would, undoubtedly, be sleeping in.

There was sun shining on the dusty street. A carriage rattled through and someone yelled to someone else to get out of the goddamn way.

Birds sang. The fresh air coming through the window tasted depressingly like spring.

Spear hungered for coffee and a sordid newspaper headline.

It didn't take long to finish off two greasy scrambled eggs in the hotel dining room, and the black, fierce coffee helped kill the taste of rancid oil. The same three cups of coffee also washed out the remaining taste of springtime nostalgia and made him ready for civilization.

Spear rose from the table, laid down his money and tossed aside Tucson's only newspaper. It had plenty of information about Indian uprisings and local street fights, but not much else. The name "Underwood" appeared nowhere on its politically safe and economically secure two pages.

Leaving the hotel, Spear met another damn gust of spring air, causing another fierce wrestle with some dimwitted spirit of the past. Lord, would he ever get the Oregon woods out of his blood? The smell of his ma's bacon on a spring morning? The splash of a salmon breaking water, headed upstream? Curse the whole mess of nature anyhow, and earth's cycles with it.

He stank and needed new clothes. Priority matter.

At Anderson's General Store, he found a lightweight white shirt and a new vest made of bleached doeskin with small pockets on each side. He picked up a wide silk tie with a permanent bow, but didn't bother to put it on just yet. His pants were dark brown. The stovepipe cavalry boots were still doing their job and he kept them. As for the Stetson, it just needed dusting.

When Spear was done, there was a heap of clothes at his feet and a brand-new man standing in the middle of Anderson's General Store.

"What'll I do with those things?" asked Anderson, pointing to the pile on the floor.

"Find a criminal they fit and put 'em on for punishment," said Spear. "What do I owe you?"

When Spear had paid, he headed for the sheriff's office. The door was open. A lawman sat behind a chunky, pine desk, wearing a head of black hair that looked as if it had been lacquered. The eyebrows, too, glistened with a kind of primordial sweat, as if the man were freshly born and slicked up every morning. A badge shone from his chest. A topaz twinkled from the middle finger of his left hand. And, when he held out his right to the visitor, Spear was surprised to see that each finger displayed at least one different kind of stone. The man was a walking vanity box.

"Welcome to town, stranger. What can I do for you?"

"Want to write my last will and testament."

The sheriff shrugged.

"Well, it wouldn't be the first time. I better warn you, I'll have to charge you for ink and paper."

"Think I can afford it."

"What's your name?"

"Spear. Brad Spear."

"Help yourself, Mr. Spear. There's all the paper you need, two cents a sheet, and I filled the ink bottle this morning. If you want a notarization, that's fifty cents, and an official seal will cost you a dollar even."

"Think I can afford it," Spear repeated.

" 'Spect you can, 'spect you can. You look like a gentleman, so I won't ask to see your money first. Set yourself down right there." The sheriff waved toward a writing desk, just the right size for a ten-year-old kid, that was up against the wall. "And don't forget your Aunt Milly. She was good to you, mister."

The slicked-down sheriff could not contain his amusement at his own quip—even though it was a gibe he'd probably repeated a hundred times—and he burbled with laughter as Spear picked up paper, ink and quill, and made for the school desk.

He'd hardly begun to write when there was a rat-like scuffling at the door, and Spear looked up to see the leanest man in the West, wearing polished, patent leather shoes, hesitating in the doorway. Spear quickly returned his attention to writing, hoping that the sheriff would forget about his presence.

"What is it, Butler? What the hell do you want now?"

Pitkin's voice was bullying, having lost all traces of the deference he'd shown to Spear.

"Sorry, Mr. Pitkin. Mr. Underwood sent me."

"Of course he sent you, Butler. You wouldn't be here otherwise, would you?" Pitkin sighed a long, exasperated sigh.

"He wanted to know—did you find out who sent that Injun to kill his whore?"

"Now, look here, Butler!" Pitkin's voice broke under the awesome strain of controlling his own temper. Spear heard the rumble of a chair rolling back as the lawman got to his feet. "There's probably ten thousand Injuns in this territory and they all look the same to me and to anyone else. I'm very sorry if Mr. Underwood got himself in a pickle. I'm very sorry that whore of his got killed. But I haven't got a ghost of a chance in hell of finding out who he is or what kind a grudge he had against your boss. So you just tell your Mr. Underwood I ain't gonna spend the next year of my life running over this goddamn territory trying to chase down some invisible goddamn Indian conspiracy."

"Yes, Mr. Pitkin," replied Butler, immediately. Spear had to admit to a twinge of respect for the ratty creature. Most would have withered under the barrage from Sheriff Pitkin. But, apparently, Butler had a card up his sleeve.

"Mr. Underwood thought you might say that, Mr. Pitkin. Mr. Underwood said I should ask whether you still like your salary?"

There was a long silence. There was the rolling sound of the sheriff's chair, equipped with wooden casters, riding back to its humble place behind the desk. And there was a voice so different from the previous, bullying tone that Spear was sorely tempted to look up and find out whether someone else had come into the room.

"Yes, Butler. Tell Mr. Underwood I like my salary fine." Another pause. "Anything else?"

"Yes, Sheriff. What should we do with the dead Injun? And Lucille?"

"Put them on a meat truck and send them to Hong Kong."

"Sir?"

"Drag 'em out to the desert and leave 'em for the buzzards." Pitkin's voice was just a half-tone higher.

"Sir?"

Butler was more like a crow than a rat. Pecking at his prey. Feigning innocent subservience. The sheriff's humiliation was a delight.

"Mr. Butler, there's an undertaker in this town. It is the undertaker's job to handle corpses. It is my job to keep the law in this town. Do you have any further questions, Mr. Butler?"

"No, sir, only Mr. Underwood wanted to know . . ."

". . . Whether I like my salary. Yes, Mr. Butler, I like my salary. Now, get out of here before Mr. Underwood loses the incompetent, stupid, useless secretary who also likes his salary."

"Thank you, Sheriff."

The ratlike tread had faded to a distant skitter along the boardwalk before Spear finally looked up. Pitkin was still staring straight ahead, apparently forgetting the man against the wall who was—as far as he knew—making out his last will and testament. Escaping from the schoolboy's chair was only slightly more difficult than getting out of a pair of handcuffs, but Spear managed the feat.

"Well, I've said about all I want to say on this here paper," Spear announced.

Pitkin looked up. "Oh. You."

Spear nodded. "Now I'd just like to put this in an official envelope and seal it up."

"That'll be . . ."

"You've already stated the price, Sheriff."

Glumly, Pitkin got out an envelope. He took an alcohol lamp from the desk, lit the wick with a sulfur match and sat, listlessly, watching the blue flame. Taking up his official seal from a rack, he heated the end of it over the flame.

Spear tucked his masterwork into the envelope, folded down the flap and watched as Pitkin pressed on the hot wax. When he'd finished, Spear picked up the sealed envelope, examined the work critically, nodded and paid his money.

"This here contains certain evidence which will lead to the certain arrest and hanging of certain known criminals in the eventuality of my death," spoke Spear ponderously, pleased to sound so much like an instantaneous lawyer. It might have been his imagination, but he thought he saw Pitkin blanch.

"I thought you was doing your will!" cried the sheriff.

"Some wills say some things, some say another," replied Spear. "In any case, this is to be opened immediately upon the circumstance of my death." His lawyerlike mouthing was getting excessive. For Pitkin's sake, he thought, he'd better put it in English.

"In other words, if someone kills me, this tells you who."

"I see," said Pitkin, calming down. Apparently he had no intention of killing Spear, so he certainly was not implicated in this document. But Spear could see the wheels of lumbering thought churning under that slick mat of hair. Now the sheriff was thinking of others. Who *would* be implicated?

"I'm accustomed to handling such documents," offered Pitkin. "I'll keep it in the safe right here."

"No, but thanks," replied Spear. He was beginning to think this sheriff was genuinely amusing.

"There's no charge for that kind of service," the sheriff hastened to add.

"Then you won't be disappointed if I take it elsewhere," said Spear. "The fact is, I have a good friend in town. The blacksmith. Calls himself Quinn. You know him?"

"Yeah. I know him."

The sheriff's tone left no doubt as to his opinion of the man.

"Well, he kind of offered to hold on to a document of this kind, and I figure he's the size of man that can take care of it."

" 'Spect he is," agreed Pitkin. The black, greasy eyebrows came together, pointing at each other over a furrowed brow. "Trouble is, it won't be legal unless it's entrusted to a duly-appointed representative of the law."

The eyes that were fixed on the envelope in Brad's hands were small, greedy and just a trifle desperate.

Brad smiled again.

"Oh, that's all right," he drawled. "I'm one of those firm believers in the old adage, 'Might makes right.' And Hal Quinn, he looks to me like a man with might on his side."

Spear picked up his hat. "Well, I'd best be off."

"Mr. Spear," Pitkin's voice was icy, "you aim on getting killed any time soon?"

"Hell, no, Sheriff," replied Spear, chuckling, his voice filled to the brim with bonhomie. "But hell, Sheriff, we all gotta go some day. Never know when that old scythe's gonna sweep through."

He tucked his duly-executed will inside his shirt, alongside the Indian knife with its "Home Sweet Home" sheath, and stepped out into the fresh, spring air.

It didn't take long to deliver his package to Hal Quinn, but Spear went to some extra lengths to have himself observed. He lingered for a short while outside the sheriff's office, strolled along looking in shop windows and then stood alongside a hitching post, whistling. At last he noticed a stir of movement as the curtain was pulled back in Room 213 of the Commercial Hotel. Without looking directly at the hotel, he took some time to scratch his forehead, tighten his gunbelt and whistle the same tune in another key. Certain that Klonner was now observing his every move, Spear crossed the street and headed around the corner to Quinn's shop.

Quinn was already at work and a brief conversation guaranteed the document's safekeeping. With the sealed envelope delivered into those brawny paws, Spear felt a weight lift from his shoulders, and he hastened out the back door of the blacksmith's shop to observe the routine which, he knew, must quickly follow. Standing in the shadow of the alley wall, Spear watched as Klonner hurried out of the Commercial Hotel, briskly swinging his loaded walking stick. After a look around, Klonner side-stepped his way into the sheriff's office. It took him about ten minutes to gather from Pitkin everything that he wanted to ascertain. And then he was off again, hoofing it around the corner to Hal Quinn's shop.

The conversation that took place there could only be imagined. Spear timed it at three minutes. And he just caught a glimpse of the dapper thief, his face reddened with frustration and anger, as he headed straight for the Antelope. It would probably require six whiskeys and a round of tequila for the poor man to sort out this predicament.

But how much had Louisa told him? Spear wondered. It might be that Brad Spear and Louisa Wentworth had shared their first and last conversation together. If so, Spear realized, he was profoundly disappointed.

After Klonner had left, Spear returned to the back door of the blacksmith's shop. He was at first alarmed to hear an obdurate rumbling sound coming through the back door until he realized that it was simply Hal Quinn, once again, laughing to himself.

The giant was waiting with tears in his eyes and a story to tell.

"What did he ask you?" questioned Spear, when Quinn's hilarity had softened to a subdued chortle.

"He said he was your cousin. He said you'd changed your mind, and I was supposed to deliver the will to him."

"Well," asked Spear, "what did you tell him?"

"I told him . . ." And Quinn chuckled again, tears reappearing in his eyes. "I told him if he could come in with his head between his legs and his ass bare and jump up and down on my anvil singing 'Cockadoodle Dandy', I would be more than willing to hand over the document he requested."

"Well? What did he say to that?"

"Mr. Spear, he said nothing. The way he looked, saying nothing. . . ." Quinn shook his head and chuckled again. "Well, there are just some things men don't say that makes your whole life worth living."

Spear sacrificed his right hand in appreciation of Quinn's services. And, once again, he felt relieved by the knowledge that the document was in safe hands. Even so, as he went out the back door, Brad Spear couldn't help wondering whether sparks, heat and long hours of work couldn't unbalance the sturdiest of men, even a man like Hal Quinn.

Klonner looked up quickly when Spear came into the Antelope and the hatred in his eyes was mixed with a kind of wonder at Spear's boldness. By now, however, Spear was feeling buoyed by the spring weather. This case wasn't going to finish neatly, but right at this point, it didn't look too tangled, either. He noted that the whiskey bottle parked in front of Klonner was already one-third gone and the man's tie was askew.

Spear nodded his greeting and requested a double from the bartender.

"Got to celebrate," he announced loudly, as the drink was delivered. "Just did my last will and testament. What a load it takes off a man's shoulders just to have that out of the way. Knowing you can die in peace—well, it's a wonderful thing."

Spear looked around, as if trying to find someone to share in the celebration. Finding only Klonner nearby, Spear raised his glass, smiling.

"Here's to, stranger," he pronounced.

The look Klonner gave him would have slaughtered a mad wolfhound. But Klonner was, after all, a dandy, and his instincts of propriety prevailed. Without thinking, he lifted his shot glass and glumly clinked.

Spear smiled again, looked down.

"Say, that's quite a walking stick you got there, stranger," he went on cheerfully. "Only trouble is, you've got to keep oiling the barrel of that thing. With a one-shot like that, once she gets rusted up, she'll never shoot like you want her to." Klonner wasn't taking this well and Spear decided to cut it short. "That's just my advice, friend—you don't have to take it. Excuse me. Looks like a woman I was destined to meet sitting over there in the corner. Must be my lucky day . . ."

Spear made his way around the astonished Klonner, who neither flinched nor turned. The woman who had caught Brad's eye sat alone at a table in the back of the room.

There were only a few men around the tables this time of morning, and the only two that weren't playing poker were doing some other kind of business—probably working out a way to rustle cattle from south to north or north to south. No one looked up as Spear crossed the room, but he knew they were noticing. And when he sat down, he took the precaution of repositioning his chair about nine inches to the right. That allowed him to look in the mirror that was set on the back wall, giving him a reflected view of the whole room.

"Mr. Jenkins?" asked the woman, as he sat down.

"No," said Spear, shifting his chair another inch, checking Klonner's position at the bar. "No, I'm not Mr. Jenkins."

To his surprise, the woman seemed almost overcome with disappointment. Perhaps he was cutting in on some love tryst.

"Who is this Jenkins, anyway?"

For the first time, he studied the woman closely. To his surprise, she had bright blue eyes, though her complexion was that of an Indian. She was badly dressed. A long, baggy cotton shift hung over her shoulders like a gunny sack and she had no ornaments around her neck or wrist. So it took a second inspection to ascertain that the woman wasn't fat. She wasn't old, either. She was young, slim—and uncertain. When she learned that he wasn't Jenkins, she sat up straight, putting her hands in her lap. The fingers worked nervously and Spear could see that her brown, well-formed arms hid great strength. She wore no undergarments and the small points of her nipples could be seen clearly through the shift.

Yes, she was Indian. But those blue eyes . . .

"Oliver Jenkins," she explained. "He's from the Indian Bureau. He was supposed to come . . . last week. . . . I have waited every day."

She spoke good English, but there was something odd about her accent, as if she had acquired her pronunciation through hard study.

"Sorry to disappoint you," Spear apologized.

"No . . ." The negative response was a non sequitur, but Spear understood. Her disappointment was so visible it was almost painful to look at her.

Out of the corner of his eye, Spear noticed that Klonner, seated at the bar, was watching them. For some reason, that brought back the conversation he'd heard recently in the sheriff's office. He didn't want to frighten the girl, but still . . .

"Listen, what's your name?"

"Emma Tom," she replied.

"Pleased to meet you, Emma. I'm Brad Spear." She lifted her eyes and that was all. "I don't know where you've been spending your time, Emma, and I don't know whether you're involved. So don't take this personally." Spear lowered his voice and leaned forward. "I recently heard the sheriff discussing a lady of the night who got herself killed by an Indian. Now, I don't know whether they're going to go hunting Indians or not, but you might be smart to keep out of town for a while. There's no sense in a pretty girl getting hurt if she doesn't need to."

At the expression of fear in her eyes, Spear was instantly sorry he'd told her.

"I can't go," she stated calmly. "I must wait for Mr. Jenkins."

Spear studied her for a full minute. The girl had courage. He had to admit that.

"Why's this Jenkins so important to you?"

"Not to me, Mr. Spear." She looked at him, and again those clear, blue eyes went through him, stirring some unnecessary, womanly emotion. "To my people."

"Who are your people?"

"The Aravaipa Apache."

"But why . . . ?"

"My father was a white man," she replied. Obviously, Spear wasn't the first to wonder about her blue eyes.

"I see."

"He was killed when I was young, but he taught me English. Chief Eskaminzin also knows some English, but not as much as I."

"So you're the link?"

"Yes. I was sent to meet Jenkins. To bring him back."

"You've been waiting a whole week! Where do you sleep?"

"Out there." She waved her hand vaguely toward the hills surrounding Tucson.

"And eat . . . ?"

"I have plenty to eat."

There was stern pride in her voice.

"Tell me something, Emma. Why is it so important to find this Jenkins?"

"Eskaminzin made an agreement, with Lt. Whitman at Ft. Grant. The chief said we would give up all our rifles if the soldiers would guard us, promise us safety."

Spear gave a low whistle. "Seems like a gallant offer to me."

"No." Emma shook her head. "We are afraid. Two weeks ago, Indians raided San Xavier, south of town. They stole cattle and horses. All Apaches were blamed, though Eskaminzin's tribe had nothing to do with it. Then, three days later, four ranchers were killed in a raid on San Pedro, just east of here. Again, Aravaipa were blamed. But Lt. Whitman knows we did not do it."

"Oh? How's that?"

"We have asked him to guard us. To watch our every movement. No force of braves could leave camp, ride more than one hundred miles, make two raids and return without his knowledge."

Spear shrugged. "Then I guess you're off the hook."

"No!" She shook her head fiercely. "Lt. Whitman will keep his promises. But he cannot stop the bad men from this place."

Her eyes darted around the saloon, though her head remained motionless, as if she were registering the evil that lurked in every corner of the room. When she spoke again, her voice was low, bitter and afraid.

"In Tucson, there are vigilantes. They are called the Committee for Public Safety." She laughed sharply, a mean laugh, without humor. "They say they will protect Tucson from Indian raiders. But no Indian has raided this town in twenty years! What is their real reason? To wipe out the Apaches. The Aravaipa, and every tribe. To drive us from this country so they can have it for themselves."

"Who are these men, Emma?"

She shook her head. "There are many."

"Who leads them?"

"Oury." The word was rounded out with revulsion. Her hand went to her mouth as though she were going to be sick.

William Oury. Spear knew of the man, had heard many stories of his reputation. An Indian fighter who was a killer. A man who murdered for the sheer joy of it.

"And you think Jenkins can stop a man like Oury?"

"He must. It is our last hope. Mr. Spear, our tribe is only one hundred and sixty, and less than a third are braves. How can we hope . . . ?"

She could not finish.

"Emma, listen to me." Spear chose his words carefully. "Underwood's favorite whore was killed by an Injun. I don't know whether he was Aravaipa but that makes no difference to Underwood. Once the news gets out, every man in town is going to be looking for some Injun to string up." Again the blue penetrated his eyes, warning him, almost accusing. "For your own good, for the tribe, go back. Stay away from here, at least until this thing blows over."

"No!" The motion of her head was almost imperceptible, but as emphatic as the rapping of a gavel. "I must meet Jenkins—before they do."

"I understand," nodded Spear. "I'll keep an eye out for Jenkins. When he comes, I'll tell him what you said. Then I'll send him to you. Do you agree?"

She stood up.

"Very well," she replied. "You will not see me again. But I will be here."

At Spear's look of puzzlement, she almost laughed. Then she touched him on the shoulders.

"In the hills by the stage road. When Jenkins comes, leave your knife by the spring in the west notch."

"My knife?" Spear looked at her in astonishment. And this time she didn't try to restrain her laughter. It was a beautiful sound.

"The one with the crystal, that was given to you

yesterday by the brother of Chief Eskaminzin. His name is Chipata."

She touched him again, lightly, on the shoulder, then turned and left by the back door. It all happened so fast that Brad had to wonder whether he'd imagined the whole conversation. A glance in the mirror assured him that he hadn't. Klonner, all discretion gone, was watching in rapt fascination. Obviously, the presence of the Indian had interested him almost as much as Spear.

Meeting Klonner's eyes in reflection, Spear could not resist a broad, indiscreet wink.

The double whiskey, followed by another double, had done curious things to his sense of pace and timing, but Spear still had the presence of mind to look at the coating of flour that marked the entrance to his room. Three-thirteen had been invaded. That much was clear. A set of scuff marks, parallel and uneven, marked the place where a trespasser had crossed the threshold.

Spear didn't bother to enter. What was the point? He would only alarm the fellow, make him needlessly waste time and effort trying to match shots with Spear's .45.

Instead, Spear leaned soundlessly against the wall, his pistol ready and cocked, listening to the scufflings that took place behind the door of his room.

He resented that. Whoever was there, going through his things, had no business taking his time that way.

Finally, the door opened. A foot appeared. A pair of eyes came around the edge of the doorjamb. And Spear pointed the barrel of his .45 toward a shiny, unwrinkled forehead.

"Welcome," said Spear.

The forehead suddenly acquired a set of parallel

wrinkles, all registering concern and—along the edges—desperation.

"First," ordered Spear, coming around the corner, his six-shooter level, "drop your gun."

There was a thud.

"Back up. Thank you."

Spear stepped in as the man retreated, picked up the fallen .44 and closed the door behind him. The shiny, wrinkled forehead did not alter its sculptured appearance. Only a set of beaded drops of perspiration indicated that the man's composure might be changing.

Spear smiled. "Who are you?" He enjoyed asking the question. So many had asked him in recent hours.

"Charlie."

"Charlie," Spear repeated, patting the man's pants legs. From the man's right sock Spear procured a knife, which he tossed on the bed. Charlie's left vest pocket held a small derringer, which landed with a thud alongside the other weapon.

"You're a regular traveling armory, aren't you, Charlie?"

"It's a rough town," shrugged Charlie. The way the words came out, it sounded as if Charlie had a throat problem.

"Congestion?" asked Brad.

"Winter cold," said Charlie. "Hard to shake."

Spear's fist came up alongside Charlie's jaw, hard enough to send him sprawling but not hard enough to break anything.

"What can I get you?" asked Spear, peering down at the long, shiny-faced figure who lay sprawled on the pine wood floor.

"Nothin'," replied Charlie, rubbing his jaw.

"You sure?"

"Yeah."

"Then what the hell are you doing going through

my saddlebags?" asked Spear, pointing to the objects in question.

The saddlebags lay on the floor, wide open, their contents strewn around in disarray.

Charlie sat up slowly, backing toward the wall. "You looked rich. You looked like you had money on you."

"Sure I did," agreed Spear. "It was the jewels on my fingers that gave me away."

"Yeah."

"Wrong," corrected Spear, holding out his hands. "See? I don't have any jewels on my fingers."

"Okay. Okay. You got me. Call the sheriff."

"Glad to," replied Spear. He picked up the bag of flour that had fallen out of his saddlebags, shook his head and replaced it. "First I've got a question."

"Sure," said Charlie.

"Who do you work for?"

"Huh?"

Charlie did a tremendous imitation of looking bewildered. Spear wasn't impressed. In fact, the man's affectation of stupidity got on his nerves. Spear's right boot, moving rapidly, caught the man on the calf and he yowled in pain.

"Sorry," said Spear. "It's my nerves. I can't stand evasive answers. Who d'you work for?"

"Me?" The man was almost squealing. "I work for myself, mister. I mean, I like money. I want to make a buck, same as anybody."

"Fine," replied Spear. He sat down on the edge of the bed. There was a long silence while he and Charlie examined each other, and all the time, Spear focused the end of his .45 on Charlie's midriff. Finally, Spear sighed.

"Let's go see Mr. Underwood," he proposed.

"No!" The man's answer was immediate and revealing. Had there been any doubt in Spear's mind, it was immediately cleared by the man's response.

"Sure. Why not?"

Charlie's eyes shifted, looking for the way out, and for the first time, he seemed to be contemplating desperate moves.

"I wouldn't," warned Spear in response to the man's unspoken intentions. "You'd only end up dead."

Apparently, the agent's voice carried conviction. Charlie didn't move.

"Now, here's the sequence," explained Spear. "You get to your feet slowly. You lead me across the street to Mr. Underwood's. You tell him there's someone to see him. And then you show me in."

"But . . . but Mr. Underwood has nothing to do with this."

"Of course he doesn't," agreed Spear, his voice dry, without conviction. "That's why it will be so wonderful to see him. It's always good to have a third party in a case like this."

"You son of a bitch," Charlie broke out. "I've got a right to see the sheriff . . ."

This time, the toe of Spear's boot made contact with a soft portion of the man's belly, and Charlie doubled up, gasping for breath.

"Yup," said Spear. "There's nothing worse than having the wind knocked out of you."

He picked up the man by his left arm, at the same time holstering his revolver. With an urgency that seemed out of character, Spear helped Charlie stumble across the room, ushered him out the door and led him solicitously down the stairs.

"Better work on your security," he advised the astonished desk clerk, as he urged Charlie out into the afternoon sun.

"Got your wind?" he asked when they were outside. Charlie dragged his way from the boardwalk into the dusty street.

Charlie nodded, sending Spear a look of sheer hatred.

"Good," nodded Spear, smiling. "Lead the way."

Suddenly desperate, Charlie turned and ran. In two paces, Spear was on him, and the hard chop descending on Charlie's right shoulder brought him to the dust. He lay amidst the horse droppings, groaning and clutching his bruised shoulder.

A crowd was gradually assembling—mostly cowpunchers standing by the hitching rails, gaping and sharing bets.

"This-here's a thief," shouted Spear. "Anyone know him?"

He looked all around, while Charlie, still clutching his shoulder, tried to regain his feet.

No one responded to Spear's query.

"Didn't think so," he went on. "That's a shame, Charlie. Looks like you've got no friends in this town. Who was it you wanted to see?"

Spear was rewarded with another look of pure hatred.

"That's right! Mr. Underwood! Right this way."

Spear gestured with his hand. Like a wounded animal, Charlie stumbled forward, aiming in the general direction of the grey-blue building that bore the sign "Underwood & Sons, Merchandise."

Spear ushered his companion into the cool, grey dimness of the first-floor office, where a gleaming pair of patent leather shoes immediately caught his attention. Smiling broadly, Spear nodded to the clerk whom he had only recently seen in the sheriff's office.

"Mr. Butler, I believe?"

The thin secretary, flattered to be so well-known, nodded briskly.

"Meet Mr. Charlie, the petty thief."

Butler's smile faded. Charlie's eyes focused on the wall and his gaze attempted to climb through a slight gap in the window sash.

"Guess you've met," surmised Spear. "Mr. Charlie would like to see Mr. Underwood."

"I'm sorry, sir," replied Butler quickly. "Mr. Underwood isn't in just now."

"I'm sure he isn't, Butler," said Spear, pulling out his .45. "So if you would please just stand out of the way, we'll go look for him."

Butler's mouth fell open. He probably couldn't help it. Still, the teeth were not well cared for, and they made a gruesome sight—mottled, as they were, with black and green areas of decay. The sight bordered on the repulsive.

"Close it, Butler," ordered Spear, as he ushered Charlie up the back stairway.

On the landing, Spear took two steps backward, pushed open the door to Underwood's office and shoved Charlie through. He heard the sound of a chair being pushed back, heard an overweight man get to his feet. Heard a voice saying, "Charlie—what the hell . . . ?"

That was all the confirmation Spear required.

Stepping in through the open door, Spear's eyes met Underwood's. The fatter man backed off, his jowls working as though he were eating something distasteful.

"Who are you?" The voice was husky, tinged with desperation.

"Chief Sitting Bull," responded Spear. "Happy to introduce Charlie. Keep him out of my room, Mr. Underwood. I'm warning you. Trespassers make me reckless."

Turning on his heel, Spear slammed the door and

started down the stairs. For a man who ran a town, Mr. Underwood was a crushing disappointment, Spear thought. Too phlegmatic to make a good impression.

At the bottom of the stairs, Spear started out the front door, then noticed that Butler still stood precisely where Spear had left him, mouth still agape.

"For God's sake, Butler, shut that trap!" yelled Spear.

Slowly, the jaw closed, meeting the upper lip.

"That's better."

Spear went out, annoyed at his own irritability. After all, it wasn't Butler's fault. He just happened to work for the wrong man. In the wrong place. At the wrong time in history.

Hell, Butler's whole existence was inexcusable. But that was no reason to get mad at him.

Chapter 4

For several long minutes after Brad Spear left the office, the loudest sound in the room was the steady dripping of the water in Underwood's cooling system. Charlie stood with his back against the far wall, avoiding Underwood's eyes and rubbing his chin assiduously. Underwood's thumbs were hooked in his suspenders. He swayed back and forth, rocking on his heels. His bulging eyes blinked, froglike.

"Good job, Charlie."

"I'm sorry, Mr. Underwood. I . . ."

"Fine job. Caught redhanded with your pants down. I don't suppose you found anything in his room?"

Underwood looked at the man quizzically, but Charlie's expression revealed hopelessness.

"I went through his saddlebags," recounted Charlie. "Wasn't much there. A change of clothes, bay rum and rose water, some flour . . ."

"Flour?" Underwood looked up.

Charlie shuffled his feet, embarrassed.

"Yes, sir, couldn't figure that one out. Didn't seem like there was enough there to make a half loaf of bread, much less keep a man alive on the trail."

"No, Charlie, I don't reckon it was for eating."

"Then what the hell do you figure?"

"I figure he spread some outside the door so he could see the mark of your big clodhoppers."

"Oh."

"It's an old trick, Charlie. Old as the hills. I suspect that's how he caught you."

"Son of a bitch."

"You're stupid, Charlie."

"Yes, sir."

"You're fired."

Charlie rubbed his jaw. Underwood crossed the room and put his face up close to the greasy, smooth features of his hired man. The way Charlie drew back—either from fear or revulsion—made Underwood smile.

"That's a terrible black-and-blue mark you've got there," said Underwood softly. "You'd better have someone look at it."

Underwood gently reached for the man's jaw, like a considerate physician examining a patient. His stubby, tender fingers lifted Charlie's head and smoothly turned the man's cheek to one side so that Underwood could get a better look at the bruise. The fat man clucked softly, then squeezed hard with his thumb and forefinger, bringing pressure to bear on the bruised area. A choked cry escaped Charlie, a half-scream that seemed to get tangled up in the man's larynx.

Underwood released him.

"Yep, Charlie. Mean-looking bruise. You'd better have someone look after that."

Without looking at his employer, Charlie turned, tore the door open and rushed out.

Underwood shook his head, crossed the room and looked out the window. Today was hotter than yesterday, with a slighter breeze to turn the windmill, and the cooling system was having less effect than it should. He sighed and wiped a few beads of moisture from his forehead.

His annoyance with Charlie was genuine. The man who'd signed himself into the Commercial Hotel as "Brad Spear" had been asking questions about Underwood. The businessman knew that. He didn't like questions being asked about himself. It put a man at a disadvantage. And he had no idea who this Brad Spear might be.

Charlie's assignment had been so simple. Go to the room, use the passkey (Underwood had a set for every hotel and boarding house in town) and find out what this Brad Spear was up to. Such a simple assignment. So ridiculously easy. And the man had failed utterly. All that Charlie had discovered was that Brad Spear used bay rum and rose water.

"Idiot!" roared Underwood, stamping his foot. With a gesture that was like a seizure, he grabbed an orange from a bowl on his desk and began peeling it frantically, letting the juices drip into the spittoon. At least the oranges had arrived. It seemed as if that was the only good thing that had happened since yesterday afternoon's stage pulled into town.

The stubby fingers clutched spasmodically at the orange, juices shot from the pulp, as Underwood recalled the events of the previous evening.

That Indian. Where had he seen him before?

Underwood tried to erase from his memory those flashing, dark eyes, the grimace of anger that suffused the face of the Indian when he attacked. Feeling the orange juice flow through his fingers, Underwood was compelled to recall, once again, the blood of the Indian flowing over his head, down his cheeks.

He shuddered.

That face. Where had he seen that face?

Then it came back to him. The year before, Underwood had made an elegant trade arrangement—guns for gold. He had no doubt about how the Indians came by their gold. The paymaster's shipment from San Francisco was waylaid in the mountains west of Tucson. Its valuable cargo disappeared. When an Indian—this Indian, the one whose face was so vividly imprinted on Underwood's memory—came to visit him, Underwood was prepared to name a high price. He'd sold the man twelve rifles and had managed to collect the entire shipment of gold in return—more than one hundred dollars per rifle. But Underwood had also made certain that the shells were faulty, little better than blanks. After striking his deal with the Indian, Underwood had alerted the Committee for Public Safety. A nighttime raid did the rest. Underwood had his gold, and the Committee had the rifles. As head of the Committee, Underwood had the pleasant duty of re-selling the rifles.

It was a business that had a bright future.

The Indian must have escaped from that nighttime raid. Lucky Indian. Underwood smiled to himself. That luck made no difference now. The Indian was dead.

Still, Underwood was nervous. There were loose ends. The murderous attack last night had been too close, too personal. No one knew where the murderous savage had come from. Or how he got into Lucille's room.

Underwood felt himself rising at the memory of Lucille's hot body, her moist depths.

There was a knock at the door.

"Come in!" he cried irritably.

"Someone here to see you, Mr. Underwood," announced Butler, sticking his head in.

"Who is it, Butler?"

"He says his name is Horace Klonner."

Klonner. Underwood couldn't think of anyone in town named Klonner. And with things going the way they were, he didn't want to take any chances. Crossing to his desk, he opened the drawer, took out a Colt New Model Pocket Pistol with a three and one-half inch barrel, and slid it into his inside vest pocket.

"Show him in, Butler."

A six-footer, the stranger was wearing a black frock coat and felt slouch hat. He removed the hat as he came through the door, and glanced quickly around the room. The strong scent of whiskey accompanied him, but he seemed well composed. He was carrying a walking stick, which he kept tucked under his left arm. To Underwood's annoyance, the man's eyes rested appreciatively on the portrait of Franklin Underwood that hung above the desk.

"Your father?" asked Klonner, as he pulled off his black gloves. Underwood could not restrain a wrinkle of distaste at the stranger's boldness, but he gave a slight, almost imperceptible nod. "Ah, yes," continued Klonner. "I thought there might be a connection."

He held out his hand and Underwood responded without enthusiasm, keeping his feet firmly planted.

"Quite a man—your father," commented Klonner with a smile.

Was this uninvited stranger trying to get on his nerves, Underwood wondered, or did he just have a natural knack for the inappropriate remark?

"What can I do for you?" demanded Underwood.

"A great deal, I believe," responded Klonner, dropping any pretense of politeness. "I trust you've never heard of me."

Underwood shook his head.

"Good." Klonner managed a thin smile. "That's

the way I like it. I, however, have heard of you. I understand that you are the head of the Tucson Committee for Private Safety."

"*Public* safety," corrected Underwood.

"Public, of course. Excuse me."

"And I am not the head, as you put it," Underwood hastened to add. "I am simply one committee member among many others."

"Of course. Do you mind if I smoke?"

Underwood waved his hand, but he was secretly annoyed. The atmosphere in his office had already become stifling, with noontime still an hour away. He didn't need the addition of cigar smoke to increase the discomfort.

Nonetheless, the stranger took his time lighting up. Without invitation, he helped himself to a chair. Underwood remained standing. It was as if Klonner had taken over his office—his office!—and Henry Underwood was helpless to do anything about it. That slight injustice got on his nerves. He could feel himself working toward a rage.

"I have a small matter to settle with an Indian tribe not far from here," Klonner began. "The Aravaipa Apaches. I believe you've heard of them?" He hesitated only an instant for confirmation. "Good. The matter does not concern the Indians themselves, but a white man who is presumed to be living among them."

"Who?" asked Underwood.

Klonner waved his hand and peered at the end of his cigar.

"The name is of no importance. I merely wish to present the situation so that you may be able to judge accordingly, and to act in your own best interests."

Some ash fell to the floor and, for an instant, Underwood seriously considered calling Charlie and having this man thrown out of his office. Then he remembered that he had just fired Charlie.

"Damn," he swore softly.

"Beg pardon?"

"You were speaking of my best interests," Underwood tried to cover himself.

"Ah—yes. You see, the gentleman in question and myself had a business arrangement. Again, the actual substance of the business is not relevant. Suffice it to say he reneged on certain promises. I am most anxious to meet with him and conclude our dealings."

"I see, Mr. Klonner. There are numerous scouts in the vicinity. I am sure they would be glad to guide you to the Aravaipa. Now, if you don't mind. . . ."

Klonner smiled and waved his hand. "You misunderstand me, Mr. Underwood. You see, I am convinced that the gentleman is content among the Indians. He will not willingly leave. As I understand it, the Aravaipa have a small camp with an insufficient number of braves. It should be an easy matter for the Committee for Private . . ."

"Public!" Underwood shouted.

"Public, of course," Klonner corrected himself softly. "As I was saying . . . for the Committee for Public Safety to resolve."

"Mr. Klonner," replied Underwood impatiently. "I think you overestimate my influence with the committee. We are not in the habit of making war on the Indians. We do not wish to inflame rivalries. We act solely on behalf of the citizens of Tucson. And only when a situation of emergency makes our self-defense necessary."

"Mr. Underwood!" Klonner cut him off, getting to his feet. He was no longer smiling and his walking stick was pointed forward at an acute and slightly accusatorial angle, as if the tip of the long, black cane would make his point of view perfectly clear.

"Mr. Underwood, I am familiar with your influence on the Committee and I know I do not underestimate your power or ability. The fact is, I do not intend to waste time on a futile enterprise. I intend to pay and pay well. For the delivery of the gentleman I have just mentioned, I am willing to pay thirty thousand dollars."

The first notice Underwood had that his whole body was in jeopardy was a weakening of the knees. This symptom was followed by intense salivation accompanied by an almost crippling wave of heat that swept its way over his body.

"Did you say. . . ?" Underwood's question ended in choked amazement. He backed toward his chair, reached behind him without looking and sat down. He found a handkerchief inside his coat pocket and wiped his forehead.

"Yes. Thirty thousand."

"How do I know. . . ?"

"Of course, I am willing to pay half now, assuming the—uh—visit to the Aravaipa can be arranged . . ."

"Anything can be arranged, Mr. Klonner. Anything." As Underwood looked up at the tall man in black, he felt compelled to speak his words with a great—and earnestly felt—intensity of conviction. Thirty thousand! The figure filled him with a kind of radiance. It was as if God had walked in the room, blessed him with great powers. All his life, at the edge of this dung hole in the desert, he had waited—waited for just such a moment as this.

"Very good," replied Klonner, his smile restored. "And the tribe of Indians. . . ?"

"As good as gone," assured Underwood, trying to

hide his trembling hands as he replaced the handkerchief in his pocket. He smiled weakly. "What form of payment?"

"I have fifteen bills here," stated Klonner. He crossed to the desk and slid the small stack of one thousand dollar bills under Mr. Underwood's inkwell.

Klonner smiled down at the seated businessman, his eyes roving up and down the supine figure as if he were some quivering, curious reptile sunning itself on a verandah.

"I would, of course, appreciate it if our business arrangement were. . . ."

"Of course, of course." Underwood waved his hand. His eyes were fixed on the money, his lips wet with anticipation.

"I regret the necessity of making myself perfectly clear," explained Klonner. He bent over Underwood, the intense, black points of his eyes coming within inches of the bloated man's face. "But I think it is essential for our relationship that there be no misunderstanding. If, through any circumstances whatsoever, the word of our arrangement should be learned by others, I will be forced to kill you, Mr. Underwood."

Underwood's jowls rippled. He felt himself quivering, almost crushed by the awareness of his own intense fear of death. It was as if that horrible Indian had leapt on him once again. But with the last, vanishing vestige of his pride, he controlled his fear. His voice, when he spoke, managed to convey a certain dignified outrage.

"If that is a threat, Mr. Klonner, you can damn well take your money and . . ."

"No, Mr. Underwood, it is not a threat. It is a statement of fact."

Underwood tried to stand up, failed and sank back in his chair. With his beady eyes fixed on the

older, fatter man, Klonner slowly replaced his black
felt hat on his head, hung his walking stick over the
crook of his arm and dropped the stub end of his cigar
in the inkwell that held down the pile of bills. With a
tight smile and nod, he turned and walked out.

The lingering smell of cigar smoke made Underwood want to vomit. His mind, however, was still on
the money. His fingers reached out to extract the wad
of paper from underneath the inkwell. Deliberately,
anxiously, he counted the pile; then again, and again.
Finally, with a mighty wheeze at the effort, he hoisted
himself from his chair, turned to Franklin Underwood's
portrait and swung back the old, white-haired Indian
fighter to reveal the dial of a wall safe.

Money safely stashed, Underwood swung the portrait back into position and stared up at his father, the
hatred burning in his eyes.

"Bastard," he whispered at the glowering physiog-
nomy. "You may have been a hero, but you never had
that kind of money. Did you, old man? Did you?"

With the last words, Henry Underwood's voice
rose one shrill, quavering half-tone. It was a voice that
bordered on a shriek. A shriek that bordered on hysteria. As the words died on his lips, Underwood sat
down quickly, his hand on his heart. He did not feel at
all well—not at all.

"Butler!" he shouted. "Butler—come here immediately!"

The figure slouched in the back of the Antelope
Saloon was hard to decipher. Judging from the intelli-
gent, cold grey eyes, the man might have been a lawyer, politician or banker. But there was something in
his demeanor which belied this interpretation. His face
was tanned, hardened, and he had a three-days' growth
of beard. Around the corners of his mouth there were

signs of cruelty and when he broke into a smile—
which he did now and then—there was nothing soft or
appreciative in his expression. He used his eyes to
assess. He used his mouth for biting words. He used
his laugh for the final humiliation.

Yet he did not sit alone. Each of the men who
drifted into the bar made sure, in an offhand way, that
he stopped by the man's table, if only to nod and say a
few words. Some wore the same kind of sweat-stained
buckskins as the man in the chair. But there were others—in broadcloth and linen—who also paused at the
table to pay their respects. During the course of the afternoon, a large number of these conversationalists
bought drinks for William S. Oury, former mayor of
Tucson. He accepted all gifts.

The conversation revolved, with few exceptions,
around a single topic.

"Understand there's been some Indian trouble
around San Xavier," began one of the men, signaling
the bartender to fill up Mr. Oury's glass.

Oury remained passive.

"There's always Indian trouble," he remarked. He
stirred in his chair, and his eyes shifted laterally, as if
he were tired of the subject. "Too goddamn many Indians. Always have been. Maybe you don't remember my
ticket when I was mayor, Mr. Godspeed."

"Oh, I certainly do, Bill," replied his partner at
the table, leaning forward. "You said we'd keep the
redskins out of town and, by God, we did. Wasn't a
damn one of them dared showed his face here when
you was mayor."

The man called Godspeed had the face of a
cherub—pink, self-satisfied and innocent. He was a
part-time judge and part-time druggist, and it was said
that his professional library consisted of two volumes,
Materia Medica and *Fractured Bones*. To make sure

the streets of Tucson stayed clean—and to empty the jail of local, petty offenders—he had instituted a work-gang system of punishment. From petty thieves to cold-blooded criminals, Tucson convicts were inevitably sentenced to cleaning latrines and sweeping the streets.

"They're gettin' out of hand again," continued Godspeed, leaning forward confidentially. "I can read the signs, loud and clear. You heard tell of the raid on San Xavier?"

"Yeah, I heard," Oury cut in. He tossed back a shot of whiskey. As the glass rapped on the table, the bartender immediately came forward to refill it.

A shadow fell across their table. Godspeed looked up, pushed back his chair and almost fell over himself getting out of the way.

"Why Señor Delgado, pleasure to see you. Pleasure. Pull up a chair, won't you?"

"I have come to speak with Oury," replied the man icily. He was a Mexican, slight and wiry, elegantly dressed in a black jacket profusely ornamented with rows of toggles and silver buttons.

Oury looked up. The whiskey was already having an effect on him and his eyes were watery. With drink, the look of cruelty on his face had deepened.

"What happened?" asked Oury.

"It was Injuns, all right," said Delgado. "I would guess . . . ," he hesitated and shrugged. There was a whip in his hand that he flipped against his calf. "Forty, perhaps fifty."

Godspeed whistled and Oury looked sideways at his table partner as though he were some kind of bug. Delgado remained standing.

"That's a large number of Indians, Señor Delgado."

"*Si.*"

"What did they steal?"

"Sixty head of cattle. We recovered most of them."

"Kill any Injuns?"

"Just one." The riding crop smacked fitfully against the tight, lace-trimmed riding breeches.

"Recognize him?"

"He's an Aravaipa. From Ft. Grant."

"See there!" cried Godspeed, banging his hand down on the table. "I told you Whitman couldn't control them."

"Shut up," ordered Oury. He looked steadily at Delgado for a moment. "You sure?"

The riding crop fluttered. Delgado refused to meet the eyes of the former mayor.

"Si!" he replied quickly.

"You better be damn sure," muttered Oury.

The crop was moving at the pace of a hummingbird's wings. *"Si! Si!"*

"Did you bring the corpse?"

The Mexican wrinkled his nose and shook his head. He reached in his pocket, drew out a string of beads and tossed them on the table. Patches of dried blood clung to the beads.

Oury stared at the beads for a long moment, then handed them back.

"I'll take your word for it, Delgado." He looked up at the Mexican. "It occurs to me the Committee for Public Safety should be gettin' organized pretty soon. How many of your men can I count on?"

Delgado shrugged, but for the first time his face was illumined by a smile.

"Forty, forty-two," he estimated.

Oury nodded. "That'll do."

The Mexican, considerably relieved, whipped his calf one more time with the riding crop, turned and strode away without a word. But his presence and the conversation had been noted by a large number of men in the room.

"Oury!" Godspeed burst out when the Mexican had left. "You can't ride on Ft. Grant. Whitman's promised protection for them Injuns. If you go up there, it'll be an illegal action against the government of the United States." There was a look of panic in the face of the pink-complexioned lawmaker.

"What do you want, Godspeed? Do you want the babies in this town to be slaughtered? Do you want the women raped?"

Oury's voice was loud and belligerent. Godspeed looked over his shoulder, suddenly aware that the clink of glasses and buzz of conversation had ceased abruptly.

"No! Of course not! Of *course* not!" Godspeed insisted, suddenly aware that his public image was on the line. "All I'm saying is—you can't ride against the cavalry."

"For your information, Mr. Godspeed, I ain't riding against the cavalry." Oury got to his feet, plunked his fists down on the center of the table as he leaned forward. "I'm riding against the thievin', bloodthirsty Injuns that stole the cattle from San Xavier. I'm riding against the same redskins that'll come in this town and rape *your* wife and roast *your* little daughter on the fire, Mr. Godspeed."

"Oury, I resent that. I take exception."

"You can take any kind of exception you want, Godspeed. Those are the facts. This town's in danger. We're all in danger. I don't care if the cavalry's protecting them, or if Satan's sister is standin' on their side, those savages ain't gonna get away with it. Now you can ride with me or you can stay in town, Mr. Godspeed. But don't come crying to me when you find your little girl skewered on a spit with her eyeballs stickin' out. 'Cause that's what they do, Mr. Godspeed. That's what them Injuns do."

Oury's voice had fallen very low by the time he said his last words, but he didn't need to speak any louder. Every man in the room was listening. All other sounds were hushed. And when William Oury picked up his hat, walked around Godspeed as if he were some pillar of manure and made his way out of the room looking neither right nor left, every eye in the room was upon him.

Brad Spear tilted the rickety, high-backed chair against the wall of the stage depot, folded his hands in his lap and tried to figure out what was going on across the street. About ten minutes before, a group of six men, all bareheaded, all wearing handcuffs, had emerged from the sheriff's office, followed closely behind by Sheriff Pitkin carrying a revolving-cylinder .75 caliber shotgun. Spear's first concern, that he might become an unwilling witness to a mass hanging was banished abruptly when Sheriff Pitkin, stepping around the side of the jailhouse, got out five brooms and handed one to each of the convicts. Then, while Spear watched and while Pitkin sat at ease on the jailhouse steps, chewing tobacco, the five men started sweeping the street.

Spear was roused from his reverie by a footstep on the porch alongside him and he looked up to see Frank Emory. The kid was still wearing the same plaid shirt and buckskin chaps he'd had on the previous day, and the smudges on his face had neither been erased nor rearranged in the intervening hours.

"Still alive, huh?" asked Spear.

The kid nodded. "You might not remember my name. I'm . . ."

Spear waved his hand in dismissal. "Frank Emory. I know. I've got a question for you, Frank."

"Go ahead."

"Those jailhoots over there?"

"Yeah?"

"What in the name of Sam Hill's blessed graveyard are they doin'?"

"Sweepin' the streets."

Spear winced. He looked up at the kid and was pleased to find him grinning. Spear grinned right back.

"Kid, where I come from, an answer like that is said to reveal weakness of the spirit and a shortage of brain matter."

"Well, mister," said Emory, unfazed by Spear's comment, "our local justice, Mr. Godspeed, has the idea that prisoners should be put to work for punishment. And seein' as how the streets always need cleaning around here . . ."

"I see," replied Spear.

For a couple of minutes, the two of them just watched as the brooms moved briskly, stirring up clouds of dust in the dry air. Then, without turning his head, Spear observed, "But that's not what you came to see me for."

"No," admitted Frank. He shifted his weight and played nervously with a brass button on his chaps. "Yesterday, Mr. Spear, you mentioned you might need a hand doing something or other. I just want to say I appreciate the offer. And seeing as how I'm not too tied up right now . . ."

"Two dollars a day?"

"What do I do?"

"First thing you can do," requested Spear, handing Emory two shining silver pieces, "is tell me who's coming out of the Antelope."

Emory glanced quickly at the well-dressed Mexican who stepped to the rail, untied a set of reins and quickly mounted an all-white horse.

"Delgado," said Emory softly. There was no love in his voice. "Enrique Delgado. Formerly the governor of Sonora."

"A Mexican with money, apparently," commented Spear.

"Si!" Frank hissed, sarcasm dripping from his voice. "He would slit his brother's throat for money."

A moment later, a tall Indian came out of the general store alongside the stage depot. He stood on the porch under the wide overhang, obviously enjoying the shade. There was something familiar about the Indian and, as Spear examined the man's outfit, he suddenly realized it was the Apache he had met on the trail, the man who had given him the knife. From his conversation with the Indian girl, Spear now knew, this must be Chief Eskaminzin's brother, Chipata. Spear dropped the front two legs of his chair to the porch and was about to call out to the Indian when Frank Emory's excited whisper cut him short.

"Holy Christ!" There was awe in his voice. "Now we got trouble."

Following the direction of the kid's gaze, Spear saw a bullish, ragged man dressed in greasy buckskins step from the door of the Antelope. Though obviously drunk, the man looked fiercely alert, like a winter bear who had just stumbled out of his cave, ready for trouble. Something about the man commanded attention. And fear: a woman in a summer frock, accompanied by her child, quickly pulled the little boy inside the door of the general store.

"Mama, I want to see . . ." The boy's voice was cut off as he vanished into the interior of the store.

"Who is he?" asked Spear, getting to his feet.

"Oury," replied Emory, glancing from the Indian to Oury and back again.

"So that's William Oury," exclaimed Spear appreciatively. "Looks like something the dogs dragged in."

"Shit," mumbled Emory, more to himself than to Spear. "I don't want to be here. I sure as *hell* don't want to be here."

It took Spear an instant to understand what the kid was talking about. But gradually, the realization dawned. Within seconds of his exit from the Antelope, Oury had spotted the Indian outside the general store. Now Oury stood his ground, his body swaying slightly, his lip curling, watching the Indian, waiting to see what he would do. Though the Indian gave no visible sign of recognition, it was obvious to Spear—and to the small cluster of men who had begun to gather in the street—that the Apache would not leave town unchallenged.

Chipata did not appear to be ruffled by the attention he attracted, nor did he seem to notice the stir he created when he stepped down to the street and started across to the hitching rail. His destination was obvious—a light-grey pinto, wearing a brand-new girth and saddle, stood with its head bowed to the hitching rail. At Chipata's approach, the horse put its upper teeth on the rail and backed, stomping its hind foot, snorting nervously.

Oury watched, a sneer spreading across his face, as Chipata came toward the hitching rail. A few uneven steps brought the Indian fighter into the street where he stood belligerently between the Apache and his horse.

Chipata stopped and looked at the white man.

"Where you goin', Injun?" Oury's voice dripped with hate.

Chipata eyed the man from head to foot, his face

impassive. Then he started around the white man. Oury laughed and stepped sideways, bringing himself between the Indian and his horse again.

"Good saddle you've got there, Injun," declared Oury, raising his voice for the benefit of the crowd that was now pouring out of the Antelope. "Too good for a low-down Injun, if you ask me. Where'd you get it?"

Chipata shook his head and, again, tried to pass his antagonist. Oury refused to give ground.

"I asked where you got it, you son of a bitch."

"Trade," replied Chipata. The simple word, spoken like a declaration of truth, was met with a derisive chorus of hoots from the men outside the Antelope.

"You got it from San Xavier—didn't you, Redskin?" Oury mocked the man, sneering. "Ain't that where you stole it, you thievin' muskrat?"

"No!" His eyes fixed on Oury, the Indian shook his head. "Trade!" Again, the word met with derision. But this time, the men's hilarity was mixed with anger. They stirred restlessly, anxious for blood.

"Fight!" demanded Oury.

The Indian shook his head.

"Come on, you bloody redskin. You want your horse? Fight for it."

The Indian waited, the subtle tensing of his body barely perceptible to those who watched.

"Come on," urged Oury softly, unsheathing his knife. Still, the Indian did not move. The group had closed in on him now, and the cacophony of shouted insults was almost deafening. Grinning broadly, Oury stepped forward, knife outstretched, pointing. The glistening steel tip approached the bare, muscular, brown belly of the Indian who looked straight ahead, peering haughtily into Oury's face, ignoring the weapon. Oury took another step and the tip of his knife pressed the

Indian's stomach, probing forward until the indentation made a shadow below the man's ribs.

The Indian's motion was so quick that Oury was lying sprawled in the dust, reaching for his knife, before anyone knew what had happened. Chipata had simply stepped aside and, with one brief, efficient motion, landed a chop to the man's neck.

Shouting, the men surged forward, ready to lynch the Indian if he attacked. Chipata watched. Waiting for Oury to get to his feet, the Indian took from his belt a long strip of narrow cloth.

Oury struggled up, shaking his head, the knife in his hand once again. The blow had made him alert and all signs of drunkenness were gone. Now there was just the rage in his eyes—a venomous anger reflected in the expressions of all the men around him.

"You'll die, Redskin," he threatened.

Chipata lifted the end of the cloth to his lips, gripped it between his teeth. The other end he tossed to Oury, who caught it. There was a moment's hesitation and a trace of fear flickered across Oury's face. But he knew the ritual, as did the other men around him. This was the Indian way to fight. To refuse was to admit to cowardice.

Oury clutched the end of the cloth between his teeth, biting hard.

Only then did the Indian unsheath his knife. Linked by the cloth in their clenched jaws, the two men circled, facing each other by necessity, two spiders locked in mortal combat.

Oury's blade licked out, whisked across the Indian's forearm. Blood spurted, leaping from the flesh wound. The crowd murmured, pressed forward.

Chipata dove for the dust, rolled, came to his feet again, the cloth still between his teeth, and his blade

stabbed, catching the white man's leg. Oury stumbled
and, for a moment, it looked as if he would go down.

The Indian's blade shot up, going for the kill, but
Oury met it with his blade and there was the clash of
steel on steel. They held for a moment, both forearms
trembling with the strain. Blood spilled from the punc-
ture in Oury's leg, soaking his buckskins, running to
the ground. With the pressure of their deadlock, blood
oozed from Chipata's wounded forearm.

They spun apart. The contestants backed up,
arms spread, teeth clenched, just out of reach, both
panting with the struggle. The cloth that linked them
had become a part of them, a part of their hold on
each other. So close to each other, only a flicker away
from death, they could neither approach nor flee. The
cloth bound them. The flashing knives held them apart.
They could circle and circle forever, until one of them
lost attention, one of them made a mistake.

Oury feinted left and the Indian slashed out to cut
him. It was a hard stroke that drew blood. The knife
came up again just as suddenly, drawing blood a second time—and Oury screamed through clenched teeth.
But the feint was a calculated slip. It gave him time—
only an instant. In that instant he pulled a gun from his
belt. It took him only a fraction of a second to cock it
and pull the trigger.

The blast of gunfire roared in the crowded street.
The bullet burrowed into the dust. The gun fell from
nerveless fingers. Oury's jaws unlocked and the cloth
fell from his open teeth. He fell to the ground,
clutching his side where the tip of Brad Spear's boot
had pounded into the fighter's ribs.

"You don't fight fair," said Spear, looking down
at the Indian fighter. He turned to the Indian, and
spoke a few words in Apache. Chipata slipped the
knife into his belt, turned and walked toward his horse.

He didn't get far. The men closed around him, grumbling for revenge.

"Back off!" The voice was above them. It was a voice that commanded attention, respect. Instinctively, now behaving as a herd, like a mass of blind sheep responding to the bark of a dog, the men turned to see who had spoken.

Hal Quinn stood on the boardwalk, a double-barrel shotgun in his hand.

"Mount up, Injun," he ordered. Chipata untied his reins from the hitching rail and with one, smooth motion leapt into the saddle. The grey pinto backed up, alarmed by the crowd that surrounded it. The Indian wheeled his horse and galloped off. The men stirred restlessly, looked at each other, then at the barrel of Quinn's rifle. Quinn waited.

When the puff of dust had disappeared from the edge of town and the sound of horses' hooves had faded in the distance, Quinn tucked the rifle under his arm, tipped his hat to the men, turned and strode back along the boardwalk in the direction from which he had come.

Oury struggled to his feet, holding his side, glaring at Spear.

"I won't forget this, stranger. You protected an Indian, mister. A murderin', thievin', no good savage . . ."

"Shut it, Oury," replied Spear. "You're drunk."

He crossed the street to the stage depot, nodding to Frank Emory who nodded back, his mouth open in amazement. Spear mounted the few steps to the porch, sat down in the high-backed chair, tipped it against the wall and lowered his Stetson over his eyes.

"He'll pay," predicted Oury, stumbling as he moved toward the Antelope.

But deep down he knew that the Indian came close to winning that fight. William S. Oury, Indian fighter, was slowing down. Getting old. He'd fought hard and this was what he'd won. Nothing. The damn savages were taking over the country and there wasn't a man left to stand up to them.

"He'll pay," muttered Oury again, shaking his head murderously. "By God, he'll pay."

The few men who bothered to listen couldn't tell whether he was talking about the Indian or that stranger in town who had just given William S. Oury, former mayor, a kick in the ribs. Most of them didn't care. Somehow, they all thought to themselves, Oury didn't seem quite the man that he used to be.

Only one man approached him at the table.

At the sight of gleaming, patent-leather shoes, Oury looked up.

"What is it, Butler? What the hell do you want?"

"Excuse me, Mr. Oury," Butler apologized. "Mr. Underwood would like to see you. I'm sorry, but he says it's urgent."

Chapter 5

"You can put him on the bed, Charlie," said Louisa Wentworth, opening the door of Horace G. Klonner's room at the Depot Hotel.

The sweat glistened on Charlie's forehead and he grunted under the weight of his load. Moving slowly, with the care of a man who knew he was drunk and didn't want to show it, Charlie carried his burden across the room and eased it down on the edge of the bed.

Horace Klonner's head flopped forward. His smart, felt hat had fallen off long ago, but Louisa had retrieved it and carried the hat respectfully in one hand.

"Here, let me help you with him," she spoke quickly. Klonner was so limp and nerveless that it was almost impossible to control the weighty flopping of his head and hands.

Louisa quickly put down the hat and removed the shawl from her shoulders. Charlie waited, jammed in a ridiculous posture, legs spread in an A-frame position, his head still caught under Klonner's limp, right bicep, the other hand reaching out to the bed for support.

"Don't worry," soothed Louisa. "This always happens when he's drunk. Horace? Horace!"

She lifted the limp head and shook it back and forth.

"Uuuuuuhhhh." Klonner emitted a low, indistinct groan and his eyelids fluttered open—but only for a fraction of a second.

"Dear, dear," she clucked.

"Uh, ma'am." Charlie's voice came from under Klonner's right armpit and the inflection of that voice implied misery. "I don't feel so good."

"Now, Charlie, don't get sick on me."

Acting swiftly, Louisa lifted Klonner's arm from around his carrier's neck and Charlie stood up quickly, taking deep gasps.

"The basin's in the corner," instructed Louisa over her shoulder, as she turned her attention to her partner. Gently, she eased Klonner down on the bed, lifting his hips to shift the limp body away from the edge of the bed. While Charlie, in the corner, heaved violently into the china wash basin, Louisa lifted Klonner's legs onto the comforter, settled his head into the goose-down pillow and loosened his tie.

"When you're through there, Charlie, would you please bring the water pitcher and the towel?" she asked over her shoulder. Without waiting for a reply, she turned her attention to the dust-rimmed shoes.

By the time Louisa had Klonner's shoelaces untied, Charlie was at her side, apologizing.

"I'm sorry, ma'am. Didn't mean to be sick."

"Don't worry, Charlie. You've performed a wonderful service. Thank you." She took the pitcher from him, poured some water on the edge of the towel and gently cleaned Klonner's face. Charlie was still apologizing.

"I usually don't drink so much, ma'am, but tonight. . . . Well, Mr. Underwood fired me today."

"He did? Is that so?" Louisa was hardly paying attention.

"Yes, ma'am. I guess I didn't perform so good. You see, I had to go in this stranger's room for Mr. Underwood and look for some things. But Mr. Underwood didn't tell me what to look for. And then the stranger, he came back and bashed me up some. A real son of a bitch, that guy was. And I didn't do nothing. I was just . . ."

"Going through his things. Sure, Charlie. Hand me that pitcher again, would you?"

"Sure, ma'am."

After repeating her ministrations and patting Klonner's face dry with the unused end of the towel, Louisa rose to her feet, crossed the room and picked up the small black bag she'd set on the chair when she came in. From it she removed a silver dollar.

"Ma'am, I couldn't!" protested Charlie.

"Go ahead, Charlie," she encouraged with a smile, pressing the silver piece into his hand. "You earned it."

He hung back a minute, looking at the sprawled figure sleeping soundly on the bed.

"You sure you'll be all right?" asked Charlie.

"Oh, yes," assured Louisa.

"Doesn't look like he can look out for you, ma'am."

"Don't worry. I'll watch out for myself."

Charlie looked down at the woman, his eyes glazing over, his forehead slick. His voice, when he spoke, was husky.

"Sure could use the company of a woman tonight. It's a terrible thing when a man loses his job. He feels like—feels like the rug's been pulled right out from under him."

"I'll bet he does," agreed Louisa, sighing. She

didn't think she could stand much more of the breath that was being aimed, intimately, in her direction. "You go home and sleep it off, Charlie."

"Ain't really . . . got a home . . ."

He was getting maudlin. She was getting annoyed.

"Then try the street. It's a nice, warm night and the 'skeeters haven't started up yet."

"Yes, ma'am." She looked away, trying not to see the humidity in his eyes. Tears! This hunk of clumsy, ignorant man was resorting to tears! Seeing there was no further use in subtlety, she shoved him in the general direction of the door.

"Charlie!" she called out. "Take that basin with you and dump it in the street."

"Yes, ma'am."

He crossed the room, picked up the basin, turned and made his way out the door.

"God bless us and hope he doesn't spill it on the way down," Louisa murmured to herself, turning the key in the lock.

She looked at Klonner. He groaned in his sleep and the index finger of his left hand twitched.

Louisa crossed to the window, parted the curtain slightly and looked out. Charlie stumbled down the steps, splashing the contents of the wash basin in the dust. With a conscientious, drunken-man's care, he set the empty china bowl on the lowest step and proceeded up the street.

He was the only person up and about. A light still gleamed from the Antelope, but there were few signs of activity. Across the street in the Commercial Hotel, Louisa noted, all the lights were snuffed.

Could she go through with it?

She had begun the evening with such conviction. It had seemed so simple. At her encouragement, Klonner had become more and more drunk. When he had gone out to relieve himself behind the Antelope, it had been a simple matter to pour the small vial of liquid in his drink. The sleeping-drug had gone to work quickly. And the nearest barmate, the garrulous, sweaty gentleman who called himself "Charlie," had willingly offered to carry Horace home for her.

Of course, she had known what was in Charlie's mind. She knew what was in every man's mind in this whole town. In the past twenty-four hours, she had seen only three other white women in all of Tucson. That observation implied a man-to-woman ratio of about three thousand to three, which meant that a lot of these males were going without what they needed.

That didn't bother her. What bothered her was the man in the room across the street. He knew too much. From the moment she'd opened the door to him, she had felt herself falling into some abyss of confusion.

It had all been so clear before. Everything had made sense. She had known what she wanted, had assumed that Klonner could deliver. Wealth, a comfortable life. No more running. No more fear that she would be deserted, left on the streets with no place to go and no one to turn to. Without Klonner, this town would have been a nightmare. All those men, wanting her, ready to pay for her body. She knew what she would have done.

Then a bitter afterthought occurred to her.

Without Klonner, she would not even have been here! The thought struck her full force as she stared down at the deserted street, listening to the man moan in his sleep.

What bound her to him? She was intrigued by Klonner's schemes. She loved his visions of wealth and grandeur, visions she shared with him down to the last detail, down to the gilt on the carriage and the gleam

of the crystal glasses. She shared, too, the wild exhilaration of their heists. She enjoyed working with him,
playing a part in the dreamlike world of make-believe
as they pulled off their jobs. And the wild celebration
afterward, as they counted their wealth, recalled the
fear and close calls, basked in the certain knowledge
that they would never be caught.

Now it was over.

Yes, over. The realization shook her. But she
could not deny it. The man across the street, sleeping
soundly, could finish their game tomorrow. She, Louisa
Wentworth, could hang . . .

No! The thought was too terrible. She looked at
the figure on the bed. What had he ever given her,
really? Promises. Schemes. A million ideas. But those
were all part of the dream. The reality of her life was
different. The reality consisted of seedy hotel rooms,
long journeys, bad food, sleeplessness and always the
fear of being caught. And always, she was sacrificing
herself to the wishes of this dandy and his dreams.

He was hopeless. For the first time, she felt capa-
ble of admitting that single, clear fact to herself. No
matter what happened—no matter how many jobs they
pulled, how much money they had—he would need to
go on and on until somebody put an end to him.

Well, she wasn't going to wait around. She was
getting out. But she wouldn't leave without her fair
share.

She crossed to the dresser and opened the drawers
one by one. Klonner stirred nervously in his sleep,
groaned, called her name aloud.

"Louisa!"

She spun around and, for a horrified instant,
gazed into wide-open eyes. Then she realized he was
seeing nothing. He would not remember. He turned
over and groaned.

Her heart fluttering, she finished her exploration of the dresser. Nothing. She paused. Then, with a sureness borne of her knowledge of this man, picked up the second pillow that was alongside his head.

It was heavy. She turned it over and it made a crisp sound like lettuce being crushed.

The seams were sewn shut. There was no way to find out how much it contained. If he woke and found the money gone, he would kill her.

If he never woke. . . . She struggled with the thought. Her head spun and she felt faint. Suddenly, she dropped the pillow on the bed as if it were loaded with some kind of explosive.

No, she could not kill him. She could leave him. Let him go his own way. Let her go hers. But to kill him, in cold blood, while he slept . . . no.

Her own way! It was time. So many choices, so many alternatives . . . and now there was only one.

"Who is it?" The man's voice behind the hotel door was groggy with sleep.

The woman struggled to find her voice.

"Louisa. Louisa Wentworth," she whispered softly.

The door opened and she slipped in. She felt his presence rather than saw it. The room was pitch black.

She heard the key turn in the lock. But he left it in place in the keyhole.

"Won't you light the lamp?" she asked.

"No."

She could not exactly trace the sound of his voice. He seemed to be all around her.

"What do you want?" he inquired.

His voice was so cold that, for an instant, she thought she had committed some dreadful mistake. How did she know what he wanted? She had no guarantee that the information she gave him would promise her freedom—or anything else. She reached into her bodice, fingering the derringer.

His hand clutched her wrist.

"How many times do I have to tell you, you don't need that!" he said. His fingers tightened around her wrist until she could no longer maintain her grip on the small weapon. Her fingers yielded. He took it from her.

"Why won't you turn on the light?" She tried to keep the pleading note out of her voice.

"Because, ma'am, I'm stark naked, and I don't think it's fitting for a lady to see me this way."

Her peal of laughter made a mockery of their whispers, but she quickly hushed herself.

"You don't need to worry, sonny," she replied. "I've seen a naked man or two in my lifetime."

"I don't doubt you have, and no offense meant. Let's keep it dark all the same . . . while you tell me what brings you here."

She hesitated only a moment. It was, somehow, easier in the dark.

"I have some information—what you wanted." She paused, rubbing her sore wrist. "Horace is on the trail of an Englishman, Conrad Carlington. You may have heard about the diamond strike in South Africa."

"Yes."

"Carlington left Vaal River with more than a million dollars' worth of uncut diamonds."

There was no sound from the naked man in the dark room.

"Spear?"

"Yes. I'm listening."

"Horace says the actual value might be two million."

"The Pinkerton office says three."

So he was a Pinkerton! That sudden knowledge,

so casually delivered, made her pause. But it also gave her confidence. Perhaps his promise of freedom was not empty after all. Now, if she could only convince him that her information was worth something—to her, to him—at least he might give her a partial cut, enough to reward her . . .

"I'm—surprised you've heard of him."

"We were notified in January, when he left the Transvaal on a ship bound for America. We have not been able to locate him."

"He's here," she disclosed softly. "He's taken refuge among the Aravaipa Apaches . . ."

". . . According to Klonner," Spear finished her sentence sarcastically.

"I wouldn't doubt him," replied Louisa. To her surprise, she found herself instinctively defending the man.

"I don't," said Spear. "Where is he now?"

"Across the way, sleeping like a lamb."

"With some help?"

"Laudanum."

She heard him stir. Her eyes were gradually growing accustomed to the darkness, but somehow that made her more uneasy than before. She could make out Spear's body as a dark shadow in the blackness, could see the flicker of his eyes as he looked at her. He was close—very close—and the warmth of his body combined with the darkness of his presence made her almost fearful. But there was a strange exhilaration to the fear, as if this danger promised excitement rather than harm.

"One thing I don't understand," continued Spear. His voice had taken on its former iciness.

"What's that?"

"Why did you tell him about our conversation?"

"I didn't." She leapt to defend herself. "He saw us talking together. He asked who you were."

"And you told him. . . ?"

"I told him you were a cowhand come courtin'." She laughed nervously. "Said you weren't much to look at, either."

"You told him I'd left a message with Pitkin." There was no amusement in Spear's voice.

"Yes." Louisa felt panic creeping through her. She had not expected him to know. She was playing too close to the line.

"I had to." She thought fast. "He started talking about getting rid of you. Said you might be in the way."

"A cowpoke being in the way?"

"He doesn't like people watching him. Or me."

"You're lying." His voice was sinister. Not threatening, just cold, cold as ice. "You're lucky. He got his warning. He didn't try to kill me. If he had—and failed—I would have gotten him first. Then I'd come looking for you. I like ladies. I treat them with respect. But I don't have special dispensations for ladies who risk my neck for me."

The darkness was terrible. The heat of him terrified her now. She was caught—caught!

The first sob ripped from her throat. She felt herself withering in the darkness before him. Her sobs came fast now, one upon the other, but she struggled to stifle them. His voice came back at her, smooth, unchanging.

"It won't do you any good, Louisa. This isn't a situation where Horace G. Klonner might win. He has already lost. He was a loser before your stage pulled into Tucson, only you didn't know it. I've promised you a way out if you help me and I'll stick to that promise. Just don't try to cross me."

"I won't. I swear. I didn't mean . . ."

"I know you won't," he said. Again his voice was soothing, calming her.

She covered her face but she couldn't stop crying. She felt so helpless. And when she felt his hands on her shoulders, she moved toward him naturally, seeking his support. She had forgotten he was naked. The touch of him shocked her.

She caught her breath. Then laughed. "Oh, I forgot . . ."

"Glad you did," he replied.

Her hands went around him, closing behind his back. She felt the strength of those muscles, the smoothness of his skin.

"I get so afraid," she said, her voice childlike. "I wonder what will become of me."

Her hands moved down over his tight hips as she nestled against him, feeling the warmth of his body against her breasts.

"When this is over," she continued, "I want to get away. I want to live in a small hotel, with dresses and shoes to spare. I want to dine out every night. Just think—if I had a tenth of those diamonds—just a few stones . . ."

Her hand reached down between his legs; she lifted him, cradled him in her fingers, felt him rising.

"Perhaps you . . . will," conjectured Spear.

He slipped the silk straps from her shoulders and, while she stood, willingly, he loosened the buttons along the front of her dress. The sensation of being opened, exposed, reminded her of being a little girl again. She recalled how she had taken off her clothes in the night, had rubbed her hands over the buds of her newly forming breasts, had reached down to the mound where the thin, silky hair was just beginning to grow. She had felt so dirty, then—so wonderfully treacherous. She had imagined a man stroking her, covering the mound between her legs with his fingers, touching and probing her.

And now this man lifted her breasts. She threw back her head, clutching at him. She felt his tongue playing over her nipples, licking gently, pulling the smooth, tender points of her flesh into his mouth as if they were his to devour. As he did so, she felt herself reduced, become small again, tiny enough to respond with budding breasts to the licking sensations of his tongue so that she was all in his mouth, held by him, suckled.

She was partially covered and suddenly she felt trapped by the dress that clung to her hips. She wanted that gone, too, and she swayed, assisting the man with her hips and the thrust of her buttocks as he pushed down the dress. It fell about her ankles. Then Brad Spear moved against her. She threw her head back and his mouth ate at her lips. His tongue probed her.

Now it was Louisa who enfolded him. She who reached down and touched his flesh, drawing it toward her, feeling the tip that had already turned moist. Now it was he who was controlled by her hands. The stature of the man above her made no difference. The hard flesh, quivering between her palms, stroked and fondled by her fingers, was the core of his sensations. It controlled the rest of the man. She spread the wetness up and down the long cylinder of flesh, her motions at once soothing him and making him tremble with anticipation. Long as it was, hard and threatening though it might be, she could enfold that flesh completely, take all of him inside her. She knew that, and the knowledge gave her power.

She pressed him toward her, forcing Spear to part her, making him enter the space that had opened for him at the core of her womb. She put him in place, nestling the flesh in the tiny folds of her caress, and lifted herself, reaching up for the kiss of his lips while her legs opened wide to accept him.

Then he was there, deep inside her. She was right. It was all of him. The sigh that escaped him told her that she possessed him now. The arms lifted her for only one purpose, to use her depths for pleasure, to play her whole body up and down over that probing height of his flesh.

She wrapped her legs around his buttocks, squeezed and clung. Her thighs could not open any wider. He could go no deeper. She felt the moistness cooling as it seeped from her, touching the cool night air. She was hardly aware of moving, yet he was carrying her, laying her down on the bed.

She lay back. His lips touched her nipples again. She was rising to him. Each penetrating thrust shook her down there—there, between her legs. He insisted and Louisa responded. The pleasure intensified with each thrust. His hands reached under her buttocks. His finger tips were moistened by her, spreading her. Still his body stroked against her, pulling her upward, upward until suddenly, as if she had been clutched in a vise of iron flesh, she felt the first ripple. Another and another wave passed over her, each closing her more tightly, opening her more fully, consuming her with the insistent throb of her own body. And just when she thought it would subside, when she was sure the terrible pleasure had passed forever, he insisted again, probing her, the tip of him leaping inside her. She felt the entire man, the height of flesh that she had consumed, take on a life of its own, pulsing, pouring forth, leaping against her as the man above her, almost lost in the darkness, groaned with pleasure.

In the hour before dawn, the air was cool, seeping through the closed window.

Louisa Wentworth looked out at the faint rim of pink that hovered on the edge of Tucson. She lifted herself on her elbows and looked down at the sleeping man, his face shadowed by the short, neat beard.

"So that's what it's like," she murmured softly, wondering if he had heard her. She hoped not, hating to admit so much to any man.

Safety. He had promised her safety, and already she felt it with him. Only a little more time, another danger or two . . .

Fear clutched her. What would she live on? Where would she go? Then she looked down at the sleeping figure again and remembered the iciness that had come into his voice the night before. If she didn't cross him, he had said. If she didn't weaken, she told herself.

She kissed his lips. Shivering, she rose from the bed, gathered the silk dress in her arms, seeking to warm it quickly before she slipped it over her head. She wrinkled her nose. Today, she would go shopping. In the general store, surely there had to be some dresses.

Then she remembered. Only three women in town.

Perhaps she would have to wear this dress as long as she was in Tucson. God willing, that would be a short time. A very short time.

She looked quickly around the room, searching instinctively for something worth stealing. There was nothing—only an old hunting knife with a chunk of glass in the handle. Guiltily, she looked over her shoulder. Had he seen her looking around that way? If so, he would know what it meant. She couldn't keep secrets from this man.

But he slept soundly, his face in repose.

As cautiously as possible, she turned the key in the lock, opened the door and made her way out of the room.

Only when she was gone did Brad Spear open his eyes and then it was to stare up at the ceiling, his mind filled with wonderment.

"Christ, what a woman," he said aloud.

He turned over and went back to sleep.

Hoby McVill's bar was a ramshackle shed that seemed to lean precariously into the prevailing winds at the edge of town. Its weathered siding and leaky roof needed constant patching to keep the rain from flowing unchecked into the one-room building. But Hoby's repairs were invariably slipshod and so had to be repeated with numbing frequency. The result was that the bar seemed to be an outdoor drinking establishment whenever the weather grew ugly. The slightest breeze whistled through the place, its high-pitched sound grating on Hoby's nerves. And this particular morning his nerves were especially frazzled.

The bar owner leaned wearily on the rough planks that spanned two wooden barrels. The sun had come up and still his last three customers remained. He was tired, bleary-eyed from watching their drunken, clumsy, all-night game of pool drag on. They'd torn the felt, were drinking slower and slower and Hoby was sick of waiting for one of them to win. Yet, at a nickel a beer he could stay awake. And there was half of Kitten's take to be considered. Hoby just wished they'd get on with it.

"Last rack," Jack "Lightning" Greenfield announced.

The two brothers, teamed against him, nodded in

unison. The twins always agreed. And now, exhausted, they each felt sure they were about to win.

Hoby smiled at the announcement. At last, they were about to stop. The bartender, deputy marshal, freight dispatcher and two-bit entrepreneur felt like he'd conquered them somehow. Waited them out. He'd made a few bucks selling the players beer and now they were quitting. Hoby shifted the worn bowler that always covered his balding head, indoors and out. Probably ought to wake Kitten, he thought.

The balls cracked against each other on the table. Paddy O'Rourke laughed. Garvey, his brother, grinned. The fat young blonde that everyone called Kitten snored in the corner. Her feet were propped on a chair as she slept, the dollar whore waiting for whoever won her.

"Feelin' cocky, huh?" Lightning Greenfield asked.

"Yep," Paddy allowed.

"Yep," his brother echoed.

"Well, wake the girl. I'm to it now." Lightning waved his cue in the air like a baton. He then seemed to assault the table, leaning over it and playing, cracking balls home with efficiency and speed. He cut into the field of pool balls like a surgeon, suddenly quick, stroking and chalking, staring, then stroking again. He ran the table in minutes, the previously clumsy player now clearly an expert. The twins had been taken. Lightning was a pool shark.

"Rats," Paddy grumbled.

"Rats," his brother agreed.

"You a professional?"

"Yah, are ya?"

"Yep," Lightning smiled.

"Rats."

"Rats."

Paddy dropped his cue to the table. Garvey did

the same. In unison they picked up their hats and trudged from the room. Hoby waved good-bye from the bar, chirping a perfunctory "Come again" as they grumbled onto the street.

"You're some kind of strange hustler," Hoby muttered to Lightning. "Why'd ya have to take so long at it?"

"Boys were buying the beer."

Hoby shook his head. "You really interested in Kitten?" He glanced at the sleeping girl.

"Not this morning. Put her on my tab." Lightning unscrewed his cue and stowed it in its case. They'd been playing for the whore, fifty cents from Lightning, twenty-five cents each from the twins. Hoby held the stakes and now wondered what he was supposed to do with the money. He was surprised the pool player didn't want it. Then it occurred to him that the man would be back, working other cowpokes, and the dollar he'd just amassed in Kitten-credit would serve as his wager in every game he played. It was a chip he'd play, pocketing the cash from here on.

Hoby didn't like it. Kitten would sleep a lot in the bar and Lightning would walk away with the real profits. McVill made a good living off the little fat girl and didn't like seeing her out of circulation. He'd have to think about all of this.

"We drank a lot of beer," Lightning announced as he snapped the lid on his cue case.

"Huh?" Hoby was trying to figure out what to do with Kitten.

"I said, we drank a lot of beer."

"Yeah, yeah. . . ." Hoby was tired. He could never really concentrate when he was sleepy.

"McVill!" Lightning shouted.

Hoby started.

"You make more money selling beer to my marks than you lose on the girl."

"Huh? What?" Hoby wondered if his mind was being read. Or maybe he'd been thinking out loud. "You really think so?"

"I'm positive. It always works that way."

"You'd be the man to know, I guess. That how you keep from getting barred from saloons?"

"Yep," Lightning tipped his hat and nearly bumped into Dufond as he left the saloon.

Pierre Dufond looked like hell. Interestingly, his appearance was infinitely better than his disposition. The man was spectacularly hung over. He'd bounced atop the burro since sunup, determined to find a drink as quickly as possible. The mescal was gone, but its debris raged in his skull. Dufond knew from long experience that only a double whiskey could ease his pain.

"We're closed," Hoby called to the ragged, red-eyed drunk that walked through the door.

"You let Indians in here?" Dufond asked, thinking about Asha-yo-mo standing outside with the burro.

"Nope," Hoby answered. "And we're closed anyway."

The gleaming silver rifle in Dufond's hand rose, its barrel pointed at Hoby's chest. The weapon, a .36 caliber Colt revolving-cylinder rifle, was nickel-plated and had a jet-black stock. It was the glittering prize he'd taken as he ran from Silver City, a lethal, beautiful reminder of his nightmare there.

"Double whiskey, quick."

Hoby shrugged his shoulders. Why not, he thought. Whiskey was expensive. He'd make more than a dime a shot on it. The sleepy bartender poured the liquor into two jiggers, eyeing the still-raised rifle. Hoby kept a .44, barrel down, in a glass beer mug on the bar and thought to himself he could get to it if he had to. But he hated the thing. It was loud. Still, as a bar owner he had to have one handy. His marshal's badge, a ludicrous emblem that was useful only when some drunk had to be shot, sat in the glass with the gun. Hoby hoped the bum standing before him would drink and leave quickly.

Dufond lifted the first shot glass, downed its contents and then tossed the jigger onto the bar. He reached for the second instantly.

"That's a dollar, sir," Hoby said, a little sheepishly.

Dufond handed the man two dollars, stolen with the burro from the Mexicans he'd shot. "Again," he ordered, his rifle aimed at Hoby.

McVill poured, amazed at the ease with which he was making money. The rifle bothered him, but the money was good. Hoby loved making money, his mind a reflexive calculator of every transaction, no matter how minute. He fussed with his bowler, watching Dufond drink, and thought about his week. Dispatcher and horse handler for the stagecoach, he'd sold a good animal on the sly Tuesday and convinced the coach company the horse had died. He'd trafficked six rolls of barbed wire for a fruit farmer on Wednesday. And that bunch of hired Mexicans had picked up two full cases of ammunition only yesterday. Not bad, he thought.

Dufond sipped at the fourth jigger while Hoby picked up his long, dark coat. As he put it on, the small circles of black ink that speckled his white shirt made sense. The coat, riddled with holes, would look ridiculous over a white shirt, the perforations in it blinking at any observer. So Hoby stained his shirt black where it showed through the holes in his coat. Beat buying a new one, he figured.

Hoby looked at Dufond's rifle. "Fancy iron," he

observed, nodding at the weapon, admiring the custom engraving on it.

"A dandy little monster, actually," Dufond responded, beginning to feel better. "Light enough for one hand and deadly at a distance." He put the rifle on the bar, certain he didn't have to threaten the bartender in order to finish his drink. Two dollars richer, Hoby was no longer complaining about his customer.

McVill studied the weapon. Very special, he thought. Worth a bunch. "Where'd ya git it?"

"Gift from a friend, in a way," Dufond answered, looking at the gleaming thing on the bar. "A dead friend." Images of Silver City, Nevada, of Brad Spear and the vicious Dr. Brockington whirled through his mind. The Pinkerton agent plagued Dufond's imagination. Spear was one man Dufond was absolutely certain he wanted to kill, a memory he couldn't escape, a lingering nightmare.

"Wanna sell it?" Hoby asked, rubbing his chin.

"How much?"

"Hundred, I think."

Dufond thought for a moment. The rifle was probably worth twice as much, he knew. And he had nearly twenty dollars on him. But the thought of selling the weapon was intriguing. "Can I think about it?" he asked.

"You can come back anytime," the bartender grinned. Sooner or later the drunk before him would need money, he thought. And when he did the rifle could be had cheap. It was the little things, McVill mused, that made the difference. Each deal, each offer, each exchange seemed almost petty, but they added up. Hoby wondered how long it would take the drunk to return.

Chapter 6

Chief Eskaminzin's face glowed red in the reflected firelight. His expression was drawn and tense as his deep-set eyes gazed steadily into the sizzling embers. One hand held a fan tipped with feathers and strung with beads. The down of eagle feathers at the base of the fan lifted and fell, prodded by the thin, cool drafts that seeped in through the door of the wickiup. Slowly, abstractedly, Eskaminzin moved the fan back and forth, then passed it to his brother, seated on his left, without looking up.

When his brother had taken the fan from his hands, Eskaminzin lifted a small buckskin pouch from the ground. The man seated across from him, Alsonchise, began shaking a gourd rattle, his hand moving steadily, regularly, in even beats. At the same moment, the fourth man in the wickiup, Nashakie, began beating a drum that stood like a stepstool in front of his crossed legs. The sound of the rattle and the drum were strangely at odds, following each, yet insistently out of step by a fraction of a beat, as though one were arguing with the other, independently answering. Their volume increasing, the drum and rattle filled the smoky interior of the small, enclosed hut with their throb and scrape.

All eyes were now fixed on the pouch which Eskaminzin held in his hands. For what seemed like a long time, he gazed at the circular, targetlike pattern of beads on the pouch. His thick, worn fingers played with the long strands of buckskin. His brother shifted nervously, anxious for the ceremony to begin, and Eskaminzin gave his brother a reproving look.

Then Eskaminzin's eyes left his brother's. He looked down to the low, curved mound in front of the fire—the peyote altar, representing those range of mountains where the precious cacti had been found.

The mountains had been generous to them. There were many peyote buttons in the pouch.

Eskaminzin took out three and laid them side by side in front of him. Then he handed the pouch to his brother, who duplicated his motions. The pouch was passed to Alsonchise, then Nashakie, each man pausing to take out the small, brownish buttons and place them on the ground. Each man, in turn, gazed at the altar that represented the source of this gift.

When the pouch had returned to Eskaminzin, he laid it on the ground beside him and began chanting. The other man picked up the chant. The rhythm of the rattle and the beat of the drum increased in intensity. Now the gourd and the drum were in perfect sync, blended by the strong, low, steady sounds of the men's voices. Like the building of waves, the rattle, the chant and the drum rose to a crescendo, ending in a crash that was like the spilling of water on sand.

Eskaminzin lifted the small, brown, lightly furred button to his lips and the other men copied his movements. The drum resumed, now low and patient. The men waited. Eskaminzin stirred, lifted the fan and passed it to his brother. He consumed the second button, then the third.

Still, they waited.

It was Eskaminzin who saw the vision first and he pointed, his arm remaining outstretched until the others could see.

The low roof of the wickiup, the curved sticks covered with dingy, smoke-stained canvas, was lit red by the glow of the burning embers. Gradually the ceiling changed its colors and dimensions. The canvas peeled open, turning on itself like a piece of rawhide curling up in a flame, and above it was sky, blue sky, a blue that glistened and glittered like lake water. Eskaminzin rose easily through the air, taking pleasure in the light that surrounded him and the warmth that was part of the blue expanse. And it was a pleasure to look down at the sleeping village of the Aravaipa while his people slept on, unaware that their chief was above them, watching over them. Enormous fish rose from the Aravaipa Creek, offering themselves, their eyes glistening with a strange light. Eskaminzin caught up two of the fish, choosing them carefully, and with enormous hands he laid them down outside the village, where his people would find them in the morning. That will feed them for a long time, he thought to himself. Those fish will feed us for the next season, and the next and the next.

Then he heard a rumbling. The gleaming sides of the fish ceased to sparkle. Their eyes went dead. They decayed instantly, turned putrid and began to rot. The stink of them rose up to Eskaminzin. He wrinkled his nose. The fetid odor was all around him; the blue sky had become hazy and foul with the smell of the rotting fish carcasses.

Through the haze, Eskaminzin saw that one of the wickiups in the center of his village had begun to disintegrate. The canvas fell from the thin, curved sticks and the fragile frame collapsed. Amidst the wreckage, a single man sat up, looked around, bewildered. It was the white man. His hair was tangled. His blue eyes looked frightened. Through the haze, through the stink and the foul fog of the decomposing fish, Eskaminzin could see the glitter of a mass of glasslike crystals that were piled and spread around the white man. The earth shook. The crystals fell down and the white man struggled to pile them up again, frantic with fear.

Suddenly, great flashes of fire shot across the now-darkened sky. A hail of screaming objects poured down through the fish-fouled mist. The white man screamed and Eskaminzin felt a scream coming out of his own chest as the wickiups were shattered and destroyed under the hail of fire. Women, running from their huts, were struck down, their bodies transformed instantly into dead, rotten fish. Braves stood up to fire their weapons and their eyes glazed over, turning into the eyes of dead fish. Babies, hurled to the ground, shriveled up to become the stinking entrails of dead fish.

Then it was over.

The sky cleared.

The white man sat alone among his pile of glasslike crystals, gazing up with blue eyes into the clear, blue sky. All around him, where the Aravaipa village had been, there were dead fish, rotting in the sun.

Eskaminzin shuddered.

The drumbeats ceased.

The vision passed.

There was no telling how much time had gone by. The other men did not stir. The coals in the fire died away to darkness and the sounds of the drum and rattle ceased.

Suddenly, a streak of orange light shot across the interior of the wickiup. Eskaminzin looked up and his eyes were stabbed with a sharp, searing pain as they met the light.

While one squaw held the covering aside, a young girl approached the chief and placed four dishes in a row in front of the peyote altar. The squaw raised the covering further and the light of the morning sun filled the wickiup. Eskaminzin looked up at the squaw and spoke, his voice stern and commanding.

"Send for the white man."

The squaw nodded and hurried away to carry out his command.

So, it had happened at last.

That was the first thought that came to Carlington's mind as he felt the squaw's sharp finger prodding at his shoulder and heard her voice. "Eskaminzin calls you."

Done, at last.

He had run to the ends of the earth and all his running was like a dream—a dream that had, as its one constant, a brown leather bag filled with diamonds.

Diamonds!

He laughed aloud and the squaw drew back in amazement.

"Oh, don't worry, ducky," he spoke. "I'm quite sane, and well-to-do. Quite a rich man, in fact."

He chuckled to himself, pulling on his trousers.

"So old Eskaminzin wants to see me, does he?"

She nodded.

"Well, just you hold on a minute. This calls for proper attire."

He opened one end of the valise just enough to reach inside and pull out what had once been a bright, red cravat. Long travel and overuse had given the edge of the garment a profile like an old man's whiskers and bits of dirt clung to most of the fabric. But Carlington gave the cravat a couple of brisk shakes, lifted his collar and began tying the cravat around his neck.

"When you're off to see the queen, you must dress to please the queen—ain't that right, ducky?"

The squaw gazed at him, bewildered.

"And if it's the chief you're to see—well, then, pay him the same respects, I say. Every man's a king in his own castle, or so they say, and I wouldn't be surprised if the same didn't go for the Injuns of Arizona."

Pulling on a seedy jacket, Carlington gave himself a final pat all over, then reached once again into the dim recesses of his voluminous leather case. After a brief probe, he found the object of his search, palmed it like a magician, slipped the object into his pocket and nodded to the squaw.

"Lead on, oh handmaiden," he pronounced. "It's off to Buckingham we must go."

Without acknowledging this final bit of insanity, the squaw willingly turned away from him and led on, not bothering to give a backward glance.

It was a beautiful morning and Carlington had to wonder to himself, once again, why people who lived in such magnificent surroundings chose to reside in such dim, awful hovels. Emerging from the smelly, dark wickiup into the morning light, suddenly breathing the clean, fresh air, he felt instantly reborn. "O! morning light, who's radiant beams o'er-bearing . . ." The lines came to him, their source somewhere among the books of a fine public school education, and he laughed to himself, looking around the encampment. So Conrad Carlington, Etonian—with firsts in Latin and Greek! So! It has come to this . . .

Yet, his facility in language had served him in good stead, he thought to himself, as he followed the broad back of the squaw through the litter of the village. In two short months he had learned the Apache language. A fascinating tongue, so different from the intonations of African speech . . .

Children were playing in the dust, attempting to pick up rolling hoops with their sticks. A woman stood by a large stretching frame outside her wickiup, tanning buffalo hide. By the creek, four braves were saddling their ponies. They carried only bows and arrows, no guns.

Suddenly, Carlington was struck by that single fact. When he had come to this village two months before, there had been rifles—plenty of them. Now there were none.

The squaw stopped in front of the chief's wickiup and stood aside. Carlington took one look into the hut and groaned inwardly. It was all familiar. The semicircular mound in front of the ashes. The drum and rattle. The telltale pouch with its storehouse of visions. The blank expressions on the faces of the elder Indians and the row of dishes, all carefully lined up, holding the ceremonial morning-after breakfast.

"Good morning, Chief," greeted Carlington.

"Be seated," replied Eskaminzin.

For the first time that morning, Carlington was worried. He had witnessed a Papago brave being roasted to death. He had seen the scalp of a Mexican tucked inside a silver-trimmed sombrero. Who could tell what these Indians thought? Their moods changed with the blink of an eye.

Carlington sat down. There were two braves standing behind him now, guarding the entrance of the wickiup. Eskaminzin's brother, and the men on either side, had knives. Carlington had no weapon.

"You summoned me?"

Carlington knew it wasn't in good taste to hurry the chief. But he hated the Indians' gloomy, sinister silence. The peyote made them this way. Carlington detested the stuff.

"I have had a vision," began Eskaminzin at last. "You are to be banished from our camp. You must never return."

Carlington felt his heart sink. The dread that had greeted him on waking was confirmed. He was a dead man.

"I have no place to go," he replied.

"You have your own people."

"My own people . . ."

Yes, for a time, perhaps. Then he would be caught and hanged. Carlington laughed in spite of himself. The chief looked up.

"I meant nothing," apologized Carlington. "I will leave your camp."

And perhaps he would escape, after all. He could throw away that leather case, be done with it. He could be a free man again.

"You were welcome here," replied Eskaminzin. "We have fed you and given you shelter."

"Yes, I know. I appreciate that."

"Now the white man is restless. There have been Apache raids on San Xavier. White men have been killed and their cattle have been stolen. This is not our doing."

"I know."

Eskaminzin took a knife from his waistband and held it in both hands, the blade pointed down. Raising his hands above his head, he drove the blade, full force, into the dirt in front of the altar. As the steel penetrated the ground, Carlington gave an involuntary jerk as if he had been struck.

"This is our land. We will stay here."

Carlington raised his eyes and gazed at the chief's steadily. For the first time, he imagined he could read the thoughts behind those eyes. The inscrutability was gone. The impassive coldness of those eyes had given way to an expression of perfect honesty. We are destined for tragedy, those eyes said to Carlington.

Suddenly, the Englishman felt very small, very insignificant.

"We have put away our guns," announced Eskaminzin. "From now on, we will use only our bows and arrows, the weapons we need to hunt. We have asked the soldiers to protect us. Lt. Whitman has entered our plea with the generals. If they are in agreement, we will never use our guns again."

"That's fine," said Carlington.

"We are at the mercy of the white man. Therefore, we cannot afford to protect you," continued 'the chief. "You are running from your own people."

Once again, Carlington felt his blood run cold. So the chief knew! Carlington's secret had been discovered. And now he would be turned over to the Ft. Grant soldiers like so much dog meat, dropped on their doorstep.

"I have many gifts still," Carlington offered urgently. "Things you can use for trade."

The chief waved his hand in dismissal. "Keep your barter. You must leave. If you do not, the white man will come down on us. We will be slaughtered and left to die like stinking fish."

Carlington looked around at the four men. Apart from Eskaminzin, none showed any sign of recognizing his presence. The peyote had done its work well. So they could read the future, could they? Carlington had no respect for their illusions—not even a curiosity about the small bit of cactus that had done this work. He only knew that he had been safe among them—for however short a while—and now he was cast adrift again, pushed out, left to wander on. Where would he go?

From the pocket of his worn jacket, he took out one clear, uncut diamond and placed it on the curve of the altar. He thought he saw Eskaminzin's eyes flicker as the jewel caught the gleam of the morning sun. Perhaps it was only his imagination. When he looked again, the chief was regarding him steadily, unblinkingly.

"I thank you and your people for your hospitality," said Carlington, rising to his feet.

Feeling very old, very tired, he turned and left the wickiup.

It was late in the evening when Conrad Carlington caught sight of the adobe house high on the hill. He squinted, only half believing his eyes. The house stood alone, with a narrow track leading up to its doorstep, but there was a broad, well-kept field near the house, and a fenced-in *cienega* with cattle milling around, gathered near the watering trough. From his vantage point, Carlington could make out a low parapet around the roof of the hacienda.

He shook his head. The house didn't belong there. No one had any business living this far outside of Tucson, not with the Indian raids going on the way they had been. No one . . . unless the fellow was very brave or very stupid.

A light flickered in the window. Carlington thought he caught sight of someone moving about on the roof behind the parapet, possibly a guard. Perhaps Carlington had already been seen.

There was no turning back, anyhow. That light in the window spoke of warmth and comfort, the kind of civilized life he hadn't enjoyed for two months or more. He could sleep in the cold and try to forage with his bare hands, but he didn't stand much chance out here in the hills.

Not knowing who lived in that adobe house, having no idea what he would find, Conrad Carlington started up the track.

A shot rang out, spitting into the dust at his feet.

He stopped.

"What the hell's going on?"

The question came from a bullish, bald man who appeared instantly at the door of the hacienda, a shotgun in his hand. He spoke quickly to the man on the roof, whose reply was muffled.

"Hello!" shouted Carlington. "Can you help a traveler?"

"All depends," responded the man in the front of the house. "But come on up."

He kept his shotgun leveled on Carlington as the Englishman started up the narrow, winding track. Carlington didn't mind. At least the man spoke English.

Then he heard the sound. At first he thought the snorting and grunting must come from the cattle on the far side of the house. But as he approached, the noise grew distinctly louder, and it was accompanied by a wallowing, wet slurping sound that could only mean one thing: hogs.

Carlington had never seen so many hogs. They filled the enclosure on either side of the trail, bumping against each other, grunting and snorting as they fought for position at the feed trough. As he came to appreciate the size and mass of this assembly—the largest group of pigs, he had to admit, he had ever witnessed at one time in one place—he was simultaneously assailed by an obnoxious odor. The stink was so strong, so overwhelming, that Conrad Carlington stopped dead in his tracks.

"Git a move on!" bellowed the man at the door.

"I'm a-settin' here waitin' for you, and my supper's gettin' cold."

Raising his hand to his nose, Carlington pressed forward, his shoes picking up great clumps of muck that lined and filled the top of the track.

Finally, the man at the door lowered his shotgun. He could see perfectly well that Carlington wasn't armed. In fact, Carlington wasn't carrying anything.

"Travel light—don't you, stranger?" asked the man at the doorway.

"I'd pay you for a night's lodging," offered Carlington.

The man waved his hand. "No reason to pay. Just tell me your business."

"Schoolteacher," replied Carlington. "The name is Conrad Carlington."

"Pleased to meet you."

The man at the door didn't hold out his hand, nor did he step aside. At this range, Carlington had a chance to observe the man more closely. He had a broad chin, squinting eyes narrowed almost to slits, and a thick, drooping mustache. The figure was threatening, but there was just a slight suggestion of good humor about the man's mouth.

"Pete Kitchen is my name," introduced the man with the shotgun. "You can spend the night and have a taste of ham, if that appeals to you. After that, we'll see."

He stood aside for Carlington to enter the house. Nodding his thanks, the traveler dipped his head and made his way through the doorway into the warm, narrow room.

Slabs of fresh ham were on plates at the table. A mixed group of Indians and Mexicans looked up as he came in, nodded as he took his place at the table. Conrad Carlington sat on the narrow bench, surrounded by the blissful smell of cooked ham, lulled by the warmth of the room. The men's voices swelled as they resumed their conversation. Conrad Carlington leaned his back against the wall and, in seconds, he was asleep, snoring steadily. It was the first time in months that he'd slept without his hand resting on a fat, leather valise. It was the first time in months that he slept soundly and deeply, without nightmares or restless stirrings, the whole night through.

Chapter 7

Brad Spear woke to the sound of yelling outside his window. Actually, it was his second awakening of the day—the first having occurred when Louisa Wentworth took her leave early that same morning. The special, morning-after flavor of a ripe woman was still in his bones, and he had to do some fierce stretching to break the special bonds of the entrapment she'd set up for him. Lingering perfume. The sound of a soft, feminine voice, murmuring. The woman's body fragrance that rose, still suggestive, from the warm depths of the bed-sheets. All these things were carefully designed to lure a man, make him rest, make him dream of the ever-lasting comfort of a woman's arms.

Damn that yelling, anyway. Spear turned over, got out of bed and pulled on his clothes. The voice had the cadence and intonation of a two-bit hawker at a Sunday fair. Yet the strident voice was somehow familiar and as Spear began to make out the words, he realized why. It was William S. Oury, man of action, respected citizen of Tucson, soliciting vigilantes for Indian slaughter.

"You yeller-belly sons of bitches," Oury yelled, "what the hell's the matter with you? We've got Apaches out there slaughterin' and murderin'. They've got you hoot owls so filled with terror, you're feared to walk out your front door anymore. I tell you, it ain't safe out here for man, woman or child."

A low murmur greeted the man's hoarsely shouted words, and some voices cried, "Hear! Hear!" Spear edged up alongside the window and pulled the curtain back a fraction to see what was going on down below. A crowd of sixty or seventy men including Mexicans and some Papagos Indians was gathered around Oury, listening intently to his fine oratory. Every couple of minutes, a few more men joined the crowd. Drifters made their way out of the Antelope. Cowpokes, hitching their horses to a nearby rail, strolled across to see what was going on.

Oury waved a newspaper in the air. "You see this newspaper here? This is the latest issue of *The Prescott Miner*, just published. Now, I know most of you can't read, especially that dumb-lookin' fella over there . . ."

Oury allowed a pause for noisy laughter while the man protested, "That ain't so. I kin to read—when I'm in the mood fer it." More laughter.

"So let me just read this to you. Do you know what this is?" His voice grew hushed, dramatic. The men's murmuring quieted down. "This is a list of the men, women and children that have been murdered since 1864, right here in our county. There's Dan Hawkins' ranch was attacked and his boy—his own son—murdered in the field."

The men nodded. They all knew Dan Hawkins' fine oats and grains, and many of them had spent time at the Antelope Saloon with the brave rancher. They'd known his boy, too, and they'd seen Dan's grief when he brought that four-foot coffin into town for the biggest funeral Tucson had ever known.

"Seems like that was the start of it," Oury went on, his voice low and sinister. "Then there was the raids on the stage stations on the San Pedro and along the Picacho." Oury referred to his newspaper again. "John Smiley, mail carrier, killed near San Xavier. Sam Johnson and his wife Abigail, killed on the Aravaipa. Two babies slaughtered while they slept. Should I go on?"

The crowd was deathly silent now.

"Maybe you gentlemen don't remember that fine Mexican girl Doña Trinidad Aguirre, who was in our civilized town just a while back."

"I remember her!" spoke up a voice sounding a little too anxious. The other men laughed. Oury didn't.

"A fine girl. You remember her walking along that boardwalk over there, saying howdy and thank you. You remember her fine, black hair and the sound of her laughing. Well, she ain't laughing anymore. She's lying in the dirt with her body violated and her throat cut. She and her family. Every one of them Mexicans that come to visit here, they never reached the border of their own country again. The Apaches cut 'em to pieces. The goddamn Apaches." Oury looked at the paper again and his voice roared. "Three hundred and one pioneers murdered. Two burned alive. Fifty-three wounded and crippled for life. Five captives. All the work of the Apaches!"

Some of the Mexican men at the edge of the crowd had turned away, their fists clenched around their daggers, sombreros low, covering their hating eyes. Spear understood. The hatred between the Mexicans and the Indians went back centuries. The latest crimes were merely another in a long series of well-remembered violations against their people. Nearly every one of these Mexicans had a friend or relative who had been killed.

"The time has come, gentlemen." Oury's voice was low and sinister. "This is the final hour, when the redskin must be driven from this country so's we can live in peace and prosperity. We've suffered all we're gonna suffer. The last baby has been slaughtered. The last of our womenfolk has been violated. Now we're gonna live like civilized human beings."

Oury waved a sheet of paper and the stub of a pencil.

"Step up here and sign your names. Sign your name if you're a man and ready to prove it."

There was some motion in the crowd, but no one stepped forward.

"What's the pay?" asked a man.

"Pay?" shouted Oury. "Ye're asking for pay at a time like this?"

The man backed off.

"Well, I'll sign up. . . ," said another man, stepping forward reluctantly.

Spear pushed the curtain aside and leaned forward to get a better look at the man who'd offered to sign.

For some reason, Oury looked up just then and Spear pulled back to avoid being seen. That single motion probably saved his life.

The first bullet that crashed through the window passed so close to the fingers of his right hand that he thought, for a moment, he had been hit. Where there had been clear, solid glass only a moment before, nothing remained but a shattered pane. Blood dripped from his hand. There were sharp prickles of pain. Spear gripped his wrist, pulled back.

Two more shots smashed through the window, the shots chewing hunks out of the pine wood floor.

His back to the wall, listening to the lead fly by, Spear extracted a single, long sliver of glass from the pad of his little finger. For all the blood, there wasn't much else to show. Mostly surface scratches.

It sounded as if all hell had broken loose on the street. The shots had come from the roof of the Depot Hotel. Whoever was up there had chosen the wrong time to fire and the wrong way to direct his bullets.

At least seventy or eighty of Tucson's best barflies—all the men around Oury—evidently considered that the Injuns had opened fire. Little did they realize that the object of the attack was nothing more than a Pinkerton agent holed up on the third floor of the Commercial Hotel with morning-after lust. And those seventy or eighty barflies, all would-be Indian fighters, charged up with Oury's fine oratory, responded with a fusillade toward the top stories of the Depot Hotel that broke every upper window on the premises.

Ten seconds later, they were scurrying like banshees at a midnight bash, swarming all around the hotel across the street, looking for the redskin who had dared open fire on them right in the middle of town. Their numbers gave them courage, but their numbers also gave them confusion, and they fell all over each other, each trying to outperform the other with acts of bravery, and the sum of their ineffectiveness was such that Spear was sure the man on the roof—whoever he was—would have ample time for a getaway.

Meanwhile, Spear didn't feel like hanging around Room 313 with the breeze blowing through the cracked pane and his hand dripping blood like a leaky faucet.

He wriggled his fingers. They worked fine. He quickly wrapped a kerchief around the wounded hand, drew his specially made .45, flung open the door and made a point of not stepping out into the hall.

It was a good point to make.

The four bullets that whistled past were adjusted to various levels of the anatomy, with the first at about head level and the fourth down about where Spear's navel would have been had he stepped into the line of fire. Though he couldn't actually see the bullets, he got a feel for their passing by the way they hissed and ricocheted, making their way down the hall.

There was a funny lapse of silence, while neither Spear nor his would-be assassin (judging from what Spear could hear) did much of anything. Each of them knew where the other was.

Then the lessons of an old shooting instructor, a Pinkerton specialist named Turner, came back to him: When in doubt, behave irrationally.

Spear behaved irrationally. He threw a pillow into the hall. It caught a bullet. He threw the picture frame that once held the "Home Sweet Home" embroidery into the hall: no gunfire. He threw his saddlebags into the hall, and again, they weren't fired at.

The time was ripe. Spear threw himself into the hall, rolled over, fired twice, heard a shot whistle past his head, fired again, heard a grunt and scream.

The gunman, his last shot used up, stumbled for the stairway. Spear got to his feet and followed him. The man was holding his stomach and his hand was already wet.

"Why?" demanded Spear as he caught up with the wounded man. Now he had a good look. The man had blond hair, sheepish brown eyes and the walk of a wounded pigeon. He coughed and blood appeared on his lips.

"You jerk," muttered Spear.

The blond man made a grab for his left boot as though he had a sudden pain in his leg.

"I didn't hit you there," observed Spear, kicking the man's hand away. A derringer flew out of the blond man's fingers and clattered down the stairs.

"Here's the deal," continued Spear. "You lie here quiet and don't bleed more'n you have to, and I'll see if I can find you a doctor in this godforsaken town. You make another play for me and I'll kill you. Okay?"

"I wasn't aimin' for you," said the man. "I—" He coughed and Spear looked away. Even with a doctor, the would-be assassin might not make it. "I thought you was someone else."

"Yeah," agreed Spear. "Some old rival in a love-feud. He stole your wife, so you were going to shoot him through the head. That's a great story, I've used it myself, but it doesn't explain who was the guy on the roof of the Depot Hotel just now. Your wife's second husband?"

The man groaned and clutched himself tighter. He didn't look well.

"Time's a-wasting," declared Spear. "You need a doc. What's up?"

"I'm tellin' you, I was just . . ."

"I don't buy that story!" shouted Spear. His frustration wasn't feigned. Didn't the goddamn fool know he needed help? "Now what the hell's going on?"

The way the blond man was propped against the stairs, he didn't have any way to fall. The hand that clutched his belly loosened its hold. The head rolled sideways and the shoulders sagged just slightly. But apart from these few signs, there wasn't much difference between the live, wounded man and the corpse that took its place a second later.

"Hell," Spear cursed softly.

He hated to watch this kind of spectacle. And he hated, even worse, being on the edge of gathering some information and then having his source cut off in mid-sentence.

Starting from the time Louisa had walked out of his room early that morning, it seemed as if everything had gone downhill, reflected Spear. And it wasn't the first time: that woman seemed to leave trouble in her magnificent wake.

The clerk was standing at the bottom of the stairs, looking upward. He stared at Spear as the Pinkerton agent approached. Brad suddenly realized he must be an interesting spectacle. Hatless, his hair still tousled from the night's excitement, blood dripping from his sliced-up hand, his gun drawn and smoking, he didn't bear much resemblance to the gentleman who had checked in two days before.

"It's okay, kid. Cold water and salt takes the bloodstains out. Merlin the Gun Wizard is up there, but he won't hurt you." Spear started out of the lobby, then turned back to the clerk and shook his head. "I wouldn't try to carry him all by yourself. He looks pretty heavy."

Unbelievably, the gunman on the roof of the Depot Hotel had escaped. Spear didn't even have to ask. It was apparent from the way Oury's crowd milled about on the street, talking fierce and doing nothing, that they'd given up the chase. A couple of men were pointing up at Brad's broken window in the Commercial Hotel, and it was just vaguely possible that they'd figured out the gunman was neither an Indian nor shooting at them in particular.

Frank Emory appeared at Spear's side.

"They're looking for trouble," warned Frank. "Didn't find the man."

Spear gazed at the kid and sniffed once, significantly.

"Don't you ever change that plaid shirt of yours?"

"Don't got no other."

"Next dollar I give you—spend it on haberdashery."

"Yes, sir."

"What did you see?" asked Spear.

"Winchester .44, right up there."

Emory pointed up to the corner of the Depot Hotel roof.

"And then?"

Emory shook his head. "I covered the back. I know he didn't come out there."

"And this gang of lunatics was hanging around the front," Spear mused. "That means he's still inside. Here's your two dollars for the day." Spear handed the kid the money. "But I'm not going to give you a chance to spend it right away."

"That's okay."

Emory grinned. Spear didn't.

"Fact is," continued Spear, "considering what we have to do next, you might never get a chance to spend it."

The kid swallowed hard. "Yeah," Emory said glumly. "That's okay."

"Good. Got that knife of yours?"

Frank Emory touched the handle at his belt, looked up and nodded. Spear tried to sweep some of the tangles out of his hair with his good left hand. He tightened the bloodstained neckerchief around his right one.

"Let's go."

The sound of a hoarse, familiar voice brought him to a halt.

"Hey there, Indian lover!"

Hearing Oury's voice, a dozen men turned around. When they saw Spear, they backed off. It wasn't their fight. This one was between Spear and Oury, and the others just got out of their way.

Oury was standing in front of the Depot Hotel and he looked mean. In the past couple of days he'd been slashed by an Indian, scared by a sharpshooter and had his pride wounded by an out-of-town visitor. It was the damaged pride that hurt the worst, Brad figured.

"Hi there, Mr. Oury!" yelled Spear.

For just a fraction of a second, the Indian fighter looked surprised. He'd expected a quick fight, not a greeting.

Spear took advantage of Oury's reaction to walk down the two steps to the street and, keeping his thumbs fixed firmly in his gunbelt, cross to stand cozily alongside Oury. Standing there side by side, Spear figured, at least they looked like friends, even if they weren't.

Oury spat. The gob of spittle landed on Brad's boot and the agent bent over to wipe it off with his bloodstained kerchief.

"Maybe you'd like to give them Apaches a hand in slaughterin' and maimin' our settlers." Oury's voice was loud enough for all to hear.

"Nope," replied Spear. "Wouldn't like that."

Frank remained frozen where Spear had left him, on the porch of the Commercial Hotel.

"Hey, Frank, come over here!" yelled Spear.

Emory pried himself loose from the porch rail and started across the street.

"Like you to meet one of the town fathers," declared Spear, as Emory approached. "This here is William Oury, first mayor of Tucson, or so I've been told. Mr. Oury, that young 'un you're looking at there is Frank Emory, and I reckon someday he'd make a mighty good mayor himself."

"They don't make mayors out of baby boys around here," sneered Oury.

"Now don't get Frank riled, Mr. Oury. He's a mean one when he's riled." Frank stood about three paces away now, doing his damnedest to look mean, and not succeeding.

"Frank," continued Spear, turning to his young friend and raising his voice. "This morning I heard Mr. Oury give a fine speech on how civilization was coming to Tucson." Spear shook his head, feigning wonderment. "One of the most convincing speeches I ever heard. A bunch of men like you and me were standing around, and they started yelling for blood, Indian blood. Trouble was, from the way they were yelling, you couldn't rightly tell whether it was civilization they wanted, or whether they just wanted to go out and slaughter the Indians. So I don't know, despite what Mr. Oury says. It's hard to tell whether civilization is coming this way after all, or whether it stopped somewhere just the other side of those mountains and won't get any farther. Come on, Frank." Spear waved his hand. "Let's go on in and get ourselves some breakfast." He turned to Oury, started to hold out his bloodied hand and then appeared to think better of it. "I'd invite you inside for some flapjacks, Mr. Oury, but I expect you better stand here awhile and keep a lookout for Indians."

Without looking back, Spear went up the two steps to the Depot Hotel and proceeded inside. Emory was two steps behind, and he burst out laughing the moment the door closed behind them.

"Christ, Spear, how do you do it?"

"Shut up," Spear replied harshly. Something deep in his gut told him the world was better off minus men like Oury, and he was left with a raw, sour taste in his mouth when a strutting cockatoo like that got away with what he was doing. Spear had little doubt the man would succeed in signing up enough cowards for his expedition. Spear was certain that a band of vigilantes would behave in a manner worthy of the sum of their cowardliness. He was equally certain that innocent people would be hurt. And the final, ghastly, greatest certainty was that Oury someday would be proclaimed a hero for his ability to strut.

"Sorry," apologized Emory. "I didn't mean—"

"Forget it, Frank," replied Spear. "We've got business."

He crossed to the main desk, which was four feet long, four feet high and decked in pine boards. No clerk was visible.

Spear rang the bell and a pair of eyes appeared just over the edge of the counter.

"One minute. One minute." The voice was high-pitched, impatient. The head disappeared; there was a moment's scuffling under the counter and Spear banged with his fist. "Mister, you better watch your step," came the voice from below.

The head appeared again, then shoulders and finally the dwarf stood well above the counter, his feet on a small stepladder obviously custom-made for this purpose.

"What can I do for you?" he demanded.

"I need the room number of Horace Klonner."

"Don't give out room numbers," the dwarf lectured.

"Yes, you do," countered Spear, laying his Pinkerton badge on the desk.

"Two-aught-four," disclosed the dwarf, but he was unimpressed. "A bully makes the badge. A badge makes a bully," he intoned.

"Napoleon was short. But don't think you're Napoleon," Spear replied, tucking away his badge.

He started up the stairs with Frank behind him. Outside 204, Spear put his ear to the wall and listened. There were two voices, both male, both held low. He let some time go by. If Louisa was in there, she would speak up eventually. She didn't.

Spear looked across at Frank and nodded. The kid was on the other side of the door, his back to the wall, his eyes staring straight into the maw of death. The kid's hands shook. Spear gave him a signal that everything was all right, and mouthed the words "Room Service" as he pointed at the door.

He had to say it twice, but Frank got the idea. Spear gave a signal. Frank stepped in front of the door and knocked.

Inside, the men's voices stopped. There was no reply. Spear gave a second signal and Frank knocked again.

"Who is it?" demanded Klonner.

"Room service."

The kid was so nervous that his voice was too soft. He almost choked on the words.

"What do you want?"

"Your breakfast, sir."

Spear nodded approval. The kid was improving.

"I didn't order breakfast."

Spear gave a signal: enough.

"I see. Very sorry, sir."

Frank was grinning, his voice dripping with politeness. Spear prayed he wouldn't overact.

Frank made noises of going down the hall. Then he returned silently, swiftly.

There was just one more second to wait. Sure enough, Klonner's curiosity was too much for him. He stuck his head outside the door, gun ready.

Spear's first motion caused Klonner's pistol to land on the floor. His second move, a hard, sharp kick to the dandy's midsection, crumpled the man. Klonner landed on the floor not far from his weapon, gasping for breath, and Frank jumped him, bringing his knife to a position in front of the man's nose. Klonner had to look cross-eyed to see it. But he saw it.

The other man in the room was just raising the Winchester to his shoulder when Spear slammed into the barrel, swinging it sideways. As Spear's fist rose through the air, seeking a weak chin with a two-days' growth of beard, he took note of a sweaty forehead and eyes that communicated glazed innocence.

"Oh, Charlie," Spear sighed. "Not again."

His fist landed where it was aimed, but Charlie's stolid face, still black-and-blue from the previous day's encounter, registered no pain at all. The rifle flew from his hands just as a shot went off, plugging a hole through the center of a mirror.

"Bad luck," said Spear, as his left hand plunged into Charlie's midsection. "Seven years."

The man responded with a sad sound of expelled air, but still didn't go down. Simultaneously, Spear realized that he couldn't use his right hand much more without causing himself excruciating pain. The knowledge that this oaf had caused that pain in the first place only made Spear more angry and he rushed on, driving his elbow into the man's ribs. The blow glanced aside.

Charlie swung around and his fist caught Spear in the side of the head. Spear heard something crackle inside his skull and reached for his .45, but Charlie was still in commission. He kicked Spear's bad hand and the gun flew from the agent's fingers. Charlie swung with his right. Spear's head lashed backward again. He felt himself falling.

Charlie's second kick landed in Spear's ribs and Charlie went for the Winchester. Spear was in agony, but he rolled fast. When the blast from the Winchester shook the room, he was a good three inches away from where the slug ploughed into the floor.

Only three inches, though. The muzzle moved. Spear had a good, last look at the sweaty man's bland, stupid countenance hovering somewhere above a long, shiny steel barrel. Spear rolled again, quickly, hoping. There was no second blast.

A moment later, a body fell to the floor. Spear opened his eyes, wondering why he still liked life so much.

Frank Emory stood over Charlie, pointing Klonner's .44 at the hired man's head. Klonner lurched over on his side, groaning. Brad Spear felt about as healthy as Horace G. Klonner sounded. He struggled to his feet, trying to understand.

"Wha'd you do, kid?" asked Spear.

"You okay, Mr. Spear?"

"Sure. Fine. Just fine," he lied.

Keeping the .44 trained on Charlie, Emory handed the assassin's Winchester to Spear. It was a nice weapon, Spear had to admit. Rubbed walnut stock, with some fine artwork etched around the grip.

"You haven't answered my question," Spear persisted.

"Karate," Emory replied.

"You don't say."

"I worked on the railroad a while," Emory explained. "Learned it from a Chinaman there. Man by the name of . . ."

"Never mind," replied Spear. "I can't remember names anyway." Looking down at Charlie, Spear was forced to realize that the life of an experienced Pinkerton agent had just been saved by a kid who was probably approaching his nineteenth birthday.

"How's his health gonna be?" asked Spear, looking down at Charlie's prone figure. There weren't many signs of vitality.

Emory shrugged. "Okay." The kid leaned down

and pressed two fingers to the man's neck. He nodded. "He'll be out a coupla minutes. That's all."

"Good," said Spear. "You're not going to believe this, Emory, but I've got another job for you."

The kid shrugged and studied the torn sleeve of his shirt, obviously pleased. Klonner, on the floor, moaned and turned over. Slowly, the thief sat up and propped himself against the wall. There was a desolate gleam in his eye.

"Be with you in a moment, Horace," promised Spear. He took out five dollars. "Some of that's for the new shirt," he handed the bills to Emory. "Some of it's to make sure you don't sleep in the street again."

Frank took offense.

"Let's just say I want you to improve your accommodations," Spear went on. He pointed to the bills. "Two cents of that is for saving my life, which is just about what it's worth, and there's another dollar in there for the next thing you have to do, which isn't much." He took out the gaudy dagger with the diamond in the hilt. "You know the spring by the west notch of the stage road?"

Emory nodded.

"You take this knife up there and place it out in the open. Then set yourself down."

"There's Apaches out that way," Emory pointed out.

Spear sighed. "If you have a piano lesson instead, I won't keep you."

"Okay," agreed Emory. "What then?"

"After awhile you're going to see the prettiest goddamn Indian girl you ever saw. You keep your hands off her, and tell her to wait. I'm coming."

"When?"

"As long as it takes. Part of that five dollars is for waiting."

Charlie stirred at Spear's feet and whined, "Henry? Henry? I didn't mean it." Spear shook his head over the groaning man, then looked at Emory. "I'll take care of this pair of nightingales. Now git."

When Emory was gone, Spear sat down shoulder to shoulder next to Klonner.

"Y'know, one thing I don't understand, Horace. Why would you try to kill me when you knew damn well your name—and the name of your female companion—were listed in my last will and testament? You know, Klonner, as soon as I'm gone, the law's going to move right in and hang you."

Klonner didn't say anything.

Spear decided to break the news. "Your blond friend is dead. Remember? The one you sent across the street to see me?"

Klonner persisted in saying nothing.

"The other thing I don't understand," and Spear's voice grew more emphatic, "is why you'd hire a bumbling cannibal like that hunk of greased buffalo over there to do the job for you."

"I didn't," Klonner protested feebly. "I deny ever'thing."

"Well, I'm sick of watching out for you boys," continued Spear, getting to his feet. "I think it's about time we got you locked up and out of the way."

Spear picked up the Winchester and motioned the thief to get to his feet. Klonner did so, without enthusiasm. Charlie was beginning to look sentient, though not cheerful, and in a couple of minutes Spear had them both standing, submissive, in front of the finely wrought barrel of the Winchester.

Something was wrong with Klonner. He kept peering over at the bed.

"What is it, Horace?" Spear demanded.

"The pillow. . . ," Klonner began, then thought better of it.

"Your pillow?" roared Spear. "Why, you soft piece of mama's lard. You mean to say, you won't go to jail without your pillow—is that it?"

Glumly, Klonner nodded his head.

There were two pillows on the bed. Spear picked up one and handed it to Charlie. The man's eyes shone with resentment, but he accepted the gift.

Spear picked up the second and suddenly he grinned like a satisfied cat. The pillow felt heavy. It crinkled. That wasn't goose down in there. Klonner held out his hands.

"That's okay, Horace," said Spear. "I'll keep this one."

With the cash-loaded pillow under his left arm, the Winchester cradled on his right, Spear steered his captives along the hall and down the stairs. The dwarf screamed at them as they headed across the lobby.

"Where are you going?" he shrieked. "You didn't pay your bill. Those are my pillows. Bring back my pillows."

"Don't worry," Spear soothed. "Pinkerton'll pay."

Charlie and Klonner both whirled around.

"Careful, gentlemen," cautioned Spear. "You don't want to make any sudden motions."

"You're a Pink?" demanded Klonner.

Spear nodded his head, feeling the depth of sadness reflected in Klonner's eyes.

"Afraid so, Horace. That's why I tried and tried to explain things to you. Don't try to shoot me, I tried to say. I get mad and vengeful and then Allan gets mad and vengeful, and before you know it you've got all the boys down your back . . ." Spear waved his hand. "It just isn't worth it, especially for a thief with a record like yours."

"You've been shootin' up there," screamed the dwarf. "You left holes in the wall."

"Putty and paste and a smattering of lye patches plaster neater than a whistle. Something my daddy taught me," replied Spear. "Come on, gentlemen, let's get moving." He gave them a prod with the tip of the rifle.

The sound of gunfire had drawn a crowd, sure enough, and the men stared at the strange trio that emerged from the Depot Hotel—the dapper jewel thief, all in black; Charlie, trudging along with an overstuffed pillow cradled in his arms; and Spear, also pillow-laden, urging the men on with the barrel of the Winchester.

Spear didn't appear to notice the crowd as he urged his captives on toward the jailhouse. But he noticed that William Oury was conspicuously absent.

Sheriff Pitkin stood up as Spear came in.

"Waaal, if it ain't old 'Last Will and Testament' himself."

"Got a pair of bushwhackers, Sheriff, ripe for hanging."

The sheriff looked at Charlie and shook his head. Whether it was a signal of pity or regret, Spear couldn't tell.

"We got a duly constituted legal authority in these parts, mister. We don't hang men without a trial and testimony."

"Didn't say you had to," replied Spear. "Said they were ripe for it."

"What's the charges?"

"Making unfriendly attempts on an innocent man's life."

"Those aren't charges."

"How about: 'Trying to gun down a Pinkerton.' "

Sheriff Pitkin looked at the ceiling, then at the

floor, then at Charlie. His head kept shaking and shaking.

"Oh, Christ."

"Lock 'em up."

Pitkin got out his keys and opened the gate.

"Into paradise, men," said Spear. He turned to Pitkin. "Let the big one keep the pillow. He needs it for security. This here pillow," he held out the one in his left hand, "needs a security all its own. Put it in your safe and give me a slip."

The jail door clanged shut.

"Who's to say you're a Pinkerton?" Pitkin asked.

"You've got a one-track mind."

"I've gotta ask."

Spear showed his identification.

"Brad Spear, huh?" Pitkin mumbled something to himself.

"What?" asked Spear.

"I said, I've heard of you."

"Good," said Spear. "So you can regale those two fellas with tales of my doings while I'm gone."

"Oh Christ. Christ awmighty." Pitkin was looking more and more unhappy. "How long am I supposed to keep 'em?"

"Till hell freezes over and the devil comes down to roost."

"That's no answer."

"Let me put it this way, Pitkin. I've got other entertainments planned. I don't know how long they're going to keep me occupied. But if I come back and those two aren't here, I'm going to skewer your hide and sell it for sentimental value. Clear?"

"Sounds like a threat."

"Then it's clear."

Spear blew a kiss to Klonner and walked out.

Chapter 8

"They won't do it!"

The face of the Indian fighter was flushed with anger. Underwood could tell from the man's expression that he'd already had his morning brace of whiskeys.

"Of course they will," Underwood replied gently. "You jest haven't talked to 'em the way you should, Mr. Oury."

"Don't tell me that! I was out there all morning, shoutin' my lungs out. I nearly got myself shot to death. And what do I have to show for it?" Oury held up a piece of paper with a few, scant signatures and one X-mark on it. "Seven names. Seven goddamn names. And you can bet on it at least two of 'em won't show when it comes to fireworks."

"That won't do, Mr. Oury," chided Underwood. His voice was still soft, unctuous, sinister. "That just won't do."

"What's so goddamn important about these Aravaipa anyway?" Oury fumed. "I can go out and shoot you a patch of Indians, any flavor you want, any *time* you want. Look here, Underwood. The Aravaipa is right under the noses of the whole goddamn Ft. Grant cavalry. Now the cavalry might turn their heads the other way, and they might not. Some say the cavalry's promised protection to the whole pack of 'em. I doubt it, but I wouldn't put it past Whitman. Heard tell he's soft on the Injuns."

"I'm not interested in Whitman," Underwood cut in sharply. "I asked you to do a job, Mr. Oury, and it appears you're incapable of doing it."

"I ain't incapable! But how the hell can I go in with seven blasted white men against a couple hundred savages?"

"What about Mexicans?"

"Mexicans!" Oury exploded. His face turned a brighter shade of red.

"Well?"

"Sure! I can get Mexicans!"

"How many?"

"Forty, maybe more. But you can't trust Mexicans . . ."

"Get 'em!"

"Now, look here, Underwood . . ."

"I said get 'em."

"Shit. Mexicans."

"How about Indians?"

"Injuns against Injuns?"

"They've been taking each others' scalps for years, as you well know, Oury. What tribe do you know that hates the Apaches?"

"Well, there's the Papagos. . . ," Oury wrinkled his face in distrust. "But I wouldn't ride with a bunch of Papagos."

"Get 'em!"

Up to now, Oury had maintained a steadily wheedling tone. But in response to Underwood's final command, Oury's voice turned sullen and mean.

"Sure. Get 'em, you say. Then I got to ride with 'em. I got to trust 'em to shoot straight and turn around and get their tails outta there when the shootin's over. The Aravaipa ain't so slow, Mr. Underwood. And I don't hanker to face 'em with a bunch of goddamn highsteppers on my side."

For the first time during this conversation, Underwood grew worried. Up to now, he'd been certain that Oury would fight, one way or another, just on the strength of his bloodlust, if only for the joy of killing Indians. But it looked as if the fighter had lost some of his spark. And with other men backing out, Oury might refuse to go it alone. Other incentives were needed. Underwood hated to do it, but apparently incentives were necessary. He turned to his desk, opened a drawer and took out a thousand dollars.

"One thousand, even, Oury. And I'll pay, in addition, a hundred dollars for every white man who signs up, twenty dollars for each Mexican and ten for every Injun. You can keep that thousand and there'll be another waiting for you when you get back. For the rest of them, it's payment on delivery."

"There must be somethin' mighty important in that Injun village."

"There is. But that ain't my business. Riding with you will be a gentleman named Horace Klonner. He's payin' your expenses, so be gentle to him."

Oury grinned. "Nope, Underwood. You're wrong there. Klonner won't be riding with us."

"Now, look here, Oury, I'm giving the orders. I'll tell you . . ."

"The reason being," Oury continued, "Mr. Klonner just got slammed in jail."

Underwood's face broke out in a sweat.

"But—that's impossible!"

"Ain't impossible. He's behind bars right now."

Underwood looked from left to right, wiped his forehead and walked across to the window. When he turned to face Oury again, his face was grim with determination, but there was a greedy light in his eyes. He rubbed his hands together.

"Very well, Oury. *I* will go with you."

Oury almost burst out laughing. Then he glanced down at the thousand dollars in his hand and controlled himself.

"I'm not sure that'd be a good idea, Underwood. We're gonna be travelin' fast and strikin' hard."

Underwood glanced quickly at Oury. Then his eyes rose to the portrait of the stern, white-bearded man who gazed down from the wall, measuring his son so sternly. Underwood's lower lip firmed with determination.

"Don't worry, Oury. I'll keep up." Suddenly, Underwood's voice took on an authority that made Oury lift his eyebrows. "Now get those men, Oury. I want to ride out of here tonight. I've got it on good authority Whitman and his cavalry are down in San Xavier investigatin' the raids. If we can get to those Injuns before they get warnin', we've got 'em in the palm of our hands."

Taking the merchandiser at his word, Oury's eyes shifted to the palm of Underwood's hand. What he saw was a pudgy appendage, pink and well-groomed, utterly unaccustomed to warfare. The Indian fighter's eyes shifted to the portrait of Franklin Underwood, then met Henry Underwood's eyes again. The pudgy merchandiser reddened, closed his fist and gritted his teeth. He knew what Oury was thinking and knew, from the smirk on the man's face, that Henry Underwood just didn't measure up.

"Anything else, Mr. Oury?"

"No, Mr. Underwood."

Their sudden politeness toward each other had exactly the flavor of corn syrup.

"Then I would suggest that you send some of

your Mexicans out to keep an eye on the camp. It would be most unfortunate if any sort of warning reached the Injuns before we did."

"Of course."

"Immediately."

"Of course."

"You may go."

"Butler!" roared Underwood, when Oury's steps had faded into the distance.

A scant five seconds passed before the clerk's scuffle was heard outside the door.

"Come in, goddammit!"

Butler came in. Underwood didn't bother to look at him.

"Find out who arrested Klonner."

"Klonner?"

"That—that dandy. That simp. The one with the cane who was in here yesterday."

"Yes, sir. Do you want him released?"

"No!" Underwood roared. "Just find out who arrested him. Find out what he's in for."

"Yes, sir."

"Get together my trail outfit."

"Excuse me, Mr. Underwood, but you don't have a trail outfit."

"Then buy one, idiot. And I want a horse, a good one. Saddled up. Get me a rifle and some ammunition. Shut your mouth. And stop looking at me like I was hog wild. Now get out of here and get started. I want everything ready by six o'clock this evening."

"This evening?"

"You heard me. I don't want to be disturbed any more this afternoon. I'll be in my private rooms. Oh, Mr. Butler . . ." A thought struck him.

"Yes, sir."

"Did you clean up the mess in that bedroom?"

"Yes, sir."

"Then I'll be using it this afternoon. Tell Desiree to get ready. I don't want anyone coming up or down those stairs today, Butler. Post a guard."

"Who?"

"Who??" Underwood mocked his secretary. "I don't give a damn who. Get Charlie, if you have to."

"I'm sorry, sir. Charlie's in jail."

"Charlie's in jail, too? My God!" Was the whole world going insane? Underwood shook his fists in frustration. "Get out of here. Get. Go on!" he roared at Butler.

The secretary quivered and left.

It was ten minutes before Underwood felt sufficiently calm to face what, he surmised, might be his last afternoon of pleasure. He had never gone Indian hunting before and he didn't relish the experience. He planned to hang back, let the others do the fighting. Then he would move in and pick up the white man—whoever it was who was worth thirty-thousand dollars to Horace G. Klonner. With Klonner in jail, events were working out nicely. It might even be an educational ride. Underwood didn't enjoy the thought of battle, but perhaps it would all prove worthwhile in the end.

Still, one stray bullet could be the end of him. He'd heard about the Indians' tricks of sneaking up behind, taking advantage of a man when he least expected it. He'd heard of the way they sliced the scalp off living men, left them screaming in pain and praying for someone to kill them.

Underwood shuddered. Not him. He'd go along, he thought, looking up at the portrait, but he'd let the others do the fighting. That's what he was paying them for, after all.

"That's what money can buy, old man," he said aloud on his way out of the room. "If you'd been smart enough to buy some protection, you'd still be alive today."

The white-bearded figure in the portrait didn't blink. Underwood left his office in a foul mood, slamming the door behind him.

By the time he reached the bedroom, however, his mood had lightened considerably. He gave the door a tap, brushed down his fringe of grey hair and stepped in.

Desiree looked magnificent. She wore two small fur pelts, one draped over her long, sloping breasts, the second covering her like a loincloth. Underwood found his way to the single, straight-backed chair that faced the bed. He unbuckled his pants, dropped them to the floor and sat down. Feeling the cool air on his genitals made him feel naked and dirty. He loved the expression of shock that came into her face, the way Desiree turned away, covering her eyes with her hand.

"I know you like it," said Underwood in a soft voice. "I know you want to look. Come here."

Keeping her eyes averted, Desiree came toward him. Under the shelter of the fur pelt, her breasts were held out to him, the pink nipples showing just below the edge of the fur.

"Come closer, my dear," Underwood beckoned her.

Now she stood in front of him, moaning her protests. "Don't make me look. Please, Henry, don't make me look."

He reached up and took her arms.

"Look!" he ordered fiercely. "Look, you bitch!"

Shaken by his arms, reluctantly obeying his command, she looked down at his naked waist and shrieked.

"You like it. I know you like it," Underwood repeated over and over. The woman shook her head. Her breasts swayed. Underwood pulled her closer, nuzzled the fur aside and took her nipple in his mouth. He rolled the tip of her on his tongue, enjoying the smooth, warm, round pebble of flesh. Her moan of protest became a sigh of pleasure. She spread her legs and sat down on his lap, lifting the fur loincloth so it covered both of them. Under the warm pelt, Underwood reached for her, his finger moving upward into her moist, soft depths. She wriggled her hips, moving closer to his groin, taking his finger deeper into her.

"Desiree," he whispered softly. "I've always hated that goddamn name, Desiree."

She shrieked as his fingers moved into her, probing deeper and deeper.

Spear smacked the rump of the big roan and she edged aside, giving him some room to check her over. There were a couple of raw places along her withers, but she'd come through pretty well, considering the hard ride on the trail. After a couple of days' rest, she was looking perky again.

"You better be fit, girl," Spear muttered under his breath. "You ain't seen nothing yet."

She flipped her tail, whacking him across the face.

"Damn it, Lil, you're dustier than a mound of hay. Host'ler!" he yelled.

A lazy voice responded from the far end of the stable. "Yeah, what's the matter?"

"Don't you ever brush down your horses?"

"Not 'nless they ask fer it."

Spear shook his head and smacked the roan's back. Sure enough, a fine haze of dust rose along her spine and floated in the afternoon air. "Hell," grunted Spear. He began brushing hard, using his left hand.

The right one still smarted from the morning's spray of glass. But at least he'd had a chance to clean up, take a bath and wrap his hand in a fresh bandage. With a little luck, he wouldn't need to use that hand for anything more elaborate than pulling a trigger. If that.

It was twenty minutes later when a well-groomed man on a better-groomed horse left the stable, headed for the east end of Tucson. Spear noticed a few curious stares as he headed out of town, but he didn't mind. He wanted it to look as though he were leaving for a spell. He'd checked out of the hotel room. He was carrying his saddlebags. His beard was trimmed and his Stetson was settled low over his eyes. A beautiful woman was looking down from the window of Room 213 of the Commercial Hotel—one glance told him that—and to all appearances, Brad Spear, Pinkerton agent, was on his way to another town.

"What's the matter there, stranger?" one man yelled from the Antelope. "Bill Oury chase you outta town?"

"Nope," Spear replied. "I'm just looking for civilization. Sure as hell didn't find it here."

The men in front of the Antelope guffawed their appreciation. The gait of the roan didn't change.

Along the next block, in front of the jailhouse, Horace Klonner and Charlie, both in handcuffs, were among a group of men applying their brooms to the street. Spear tipped his hat.

"S'long, gentlemen. Keep things tidy while I'm gone."

Pitkin, wielding his shotgun, looked up at the sound of Spear's voice. Spear held up Lil long enough to say a word to the sheriff.

"Don't worry. I'll be back to prosecute. Keep an eye on those two."

Pitkin glared at the Pinkerton agent but made no comment.

Spear was about two miles outside of town when he was struck by the certainty—as sure as birth, death and drink—that the two sweepers wouldn't be around when he got back. He sighed . . . just one more detail to look after.

It took him longer than it should have to find the west notch in the Santa Catalinas Mountains and, when he did, the sun was almost down. The dry mountainside was turning orange, preparing for the final burndown of the day, and killdeer swooped low over the trail, perching on the saguaro long enough to belt out their self-naming cries of alarm. The trail through the notch was both ambiguous and deceptive. Respectable-looking tracks ended up in dry creek beds, while disreputable sluices of dried mud turned out to be bona fide sections of the trail washed away by spring floods. Spear let the roan have her head, trusting her to find her way in the fading light as they made their way up toward the notch.

He heard the spring long before he saw it. An anxious sound, maddeningly steady, sought him out and followed him turn by turn. The roan had already dipped her head to drink before Spear realized they were there. Black and melodious, the spring came down through a low set of bluffs and wandered toward the dry country, trickling into oblivion somewhere below.

There was a low whistle and Spear clucked to the roan. She whinnied and another horse answered. Spear dismounted, leading the roan. He saw a figure ahead. Frank Emory was standing at the last bend before the notch, waiting for him.

"Christ, I thought you weren't gonna show," the kid complained.

"Is she there?"

"Yep. Givin' me the creeps, too." Emory's voice betrayed nervousness.

"How so?"

"She's been sittin' there the past five hours, doin' nothin', just staring at me with them blue eyes. Christ, Spear, them ain't Apache eyes."

The last vestige of evening light revealed Emory's shiver. Spear laughed.

"What's the matter, kid? Never had a girl stare at you before?"

"That ain't no girl," replied Emory. "She's some kind of coyote. Christ, I was afeard to take my eyes off of her. Thought she'd be at my throat any minute."

"Sounds tough."

"Where we goin' now?" asked Emory, wincing under Spear's sarcasm.

"Different directions," replied Spear. "I'm going on with Emma. You get on back to Tucson."

The kid shuffled his feet in the dust and hunched his shoulders.

"Well, you can have her, far's that goes. Still, it don't seem fair to git rid of me just when the fun starts."

Spear let his voice turn nasty. Something about this situation reminded him of being a father, which he'd never, ever, wanted to be.

"Fun? Who said anything about fun?"

"Well, no one—I just figgered . . ."

"You just figgered wrong. If you think some people are going to die, you're probably right. If you think there's going to be some shooting and stabbing, you're probably right again. But don't go getting that confused with fun. You understand?"

"Sure, sure."

"No, you don't understand." Spear spat viciously.

"No one in this damn whole entire territory understands."

Just the sound of his voice made the roan start. She stepped back as if she'd seen a rattlesnake, whinnying, the whites of her eyes showing.

"Easy, Lil. Easy," Spear gentled her. He turned to Emory again. "All right, kid. I'll tell you what you can do. Get on that horse of yours and ride down to San Xavier. See if you can find Lt. Whitman. If he's not there, keep on riding till you find him. Then tell him to get back to Ft. Grant before he finds himself noncommissioned all of a sudden."

"You're gonna warn the redskins?" Emory demanded. Spear could see the whites of the kid's eyes, widened in amazement.

"It's those goddamn questions that get you in trouble, Emory. Every goddamn time, it's the questions, questions, questions."

"Okay, okay."

"Do it?"

"Yeah."

"Now get your pony and get out of here."

Emory lunged off into the darkness, his feet kicking chunks of clay.

"And change that shirt of yours!" Spear hurled after the retreating figure.

"Sure, sure."

But the boy's voice was already muffled by the distance. Spear shook his head and gave a tug to the lead rein.

"Come on, Lil."

She pranced, following him up the gully. As they rounded the bend, Spear heard a slight shuffle up ahead. The rein jerked in his hand.

"Easy, girl, easy," he whispered. Then, aloud: "Emma!"

"Here." She joined him at his side.

"Did Jenkins come?"

"No," Spear replied.

"Why did you send the boy for me?" The resentment made her voice brittle. And her tone was laced with disappointment: she had hoped for the Indian agent so long that she'd blocked out everything else.

"Emma, there's an Indian fighter down there, William Oury, has the men riled up to attack your village. If you want Eskaminzin, Chipata or any of the rest of them to make it out alive, we better give them fair warning."

"Whitman is there. He will protect them."

"Sorry," corrected Spear. "Whitman's not there. Whitman's hightailed it to San Xavier to see about the Indian troubles down there."

There was a long silence. Spear reached out his hand and touched an arm that was warm, smooth and soft.

"I will go alone." Her voice was almost inaudible in the darkness. "It is no business of yours."

"Right and wrong," replied Spear. "What happens to your tribe isn't my business. But there's a white man sitting here with stolen goods. I'm interested in his welfare. Have to be." He sighed. "It's my job."

"We will go tonight."

"Yep. That's the idea."

She turned and started up the trail, wasting no time.

"Come on, Lil," Spear urged. "Better follow the lady before she leaves us behind."

It had been an hour since he left Spear and the Indian girl, and Frank Emory was having trouble picking his way down the steep slope. He leaned back in the saddle, bone-tired, bracing his feet in the stirrups.

His pony had bad lungs, and the gelding wheezed and snorted like an old steam engine. Just like old Cranby, the son of a bitch, to give him the worst horse in the stable, Emory thought to himself. It seemed like the old hostler did nothing but sleep all day, and the only time he roused himself was to perform some evil service.

Emory pulled the gelding to a halt, giving it a chance to catch its wind or die on the spot, whichever came first. It was during that brief interval, after the horse stopped but before its next wheeze, that Frank caught the sound of a footstep on the trail.

"Shaddup, you critter," he hissed to the horse. But the gelding only wheezed harder. Damn that Cranby anyhow.

Frank dismounted quickly, tucked the gelding's reins under a boulder and slipped into the sagebrush. He was freezing and his blood temperature didn't rise any while he waited. Those two years of driving spikes on the railroad had made his muscles tough, but a lot of nights in cold, damp shacks had given him a deep and abiding hatred of any air temperature below seventy degrees Fahrenheit. And now he was in the middle of a frigid bath of cold, mountain air that came sluicing down the trail, headed for the valley.

He'd been right about having a visitor. A figure appeared on the trail, halted, then drew closer. The man moved stealthily, approaching the gelding like a mountain lion stalking a helpless goat.

Frank crouched, his knife ready. A dash of light from a scimitar of moon revealed the man who approached was slight, bowlegged. There were flashes of white on his leggings. His gun was drawn and he moved around the edge of the sagebrush, his back toward Emory.

The crackle of sagebrush gave away Frank's position, but he was already in motion, his hand coming down hard on the man's neck, his knife plunged forward. There was a quick gasp. The man collapsed. Emory hardly had time to pull the blade out of the sagging body before he saw the second man, plunging down the gully on his right.

Emory spun around. A blow caught him behind the ear, sent him flying. The knife fell from his limp fingers.

He awoke surrounded by men and horses. The men were Mexicans. One grabbed him by the throat as soon as his eyelids fluttered open.

"Where is he?"

"Who?" Emory managed to gasp.

"The man who followed you up thees mountain. Whar ees he?"

"I don't know what you're talking about, you lousy bandito."

The blow of the rifle butt across Frank's face broke his nose. The pain made him scream. Blood gushed from his nostrils.

"Whar ees he?" The grip on his throat tightened.

"I . . . don't . . . know," Emory managed to gasp through the haze of pain.

The next blow came so fast, Emory caught only a glimpse of the grinning white teeth, then the flying pistol butt. It landed and he was released from his pain into the nerveless world of unconsciousness. "I've got to warn him" was the last thought that occurred to Emory before his senses failed completely and he collapsed on the cold, dry mud of the streambed.

Chapter 9

The sliver of moon wasn't nearly big enough to steer by and its light suggested the wrong notions of space, depth and distance. The edge of a canyon rim that looked only a few yards away seemed to recede deeper and deeper into the void of the night sky as Spear and Emma struggled along the trail. Gullies that appeared to be three or four feet deep yawned into steep arroyos at their approach. More than once, it was Lil who averted disaster, shying away from the rim of a dangerous gulch just when they were about to plunge over.

The treacherous trail worsened as they ascended. Caught between the sides of an ever-deepening canyon, the darkness concentrated all around them. The sound of their stumbling feet and the clatter of the roan's hooves echoed off the canyon walls, mocking their progress. Cholla cacti caught and clung to their skin, tiny hooked barbs seeking purchase in human flesh. Doves swooped from the thickets of paloverde and mesquite, and their cries of "whoo-whoo" haunted the travelers as they struggled up toward the ridge. For a distance, the stately saguaros accompanied them, their curved trunks upraised as if in reverence to the night sky. But soon those cacti were left behind and there were no identifying landmarks, nothing but the clinging brush mounded in all directions, the bare scarps always receding, the dry, pebble-strewn gullies.

Few words were exchanged between the white man and the Indian woman. Emma seemed tireless, climbing quickly up the tortuous trail, stopping only to wait for the man and his horse to catch up. When she took the wrong turn and their trek brought them to the blank face of a steep, canyon wall, she would whirl around, whisper, "No," and lead back the way they had come. She seemed confident, immune to discouragement.

It was only when they came to the steepest part of the ascent that Spear sensed her determination flagging. Three false starts, each leading up a steep, dangerous incline, each coming to a dead end, left them stymied. There seemed to be no other way over the ridge but the three, gravelly trails they had attempted. Yet all three were impossible.

Had they taken a wrong turn hours ago? If so, how could they ever find their way back through the darkness, following the twistings and turnings of the labyrinthine gulches? From where they stood, peering upward, there appeared to be nothing but that relentless, jagged edge of mountain, forbidding them to trespass.

Emma stood motionless, staring upward, her eyes trying to pierce the darkness. The frustration was monstrous. It was as if the mountain had forbidden them to go any farther, and she could not help but wonder if it was a sign.

How could it be? What destroyer, or evil purpose, could be keeping her away from her people?

She could not fathom it. Yet there was evil in this mountain, emanating from the canyon walls, rushing down on her with the cold, whistling breeze that stirred the mesquite. The evil was mingled with the "whoo-

whoo" of a dove that spoke much too early, long before morning. It was in the wings of the bats that fluttered suddenly across the valley.

There was a whinny behind her. She drew back, stood close to the warm flank of the horse.

"Bad," she said.

"That's three draws," Spear remarked. His gaze, like hers, sought a break along the ridge of the canyon. "I figure we better draw an ace next time or spend the night here."

"No!" Her hand clutched the mane of the horse. "We must go on. My people must be warned."

"They're only half your people, Emma."

The moment the words were out of his mouth, Spear wished he hadn't said them. She was so quick and nervous, like a jackrabbit. His one shot jerked her around as if she had been hit.

"They are! I have no other. I want no other. Do you think I can go back there?" Her trembling hand pointed down to the moon-tinged valley. "You think I have a home with those drunks and bandits, those wild men?"

"I'm not asking you to go back," Spear replied. But her loyalty disturbed him. He knew what was coming for the Indians. Maybe not this time around. Maybe not the next. But eventually. He'd seen it before—the inevitable. Sometimes it was cavalry. Sometimes pioneers. Sometimes rabble-rousers and fortune-seekers. But they always won, whoever they were, as long as they carried guns and moved West. He couldn't tell that to this woman. He couldn't promise her anything. But somehow, he thought, she ought to have a way to survive what was coming.

"I'm just saying you have a life for you outside of that tribe that's holed up on the creek. This country's a whole lot bigger than the Aravaipa and this range of hills."

"No," she disagreed quickly. "Our country is small. Once it was large, but I have seen it shrinking and shrinking until now . . ." She tugged at the horse's mane. "There is something wrong here. I can feel the evil in this mountain."

"Sure is," agreed Spear. "There's every flavor of scorpion, rattler, mountain lion and gila monster you want up here. There isn't anything that doesn't stab, sting or bite. If that isn't evil, I don't know what is."

"You are mocking me."

Her line of reasoning was beginning to get on his nerves.

"Sure am. We have enough troubles without some Indian evils breathing down our necks."

The moonlight was sketching out some odd clefts of rock in a cut to the south. It was the wrong direction. But they'd tried every other way. If this next one didn't do it, they'd have to turn back.

"Up there," Spear pointed. "Could end our streak of bad luck."

She nodded and they started up a rocky draw scattered with scrub and mesquite. But bad luck wasn't through with them yet. A set of clouds, as hostile as a curse, scudded across the slice of moon, dimming what little, precious light it had to offer. The trail grew steeper. The gravel moved under their feet and they had to grab chunks of prickly scrub to hang on and make their way upward. The roan plunged ahead, but things bothered her—the skittering of a lizard, the sudden hard thumping of an owl's wings as it took to the air. Spear had to keep a firm hand on Lil's bridle to steer her up the grade. If she took fright and bolted, she would have a straight nosedive to the canyon below.

The draw leveled out for a stretch and they stopped to catch their wind. The clouds thickened. Spear looked around, wondering if they'd come to another dead end, trying to make out shapes through the darkness.

Ahead of them, the scree ended in a sheer wall of rock. But off to one side, there was a cutoff leading to a trail that hugged the wall of the sheer mountainside. It was narrow. It might end in a drop. But if there was a way out of this bear trap, that was it.

Emma saw it at the same moment.

"I will lead," she said. "Keep the horse behind."

"Don't worry about Lil," replied Spear, none too confidently. "She's having a fine time."

So was he, for that matter. Just fine. The part they'd just traveled could have been done in twenty minutes by daylight. Working this way, it had taken them about three hours.

Emma edged her way along the trail, keeping close to the wall. At least there was no wind here. And the steep canyon seemed to be devoid of any animal life. There were no sounds. Emma's footsteps, muffled in moccasins, could scarcely be heard, though she led Spear by only a few yards. Lil was either too exhausted or too respectful to shy away. And there wasn't much to shy at. Just that black void. That black, black space off to the left of them, filled with nothing.

If it hadn't been for the steadiness of the silence, Spear might never have heard Emma fall. As it was, the noise was little more than a swift change in her regular soft footsteps, a hiss of gravel, and a sharp little cry, not much louder than a deep breath.

The suddenness of the motion, the complete, awesome disappearance, left Spear riveted, motionless. His first instinct was to calm the horse. His hand flew to her muzzle and he held her, stilling the tremor that ran through the roan's body. Then Spear edged forward, dropping to his hands and knees to feel into the darkness. His hand reached into space. He sought the wall of the canyon.

Emma was gone. Without a cry or whimper. Utterly gone.

Spear's hand, against the steep wall, veered off to the right. He lowered it to the trail bed. So this was the turning. And she had kept going straight ahead. Her feet had betrayed her only once.

The clouds broke and a band of light shot down the silent valley. Around the turn, the trail was clear, gradually widening, leading uphill to the crest of the range. If she had only made that turn . . .

Suddenly his ear caught a sound, as slight as the beat of a wren's wing. Still on his hands and knees, he peered over the edge of the trail. Though the moonlight had blinded him momentarily, gradually his eyes penetrated the shadows, saw the fluttering of a hand.

"Emma!" The sound of his own voice astonished him. Why should relief and hope spill over this half-Indian girl?

"Aiiiyeeee!"

It was the cry of someone trapped, in despair. It was an Indian's cry, a man's cry, coming from a woman. It spoke of the end.

"Listen! Can you hold on?"

"You cannot save me. Go on. Go on to the village."

"Don't give me that rot. Can you move?"

There was some motion. A few pebbles fell, dropping endlessly, pinging into the void below.

"Yes."

He could just barely see her now, clinging to a narrow ledge. Her arms were wrapped around a scrubby sycamore—one of those ridiculous, rock-clinging trees that somehow had seeded itself and taken root, defying all reason and all the forces of gravity by growing on the cliffside. One leg angled over the edge of her narrow perch, the foot twisted.

"Lil's going to haul you off there." Spear voiced a confidence he came nowhere near to feeling. "I'm going to lower a loop. Put it under your arms, so the knot's under your chin. I'll let you know before we start hauling. But you're going to have to help."

"Go on," she replied. "Leave me." There was no hope in her voice. "It is the mountain that wants me. You must warn my people."

"Shut up!" Spear yelled. "There's nothing in this goddamn mountain but a bunch of stone." But as he looked around at the bleak sheer walls and the clouds settled in front of the moon again, he wondered how sure he could be. Then he buried all feelings.

"You ready?" Her reply was a long time coming, and very soft.

"Yes."

With a hand on the roan's flank to keep her calm, Spear unlooped the length of rope from the pommel and tied a bowline on a bight, forming two loops and knotting them so they wouldn't slip. He took off his vest and laid it down on the rocks at the edge of the trail to prevent the rope from chafing. It was a ten-dollar vest going to hell, but at least the rope would slide smoothly over all that Chinese silk. Carefully, soothing Lil with his voice and hands, Spear urged the big roan around the corner of the trail and fastened the free end of the rope to the pommel. From the way Lil stamped her foot, Spear knew she'd been used as a cow pony before. She knew the routine.

"Easy, girl. This isn't an ordinary calf."

Spear draped her reins around a rock, made his way back along Lil's flank carrying the bight of rope.

He lowered it into the darkness and caught a glimpse of a hand reaching up. From the quickness of Emma's gesture, Spear knew she was with him again. Old evil mountain was going to lose this one. Maybe.

He gave her a couple of seconds.

"Ready?"

"Yes."

"I'm going to be at Lil's head. So if you get tangled, you better holler good."

"I will."

Spear wasn't so sure. From what he'd just experienced, it seemed like the Indian girl's notion of bravery was to go flying off into the darkness without a grunt or a holler. It was an eerie notion of bravery.

"You sure you remember how to holler all right?" Spear asked.

"I remember."

A strange noise floated up from that twopenny ledge with its life-supporting sycamore, and Spear suddenly realized that Emma Tom was laughing at him. Jesus Christ.

"Okay, smart gal," he said irritably. "Here goes."

He returned to Lil's head, retrieved the reins and tested the knot on the pommel. Step by step, backing slowly, he drew Lil forward, soothing her with his voice, keeping her muzzle straight. He felt her muscles strain as the rope tightened and for one, awful instant he thought the line was going to give. Every fiber strained as the rope took Emma's weight and, for a long, terrible moment, Spear was sure it would give under the strain. Then he heard the hiss of the hemp sliding over his silk vest.

Step by step, Lil moved forward, the warm breath flaring her nostrils. From the girl on the cliff there was no sound of life. The horse might have been pulling dead weight. Spear backed along the trail, guiding the roan.

He didn't have to test the slackening of the rope. It registered in every muscle of the fine horse's body. Lil stopped, breathing hard.

"Good girl. Hold it there."

Spear slipped the reins over a boulder and moved fast. Emma was already half over the edge, but struggling, her arms straining to pull herself up.

"I can't . . .," she gasped as Spear reached her.

He sat down hard, pulling against her weight. There was a moment of imperfect balance. She was pulling at him, drawing him down into the canyon and for one, panicked instant he wondered whether she meant it this way. Had she really resigned herself to this mountain? Was she prepared to drag him with her?

"Get . . . your . . . ass . . . up . . . here!" he panted, digging his heels into the hard mud of the trail.

Stones shot off into the darkness. There was a sudden lunge, a giving way. And she lay beside him, gasping, on the cold ground.

"For a featherweight," Spear managed, "you sure feel like a ton of bricks. Come on."

"My foot."

"Well, you had to damage something."

But they managed. He put one arm under her shoulder and she braced herself against the side of the trail with her free hand. They did a lot of stumbling and there were places where she had to crawl on hands and knees. But after another thirty yards, the trail widened and smoothed out, and Spear could help her up on Lil's back.

When they broke the top of the ridge, Spear was walking ahead with the lead rein in his hand and Emma was riding high in the saddle, one foot in a stirrup and one dangling. The clouds moved in their favor once again and for a couple of minutes that shook Spear's notions of heaven and earth and the stretches of this place, he had a good, long look at the San Pedro River valley, the Gila, the Aravaipa, and the miniature, black dots in the distance that were the wickiups of the sleeping Apache village.

He looked up at Emma. "Goddamn," he muttered.

She was crying like a baby.

It was a risk, but Spear built a fire. He had to. Emma was shivering as if she were going to rattle apart and he didn't have anything more than the thick, old horse blanket to cover her with.

They had found a sheltered arroyo just under the ridge, protected from the wind, where, miraculously, there were a couple of patches of soft grass. For anyone to see the fire, he'd have to be standing right above them on the ridge.

As for the smoke, nothing could be done. Emma had to get warm.

Lil was grazing nearby, unbridled and unsaddled, with a tether rope around her neck.

"Come here," urged Spear, pulling the blanket up around Emma's shoulders. She shot him a look that had fire in it. "Damn your pride," he muttered. He got up, dragged over a couple of branches of mesquite and tossed them on the fire.

Her eyes followed him. She hadn't wanted to stop.

"You saved me," she said.

"Hell. Next time you take a dive, do me a favor and shout."

She hunched her shoulders, stared into the fire and pulled the blanket around herself.

"I'm cold."

"Goddamnit, I know you're cold."

Spear sat down beside her, pried loose an edge of the blanket from her fingers and pulled it around him. She looked up at his face, reached up and her fingers touched his beard.

"What're you staring at?"

The fire blazed up, giving them real warmth now. It was beginning to get comfortable.

Her hand moved up farther, to his cheek, reached toward the back of his head and pulled his lips toward hers. It was what he needed. She tasted good. Her lips had the smooth texture of warm butter, spread thin, and there was something in the way her hands tugged at his neck that made him want to lie down beside her. He did what he wanted, still not real sure about the outcome.

The blanket covered them better prone. The base of Emma's neck smelled like warm pine wood, but that could have been the smoke that lingered around them.

"Wish you'd say something," Spear told the small, delicate hollow in her neck.

Somewhere near his ear, her voice was laughing.

"You must make love to me," she responded.

"I must?"

"You must. It is the only way to be warm."

She was right. The moment he laid his hand on the round, soft globe of her breast, he realized the truth of her words. He also realized why she was so cold. Apart from the cotton shift that she wore under her buckskin coat, she had nothing on. His fingers moved down to her ribs. He lifted her in his arms and she helped herself rise toward him, as light as a little child.

"My foot," she whispered.

"Huh?"

"Be careful of my foot."

"Of course."

He sought the long, smooth stretch of her leg, letting his hand drift upward to her thigh. It was mysterious there, dark with her animal warmth, and he had to reach no farther. She eased down, her legs spreading, and he felt her hair brushing against his hand. The wet lips of flesh kissed his hand and kissed again. Amazed, he remained motionless. Nothing was asked of him except absolute stillness, while the warm, hungering part of her body nipped at him, calling his fingers, one by one, into the moist, warm darkness.

But then she wanted more. Her hand reached out, touched the bulge in his trousers, and she pressed.

"Give me this," she demanded.

Spear unbuckled, lowered himself gently to where his hand had been, and again she played the game. This time, she was playing with a part of him that was so sensitive to her touch and movement that his response was uncontrollable. Emma cradled and licked him with her body, pulling him into her for an instant, giving pressure, then releasing. She rippled along his length, but it was only the tip that recognized her careful inner touch, responding with gentle, meaningless pulses to the pressure of her muscular body. He was aware of her sliding down, down, embedding herself on him long enough to squeeze and torment him, then rising suddenly, freeing herself, turning away.

"What?" He felt chilled and lost.

She rolled away, but her hands reached behind her, guiding Spear once again to that female opening that seemed so alive and responsive. He came close, but she would not let him enter. Instead she guided him downward until his moist organ pressed at the tip of her pleasure. Her hands, reaching back, held his hips now, guided him up and down as she rose—curving her back until her tight, soft buttocks pressed against him, then rising on her knees, so the whole length of him stroked her opening, pushing her toward fulfillment.

Until now, the playing of her body had been a pastime, an amusement. But an instant passed that was almost like wonder, an instant when her body, upraised, held still, quivering. Then the playfulness was gone. There was only greed, wanting him. The upward thrusting hips, the clutch and pull of her moist flesh was no longer casual. Emma needed him. Her body begged for him to plunge into her.

Spear obliged, then withheld.

"Please. Please." Her face turned aside. Her cheek was buried in the blanket. Her voice begged. "Please."

Slowly, spreading her, easing deeper and deeper into her open, warm body, Spear entered again. Emma clutched at him inside, every fiber of her body begging him to speed the pace. He refused. His long, slow thrusts commanded her. He controlled her, slowing and pacing her as she begged him for more.

Brad Spear's hands held her hips, slid up her smooth waist and found her breasts again. He felt the weight of those breasts in his hands, lifted them gently, the small, delicate nipples between his fingers.

Then his fingers drew down, stroking toward her thighs and he buried his fingers in the fur at the base of her smooth belly, so close to where their bodies were locked, hot and moist. Emma groaned as he touched her. His fingers caught her moistness and spread it over her, down her thighs, as he pulled her taut against him.

New sensations lapped at him, licking the tip of his body. Something collapsed in his chest, fell through his belly and surged forward. At the same moment, her scream bit into his ears. She heaved upward and heaved again, spreading. The moistness spilled. Spear shot forward violently, filling her insides with his thrust of pleasure. Each throb answered all the playful teasing she had given him. The tip of his member thrust at her as she rippled against him, responding with waves that were savage and relentless.

The falling of her body was as slow and gentle as her rising. Still inside her, Spear felt her buttocks soften, press against his groin as her body tugged, kissing him as he left her. She turned on her side and Spear was with her, holding her as she curled.

The fire had died down to embers. Spear pulled the blanket more tightly around them.

"You're right," he agreed. "It's the only way to stay warm."

"I've been working too hard," Hal Quinn thought to himself, as the banging began again. That noise. He couldn't get it out of his head.

At first he'd dreamed of a row of men driving spikes along the rails, all their hammers crashing down simultaneously. Then it had been some jailbird trying to escape, banging at a jail door. Finally, it was Quinn himself, at his own anvil, clanging and banging away in the middle of his dreams.

But now he was half-awake, and the banging continued. He threw the covers aside and sat up. The noise stopped. He lay down, and it resumed.

"Hell's blazes!" he roared, jumping out of bed. The pounding continued unabated.

Grabbing his shotgun from the pegs on the wall, Quinn went to the door.

"Who is it?" he yelled.

"Hal!" The voice was choked, almost sobbing. "Hal, it's me—Frank Emory."

"Jesus Christ, son," exclaimed Quinn, lifting the bar from the door. "What the hell're you . . ."

He stopped in midsentence, as Frank fell forward. Quinn dropped his gun, caught the boy by his arms and helped him stagger to a chair. Seated, Emory slumped sideways. Quinn left him long enough to bar the door and shutter the window. Then he lit a lamp.

"Holy mother o' God."

The boy's face was a mess. Blood had spread in a delta and dried that way, covering the lower part of his face. It was crusted on his lips and teeth. His nose was skewed to one side, his cheeks puffy and torn. The boy's eyes were circumscribed with a color that resembled the purple-black of a martin's wing.

"Be right back."

Quinn let the boy's head tilt forward. He left the room and came back carrying a wash basin and towel.

"Don't know what to do with a nose like that." Quinn dabbed gently at Emory's face with the moistened end of the towel. "If you got the chance, you'd best start over 'nd sprout a new 'un."

"Hal," the boy tried. The way it came out, the name sounded more like Owl. He made another attempt.

"Hal, they're after him."

"Sure," said Hal. "Now say it again, and try t'make sense."

"Spear. The tall guy w'the beard."

"I met the man."

"The Mexicans're after him."

Quinn paused in his ministrations.

"What for?"

"Spear—," Emory winced and touched his nose gingerly. "Spear an' that Injun girl are going to warn the Aravaipa. Them Mexes—I think Oury hired 'em. They must've followed him out of town."

"Oury rode outta here tonight with a band of 'em—Mexicans and Papagos. Must've been over a hundred."

"They're going to raid that village." Emory talked fast, his words tumbling over each other. "They sent out some of 'em to get Spear and stop him."

"And they found you instead," Quinn finished for him.

"Yeah." The kid shook his head ruefully and rubbed his neck.

Quinn sighed. "Looks like I got some riding to do."

"Where you going?"

"If they caught up with you, they likely found that Pinkerton man."

"No, I don't think so. Spear and Emma had a good start on that trail."

"Which 'un?"

"Over the Santa Catalinas."

"At night?" Quinn's voice was incredulous. Emory didn't answer. They were both struck by the same thought, a sense of futility. Oury and a hundred men, well-armed, riding fast, against one lone man and an Indian girl. The odds were impossible.

Quinn grunted. "Gotta do the best I can."

"Hold on." Emory stood up, then gripped the back of the chair as he almost fainted. "I'm going with you."

"You're going t'bed t'dream your nose gets straightened out."

Emory managed a feeble grin. "Hal, you gotta take me."

Emory pulled himself up straight. With some hard concentration, his knees stopped wobbling.

Hal Quinn studied the boy for a minute, then shrugged.

"Well, if I gotta, I gotta."

Emory grinned, relief lighting his face. Then a cloud passed.

"We gotta tell Whitman. He's down at San Xavier."

"Jesus Christ!" Hal Quinn never had liked the cavalry and he resented the stupidity of any chain of command. Given the situation, he felt justified in both prejudices right now. With Whitman at San Xavier, the whole Aravaipa camp could be wiped out without a shot being fired in defense.

"You're still coming with me," he reassured Emory. "I'll wake the O'Rourke twins and send 'em on their way. That way Whitman'll be sure to get the message—twice."

Emory grinned, rubbing his jaw.

"Feel better?"

"Guess so." Frank Emory looked sheepishly down at the brown, dried crust that was caked along the front of his shirt.

"Never mind," said Quinn. "I'll give you a clean 'un."

"Appreciate that," Emory thanked him. Then he grinned. "So'll Spear."

Quinn peered at the kid quizzically, but Frank Emory just chuckled. He never did bother to explain.

Chapter 10

Brad Spear stirred, stretched and rolled over. Every minute muscle, from the small of his back to the tip of his metatarsal extensors, ached. He unglued his eyes. The fire was out.

Emma stood on a rocky ledge, peering out into the valley. The sun was barely up and their arroyo held some damp mist.

Spear shivered. At this moment, Emma turned and gestured impatiently.

"Come here."

Creaking in every joint, Spear rose, glanced over at Lil and shook his head. The roan was silent, munching.

As Brad came alongside Emma, his eyes followed hers. Far below, the Indian camp was already stirring with activity. Smoke drifted above the wickiups. Emma pointed. Spear squinted. He caught some movement at the edge of the village. Spear went to his saddlebags and returned a moment later with the binoculars. The glasses weren't a whole lot of help. But he could make out the braves, mounting up.

"Shit," Spear muttered.

"They are leaving?" Emma's eyes had already interpreted the distant movement.

"Only the braves," replied Spear, trying to focus the glasses better. He nodded in confirmation, handing Emma the binoculars. "Yep, they chose a fine day to go hunting."

"If they come this way, we'll warn them." Her voice was alive with faith.

"No such luck." Spear turned away, not wanting to read her expression. The Aravaipa braves—probably three-quarters of the men in the village—were already strung out single file, headed north.

By the time Emma joined him, Spear had the bedroll on Lil's back and the saddlebags tightened down. Emma handed him the binoculars without a word.

"Trade," Spear handed her a chunk of dried pemmican. "Here's breakfast."

It was awful stuff. He tried not to think of scrambled eggs and ham.

"How long?" demanded Emma.

She still had a limp and Spear glanced down at the swollen foot.

"Lady, we'll go just as fast as we can and no faster. Part of it's up to Lil."

He smacked the roan on her neck and she looked around. Sated with valley grass, reasonably satisfied with a few hours' sleep, she made no objection when Spear hoisted Emma up on her back.

Spear grabbed the lead rein and started down the trail. As soon as they broke from the arroyo, it was easier going. On this side of the range the trail ran a lot easier. Spear could almost trace the course of the trail with his eyes. There were some bad twists and a couple of places where the trail disappeared around ragged outcroppings, but the fall was gradual. With luck, Emma wouldn't have to do much walking.

The universe, the season and the vagaries of the atmosphere had somehow conspired to produce a wash

of sunlight and a burst of morning freshness that
dazzled. Even chewing on the ghastly pemmican, Spear
wasn't immune to the pleasure of watching what happened to the four hundred square miles of spectacle
around his feet and overhead. Birds were rousing.
Damn spring flowers got their show in order. Lil
plodded on and Emma kept her eyes fixed on the village.

Their progress seemed imperceptible. The trail
was gradual all right, but it wound down slowly. Just
when it looked ready to level out and go straight, it
switched again. The trail had been used before, but
never for speed.

Finally, Spear could make out the movements in
the village. The sun was high now. He was beginning
to sweat. He stopped only a second to push back his
Stetson, wipe his forehead. Lil pushed against him,
urged on by Emma's heels.

Christ, that girl was in a hurry.

So was he, for that matter.

There was still no sign of Oury's men. Going by
the long road, they could be two days behind—or two
hours. It all depended on when they left, how fast they
traveled. To clear the village, get the Indians safe inside the Ft. Grant stockade, wouldn't take more than
an hour. But the Aravaipa would need at least that
much warning.

Another switchback. Still no sign of Oury. Emma
was digging her heels into Lil more frequently and
Spear had to break into a dogtrot to keep up.

Too fast. With the haste, he felt a bad panic playing along his spine. Move too fast and you get in trouble. You make mistakes.

The sun was blazing now, his throat was parched.
Spear could make out Indian women by the creek,

washing. He saw their horses grazing. A single sentinel strode the Ft. Grant stockade, smoking a big stogy.

Off to the west, Spear caught a flicker of movement, the flash of silver glinting in the sun.

"Whooa." He pulled back on Lil's reins. The horse stamped, confused: Emma's heels were digging into her while the man was pulling back.

"What is it?" Emma's voice had panic in it.

"There." Off to the west, Spear saw a cloud of dust rising from the road. It might be the cavalry, returning from San Xavier. Might not. Spear probed the saddlebags for his binoculars.

There was no flag at the head of the riding force. Spear uttered one word. "Oury."

They had one more switchback before the trail leveled out. But the last turn was treacherous, leading down between sheer, clay walls ragged with sage and scattered with boulders. The trail was bad for a horse, filled with gravel, prickly with cacti.

As they entered the divide, Spear held back on Lil. "We've got time. We've got time," he repeated, wondering whether the horse as well as the rider knew he was lying.

Emma was strangely alert, almost detached. She didn't look at Brad, the horse, or the village below. Her eyes scanned the ridge of the divide, glanced from boulder to boulder.

"What is it?" asked Spear.

"Go on," she hissed.

The next twenty steps of the trail were treacherous.

Spear concentrated on the rocky incline. He didn't see Emma draw the Winchester from the scabbard or hear the click of the lever as she cocked it. Then the trail leveled out and he paused for a minute, looking up at horse and rider: Emma was sitting calmly in the saddle, the rifle at her shoulder aimed at a point somewhere among the boulders.

"What the——?" He didn't get a chance to finish.

The movement of the gunman's hand, the sound of the pistol and the crack of the rifle came simultaneously. A man fell from behind the rock, blood spilling from his forehead. Lil reared up, but Emma managed to cling to the roan's neck, the rifle still in her hand.

There was a flash of movement off to the right, and Spear whirled around, drawing his .45. He caught sight of a grinning Mexican, the face gleeful with anticipation. Spear's first shot wiped away the glee. The second brought pain. The Mexican's pistol fell from his hand and he fell forward, trying to reach it, crawling on his hands and knees, getting nowhere. Spear let him crawl.

Emma pumped two more shots into a boulder about twenty yards away. The shots weren't doing any good, but Spear understood. More Mexicans.

How many were there?

In an instant, Spear was on Lil's back, snug against Emma, his .45 covering the left of the trail while she covered the right with the Winchester. The good horse lumbered under the added weight, but managed to break into a canter.

Shots pinged off the rocks around them and Spear felt something hot slice at his leg. Reaching around Emma, he pulled the reins hard left, bringing Lil behind a bluff.

"Hold her!" yelled Spear.

Behind the steep, high wall of the bluff, they were out of range. The men above them—Spear still didn't know how many there were—would have to move into new positions.

Emma slid from the saddle. There was blood on

her shoulder, seeping from a small hole in the hollow that Spear had kissed the night before.

A shot blasted down, kicked dirt from the bluff and sped by. The attackers were moving around. There wasn't much time.

Emma touched her shoulder, looked at the blood on her finger tips.

"Go on!" Spear commanded. She shook her head. "You have to. Emma—go! Now! Warn your village."

"I cannot." She shook her head firmly. "I cannot leave you."

"No?" he demanded. "Well, what the hell did we come here for? You want to sit here and play games while your people die?"

She lowered her head, as if ashamed. "I will stay."

"Get out of here!" Spear's tone was vicious. "I'll cover you six shots' worth and then you're on your own. Take the rifle."

"No!"

"Look!" Spear seized her by the shoulders, spun her around. For just an instant, there was the imprint of a panorama that would stay with him forever. The oblivious village. Women washing. Children playing. The cloud of dust along the road, growing larger, men visible through the haze.

"Now, go. Get out of here."

Spear turned away from her, loaded quickly. He didn't have to look around to know Emma was ready. Another shot spun off the clay wall, dust spurting. Spear glanced over his shoulder, caught a glimpse of Emma in the saddle, her body pressed flat alongside the horse's neck, clinging there, ready to ride.

"Go!" He slapped the roan hard, spun around and fired six times, exposing himself to the answering fire, dodging and rolling to draw the shots to himself.

A fusillade of gunfire followed Emma, but she was out of range almost immediately.

Spear backed up, crouched behind the bluff. You're turning into an edgy old man, he thought as he watched his fingers shake while shoving the bullets into the empty chambers. What once took him six seconds to perform now took six and a half. Even allowing for the jitters, he had ample time to get ready. The men above him were moving slowly, taking their time, selecting positions.

He was one man, alone, with two dozen rounds left and no horse to ride out of here. At best, he could only delay them.

With his back to the bluff, Spear stepped sideways and started to climb. A head appeared above him, looking in the wrong direction. Not far wrong. Spear flattened against the bluff. The man would have to look straight down to see him.

The man above called out in Spanish. Two voices answered him.

Spear saw the head again and this time he fired. There was a shrill scream and a body plunged end over end, bouncing from the cliff, landing at his feet. The eyes peered up at him, the mouth moved.

It was an Indian, and Spear recognized the markings of a Papagos on the man's face.

"Shit," he muttered. It was incredible. Somehow Oury had induced the Papagos to go along with him.

Two voices, calling in Spanish, bounced from the walls of the divide, closing in. His time was running out. One glance told him that Emma was safely away, finally nearing the village.

Spear could also see Oury's vigilantes as they charged along the road, now riding at a full gallop. Emma fired her rifle in the air.

The alarm was raised. But Oury's men were closing in fast.

Spear looked down. The Papagos was still staring at him. His lips still moved. Spear moved fast to find cover—and get away from those eerie eyes.

At the end of the bluff, there was a narrow crevasse. Not much. Barely wide enough for a man. If the two bushwhackers came at him from both ends, he'd be caught and trussed in the middle. There was no alternative. Through that crevasse was the only way to get above them.

He made a break as another Papagos came around the bluff. An arrow tore past Spear, clattered on stone. Spear fired as the Indian took cover. His shot went wide.

Reloading as he ran, Spear started up the declivity, stumbled and fell. He lay behind a rock where he had fallen. He had to. Bullets were spraying all around him. Rifle bullets, landing hard.

He glanced down. Emma was in the village. The alarm was raised. His job was done.

For a brief moment, the hail of bullets ceased. One gunman above him had to reload. Spear didn't pause to think. He had one break and he took it, scrambling up the crevasse.

He was almost to the top when an arrow coming from below soared past his shoulder, clutching at his sleeve. He sat down hard, faced downhill, leveled his pistol with elbows on knees and fired.

The shot pierced the man's throat. The Papagos fell, gurgling.

Spear turned. Not fast enough. The blow from the rifle butt caught him on the side of the head, hurling him against the wall of the chasm. Spear struggled to recover his sight, but the world was whirling, churning with agonizing pain.

His finger still worked. He pulled, pulled again. He heard the roar of a gun going off. Through the bleak, grey mist that spun around him, as if printed on the label of a patent medicine bottle, he vividly saw the words "Soothes Pain."

A heavy object, lumpy and warm, fell on top of him and he thought, so this is what death feels like.

The moment she entered the village, Emma was surrounded by screaming women and children. At her shots, the few men remaining ran at once to the edge of the cluster of wickiups, readying their bows and arrows. The sight of those few, brave warriors—some of them childhood friends, all known by name—almost made her laugh. Their chief was out hunting, his brother with him. The guns were safe in Ft. Grant's stockade. And here they stood, these meager, few toy soldiers, trying to defend their women and children. It was pitiful. Laughable.

It was horrible.

"Go to the stockade!" she shouted. "To the stockade! Go—or you will be massacred!"

The women ran for their belongings, screamed for their children. There was no order, only chaos. Emma caught a glimpse of the sentry standing calmly atop Ft. Grant, staring down at them as if a colony of ants had gone mad at his feet. He lit a cigar.

She rode to the wickiup that had been her home. Her mother was waiting for her with the two young ones in her arms. Without a word, her mother lifted up the children and Emma took them. Too shocked by the uproar to do more than stare around them in disbelief, the children were calm. Naiche, only three years old, was crying softly to himself.

Emma looked down at her mother, but no word

was exchanged between them. Her mother waved her on. The roan stamped her hooves, backing.

"I will return for you, Mother!" Emma shouted above the melee.

"Go. Take the little ones. Leave me."

A shout went up from the few warriors at the edge of the village. The first of Oury's men had appeared, brandishing their rifles.

"Go! Go!" ordered Emma's mother.

Emma looked down at the little ones, dropped the rifle to her mother, wheeled the roan and galloped toward the stockade.

Some of the Aravaipa had already reached the doors of the log fort. They pressed against the tall stockade gates, pounding, begging to be let in.

Emma looked up at the single guard who peered over the parapet, smoking his cigar.

"Massacre!" she shouted in English. "Please! Please! You must let us in!"

"Against orders!" he shouted down.

The women held their children up for him to see. They howled, their keen voices rising above the sound of gunfire that now came from the village. A village that had no guns.

"Let us in!" Emma shrieked at him. "Let us in!"

Slowly, the barrel of a rifle appeared over the parapet. "Git away from thar!" he shouted.

"Please! Please!"

"Git away! I got orders to shoot!"

"No!"

The roar of gunfire filled the air. Emma glanced around, saw the men riding through the wickiups, firing randomly, cutting to left and right with their swords, swinging their rifle butts like clubs.

"Git away!" yelled the soldier above.

He fired once. A baby dropped from the arms of Singing Dove, and the woman screamed.

Perched on the saddle in front of Emma, clinging to the mane, Naiche and Chisa were becoming hysterical. Screams racked their little bodies, each cry piercing Emma and punishing her. She wheeled the roan and, cradling the children in her arms, dug in her heels.

Pursued by the roar of gunfire, lost in the thunder of hooves, she was carried across the bare plains, up along the creek, past the field full of rabbit warrens, across the shallow ford. She passed the deep hole where she had fished for trout, followed the fern-covered bank to the trampled ground where the deer gathered with their fawns to water and graze. The roan slowed, cantered through the sagebrush to the shallow valley where the prickly pear, senita and hedgehog cacti were blooming. Beyond was the field of wildflowers, lupine and mustard flower blooming blue and yellow. Honeybees rose from their blossoms. A butterfly with black-tinged wings floated down from an acacia.

The roan slowed to a walk, then stopped, her head hanging, breathing hard. Emma looked around her. The gunfire was distant now. Grey-black smoke rose from beyond the low hill that hid Aravaipa Creek. The screams were distant.

Chisa looked up at Emma. The girl was almost seven summers. Her eyes were a dark, serious brown.

"Where is our mother?" asked Chisa.

Emma would hide nothing from her.

"Gone. You must take care of Naiche."

Instantly obedient, Chisa reached her arms around her brother and hugged him.

"Don't cry, Naiche. I will take care of you."

Emma dismounted, lifted up her arms and almost screamed with pain. She had to stand by the horse, bracing herself. Riding since early that morning, her injured right foot had become stiff, almost useless. The flesh wound in her shoulder was stiffening. All her strength was needed to lift Naiche to the ground. Chisa was too heavy.

"Come, sister," she said gently. "I cannot lift you. You must help yourself."

The little girl slid easily from the neck of the horse, hung on just a moment with her fingers clutching the mane, then dropped into the dry grass. At once she turned to Naiche, took his hand and led him toward a patch of soft grass. He sat down and looked at his sister.

"He is hungry," Chisa interpreted for Emma.

Emma nodded and reached into the saddlebags. Her hand touched the hilt of a dagger and she lifted it out. It was Chipata's, the knife with the crystal that he had given to Spear on the trail. The blade was wrapped in a cloth with threaded lettering.

Her eyes clouded. When Chipata returned from the hunt, he would find his village gone.

She slipped the knife into her waistband and fished into the saddlebags again. There was only a thin, short strip of pemmican left. She broke off a piece for Naiche and gave the rest to Chisa. The girl would feed it to her brother, little by little, while Emma was gone.

Already the sound of rifle fire had died away. The smoke of the burning village had thinned.

"Chisa." Emma took the girl by her shoulders. "I am going back to see what has become of our mother. You must stay here with Naiche. Take care of him."

The boy would not be distracted. He stared up at Emma.

"Here," she spoke quickly. She handed him the cloth that she had unwrapped from the blade of the knife. Perhaps the colors would amuse him. He looked at it, pressed it to his face. When Emma got to her feet, he had already laid it on the ground. With one finger he was tracing the letters, not understanding: the round O's in HOME, the long, sticklike dashes in the E's of SWEET.

"Do not leave this field," ordered Emma sternly to Chisa. "I will be back soon."

"When?" asked Chisa. There was no concern in her voice. She only wanted exactness.

"Before the sun falls," Emma replied.

She prayed she could keep her promise.

Satisfied, Chisa turned to the boy, helping to guide his hand as he traced the letters on the cloth. Emma limped to the roan, raised her good foot to the stirrup. Excruciating pain shot through her right leg as the weight was brought to bear. She could use only one hand to lift herself. With enormous effort, she rose in the stirrup, swung herself into the saddle.

"Yes," she soothed, as the horse stirred under her. "Again. But soon you will rest."

Taking a last look at the children, she turned the roan toward the burning village.

The sentry was still standing on the parapet of Ft. Grant, smoking a cigar and looking curiously down at the scene in front of the stockade doors. Women were sprawled there, with children's bodies scattered about them like chunks of stone. The sentry looked up as the Indian girl on the roan rode past, but he did not call out.

Small fires burned steadily in the village. Most of the wickiups had been burned to the ground, but a few were still standing, slightly charred.

There was no human sound. A large, saddled white horse stood near Eskaminzin's wickiup. Though the hut was charred, it was still standing, almost intact,

amid the ruins. The horse wore a brand-new saddle
and looked as if it had been ridden hard.

Emma paused at the edge of the village and dismounted. She limped as she walked through the remains, but she felt no pain. She could feel nothing.
Around her were the bodies of the women and children. For the first time in her life, she was afraid—
fearful that one of the bodies would rise up and beg
something of her. There was nothing she could do.
Nothing. These were not the people she had known.
These were only bodies.

She limped on. Her mother's wickiup was only a
circle of charred sticks. Her mother lay face down, the
rifle clutched in her outstretched hand. Three Mexicans
and a Papagos lay a few yards away, their bodies in
odd contortions, blasted to the ground by her mother's
close rifle fire.

Emma turned her mother on her back so she
faced the sky. She closed her mother's eyes, drew her
legs together and lay her mother's arms at her sides.
Clawing with her fingers in the dirt, Emma picked up
dust and spread it over her mother's breast.

Emma was about to begin the prayer when a
movement made her look up. The white horse had
shifted position alongside the wickiup and Emma was
suddenly aware how wrong it was to see such a horse
in this dead village. Surely, even in their haste to get
away, the attackers would have taken the horse with
them when they left.

Rising silently to her feet, Emma drew the knife
from her belt. Limping, but unaware of any pain, she
walked forward.

Now she was certain of some other presence.
Someone was inside Eskaminzin's wickiup. There were
sounds of a man digging. As she approached, she real-

ized that the grumbling sound was the man talking to himself.

"Diamonds! Diamonds! Well, of all the goddamn . . . Couldn't be just one of them. Must be hundreds buried here. Now where'd that heathen put 'em? Where the hell?"

The man, crouched in the dust, looked up as Emma's shadow blocked the doorway.

He was fat. His white features were rubbery with exhaustion. Sweat dripped from his jowls and his grey fringe of hair was plastered against the dome of his head. In one pudgy hand was clutched a gleaming crystal like the one in Emma's knife handle.

She recognized him. The merchant. She knew him by reputation, too. His father, the Indian fighter, was known by legend.

"What the—?" His eyes widened in stark fear. He stepped back, almost tripping over the crescent-shaped peyote altar. "Now look here, girl. I didn't do this to your folks. I didn't have nothing to do with it."

Emma took one step into the wickiup, the steel point of the dagger pointed at his stomach.

"Here." He held out the diamond. "You want this little gem?" He tried a smile. "It'll set you up for life."

She took another step. He put the crystal in his left hand, offering it to her, allowing his right hand to creep toward his pistol butt. The effort at secrecy was ineffectual.

"Now, see here, I wouldn't come any closer, if I were you. I'm warnin' you."

She took another step.

He reached for his gun. Before the barrel was out of the holster, the blade of the knife tore through his stomach, turning.

"No," he declared simply, looking up into her

eyes. He looked exhausted. In his eyes was the astonished expression of betrayed innocence.

The knife left his stomach and plunged in again,
hooking his soft flesh before he could fall.

He shook his head, gagged. Emma pulled the
knife away and stepped back. Henry Underwood fell
over the altar, vomiting blood.

Chapter 11

Walking through the center of Tucson that fine April afternoon, Louisa Wentworth was fully aware of the attention she attracted. She didn't mind. In the back of the general store, the previous day, she had found a brand-new corset with fancy trim and ruffles, originally ordered for some cowpoke's Mexican sweetheart who hadn't stayed around long enough to pick it up. It had fit her almost to a T. Along with the corset and petticoats and all-white frock with light-blue trim, she had received a full and not particularly surprising account of the Mexican girl's abandoned ways and the grief of the cowpoke whom she'd demolished for good.

After thanking the storekeeper for the wares (certainly not for the lengthy story) paying him lightly for the feminine accessories which he'd already written off as a total loss, and gathering her acquisitions in a bundle, Louisa had returned to her room for some judicious refitting and sewing.

Now the sun warmed her bare arms. The starched, white bodice showed off her good figure and the movement of her hips gave added emphasis to the swirling skirts that almost touched the dusty street. She mourned the lack of a parasol. But the heat was tolerable and she didn't have far to go.

Sheriff Pitkin looked up in amazement at the apparition that appeared at the jailhouse door. He was, for a moment, so totally nonplused that he forgot to get to his feet. Louisa reminded him.

"Ain't like a gentleman to stay on his fanny when a woman comes in the room."

"I'm—sorry, ma'am." His body finally obeyed the rules of etiquette. Looking around desperately for some place for her to sit, he was momentarily thrown into a state of confusion again. There was only the school desk, a saddle horse with some grimy blankets thrown over it and a rickety armchair that was losing pegs at every intersection. He dusted off the chair, however, picked it up and put it down, pointing it in different directions.

"Ain't often we get ladies comin' in here."

"Apparently," Louisa nodded in very slight gratitude for his attention and duplicated the dusting with her own finely embroidered handkerchief. When she sat down, she stared directly past the sheriff toward the two prisoners occupying the nearest cells. Each of them clutched his respective bars. Each fixed her with his eyes. The one in the left cell, a man with a greasy forehead and gleaming pink complexion, rewarded her with a look of unadulterated admiration. The one on the right, with the drooping mustache and a definite air of ruined prosperity, gave her a look that burned with resentment. To each, however, she returned equal nods and smiles.

"I'm—er—sorry, ma'am, that our conversation must be conducted in such company," Pitkin apologized. "Unfortunately, as you can see, we all are limited to the confines of this office until sech time as the territory shall see fit to construct a more ample jailhouse, separate, as it were, from the office of the sheriff."

Louisa Wentworth rewarded this effort with icy indifference.

"Now, then, ma'am. What can I do for you?"

"Leave me alone with the prisoner."

"Beg pardon?"

Her request so alarmed Pitkin that he really did not think he had heard her correctly.

"I asked, Sheriff Pitkin, to be left alone with the prisoner."

"Uh—which one, ma'am?"

"It should be obvious, Sheriff Pitkin, that if I am left alone with one, I shall, of necessity, be left alone with both of 'em, since they're standin' there right next to each other."

He looked around, as if to confirm her observation.

"Yes, that's so."

"That *is* so."

"Yes, it *is* so."

"God awmighty." Lousia shook her head in disgust.

"Beg pardon?"

"Sheriff, would you lift up your tail and get the hell outta here!"

Having reached the limit of her patience, Louisa saw no particular reason to conceal that limit from him.

"I'm sorry, ma'am, I can't do that."

The last trace of pleasantness left her eyes. She hadn't expected any opposition from this man and didn't appreciate the little he was putting up.

"Why can't you do that, Sheriff Pitkin?"

"I ain't allowed to leave the pris'ners fer any reason."

Louisa stood up and approached his desk, letting

the sinuous part of her figure above her hips and below her breasts tell him everything he wanted to know.

"This is for no reason at all, Sheriff Pitkin. This is to please me. An' you know how grateful a woman can be when she's pleased—don't ya, Sheriff?"

He stood up, cleared his throat and let his eyes rip some of the seams she'd just sewed up. Then he recovered himself. The man, she appraised, did have a sense of dignity, however quaint.

"May I take it, ma²am, you are familiar with one of the pris'ners?"

"You may take it any way you please, Sheriff Pitkin."

"I see." He cleared his throat, extracted a pocket watch from his waist and flipped open the gold cover. "You may have ten minutes in privacy."

"Ten minutes should be sufficient, unless it takes longer, in which case I will let you know."

"Yes, of course."

He scanned her body again.

"I am not carrying a weapon, Sheriff Pitkin."

"No, of course not. I would not suggest . . ."

"Then don't suggest. Go!"

He went. She heard the door close behind her and smiled at Horace G. Klonner.

"Goddamnit, Louisa, where have you been?" Klonner burst out. His face worked with anger. "I've been in this damned cell since yesterday afternoon."

"Now, now, Horace, you haven't been stuck in your cell all the time. After all, honey, they let you out to sweep the streets." Her laughter tinkled around the room.

"Miss Wentworth . . ." Charlie reached out his hand, a genuinely pitiful look on his bruised face.

"Shut up and go to your corner, Charlie," she

shot back. "I ain't got much time and I certainly don't want to waste it talkin' to you."

Drawing back his hand as if he'd been struck, Charlie turned sorrowfully and sat down on the corner of his bed facing the wall.

"Get me outta here!" ordered Klonner.

"But darling! How on earth am I gonna do that?"

"Think of a way," he growled. "You made your arrangement with Pitkin all right, judgin' from that conversation. So why don't you just use what you got to get me outta here?"

"Horace—how could you suggest—?"

"Goddamnit, bitch, what's gotten into you?"

Louisa's face hardened. She took about three steps toward him and stopped just out of reach, fixing him in her glare like a bug on a pin. Just her expression made him draw back, suddenly wary. Her expression was nasty and Klonner figured she probably had the derringer with her.

"Just this, Horace. I finally figured it out."

"What do you mean? What the hell are you talkin' about?"

"All your dreams, Horace. Your great plans. You've always got something up your sleeve, don't ya? And I always have gone along. I figured you knew what you were doin'. All I had to do was go along, do like you said, and someday all those dreams would come true. We'd be rich—loaded. We wouldn't have to run anymore like a couple of two-bit thieves."

"Louisa, it's true. Don't you realize? We're on the edge of somethin' so big . . ."

"Shut up, Horace. I've heard it before. It's a nice idea. But somehow it never works out the way you promise it's gonna. Somehow we always end up runnin'. I take the risks and you get caught and then it's my turn to get you outta trouble."

"Listen, Louisa, I swear. All you gotta do is spring me from here . . ."

"Sure, Horace. All I gotta do is sleep with that greasy sheriff, so you can get away. All I gotta do is run another thousand miles with you, bribin' hotel clerks and sweet-talkin' liverymen to make your way easy. All I gotta do is lie down an' let you take your pleasure on me any way you want . . ."

"Miss Wentworth—" A pleading voice from the adjoining cell broke through Louisa's tirade and Charlie's face appeared at the bars. "Miss Wentworth, you ought ta come with *me,* Miss Wentworth. I'd treat you good. I wouldn't do that kind of stuff to you . . ."

"You're sweet, Charlie."

"I know, Miss Wentworth. That's what I'm sayin'. If'n you'd only marry me . . ."

"Sweet," she continued, staring at him as if he were a chunk of overripe buffalo meat. "But you're a pig. And your breath smells like the back end of an unwashed baby."

Not quite surprised at her judgment of him, Charlie nodded his head in partial agreement and retreated to his plank bed, where he put his head in his hands.

"Did you come here to kill me?" asked Klonner sullenly.

"No, darling, I won't do you any favors," Louisa replied. "I just came to say good-bye."

"Where you goin'?"

"Oh, there's lots of places to go, Horace. When you don't have to run all the time, there's lots of places a woman can settle down and jest be herself . . . as long as she don't have to answer to a man who's full of himself all th' time."

"You think so—huh? Well, you jest wait till that purse of yers runs dry and maybe you'll remember who kept fillin' it."

"Or maybe I'll fill it myself, Horace. At least I won't have some swine takin' my half and stuffin' it in a pillow somewhere."

He winced. His expression of pain was her first real pleasure of the afternoon.

"Incidentally, Horace, where'd they put that valuable pillow of yours?"

"Louisa, listen." He gripped the bars again. His eyes lit up in animation. "Come here." He lowered his voice to a whisper. "Diamonds, Louisa, millions of dollars' worth. I told you where they were. Well, there's a raid goin' to that Injun village right now. They'll bring back that old man, Louisa, but I doubt they'll find the diamonds on him. He's got to be too shrewd for that. We still got a chance, Louisa, a good chance. Get me out of here. For God's sake. They're probably raidin' that village right now. We got to get to that old man 'afore someone else does. Louisa, listen to me . . ."

Louisa cut him off. "You didn't answer my question."

He bowed his head, loosened his hold on the bars.

"All right. Don't listen to me. Get me out of here."

"No." Something in her voice made Klonner look at her hand. The tiny pistol stared back. He backed up one step, then another. "Where's that pillow full of cash, Horace?" she repeated softly.

"It—it's in the sheriff's safe."

The derringer in her hand wavered.

"No—" His voice grew shrill. "No—please, Louisa, I swear, I'm tellin' the truth." He backed another step. "Don't shoot. Don't kill me," he whined.

"I won't kill you, Horace," she said. "That would be murder."

She slipped the derringer back into the front of her dress and dabbed her lips with her handkerchief.

"Good-bye, dear Horace. Good-bye for now and always." She turned to go.

Pitkin was leaning on the rail outside the jail-house, picking his teeth, when Louisa Wentworth came out the door. If Pitkin had been listening in, he gave no sign. He turned to Louisa as she came out the door and his lips were wet with expectation.

"Everything go smoothly, miss?" he asked unctuously.

"Very smoothly, thank you."

"Waaal." He rocked on his heels, content. "I expect we should meet for supper."

The expression in his eyes turned her stomach.

"I expect we should, Sheriff. But we won't."

His face turned nasty. "Now, see here, miss. I lived up fair and square to my part o' the bargain . . ."

"Sheriff Pitkin—may I please see your thumb?"

Bewildered, he had no recourse but to hold his thumb in the air for her inspection.

"Why, sure, miss. But I don't see . . ."

"Now, Sheriff, why don't you take that fine thumb o' yours and see if some inspiration don't lead you t'do something with it after I'm gone."

With a nod to the sheriff of Tucson, Louisa Wentworth turned on her heel and, with delicate steps so as not to get dust on the hem of her fine, new white dress, made her way up the street toward the general store.

It was a full ten seconds later when Sheriff Pitkin realized he was still holding his thumb in the air. He quickly lowered his hand, jammed it in his pocket and went into the jailhouse, muttering under his breath.

Outside the general store was a wooden-wheeled wagon with a freshly painted sign hung on the back: "Pete Kitchen's Fresh Country Hams." A pair of enormous oxen stood in their traces at the head of the wagon. Mounted on the bare planks of the general store's broad porch, the sole creator and proprietor of the territory's finest ham, bacon and lard was overseeing the disembarkment and, at the same time, extolling the virtues of his products.

"Men—you never tasted a ham like this 'un here. Big ol' sow pig got so large, it took me six men jest to hoist her in the tree and drain her." Kitchen gave a jab to a side of bacon as it went by, borne on the shoulders of the general store owner who had sold Louisa her corset and frock earlier that day. "Hold it there, Big Jim." The store owner stopped in mid-stride. "There's something I want to point out to these men here. Now, you take any ordinary side of bacon and what do you find? Streaks of fat. Mottlin's of color you can't rightly understand unless you know your bacons, which most of you don't. Now look here—turn around, Jim, don't be bashful." The store owner turned obediently, displaying the far side of the porker's hide. "Now see here," Kitchen continued. "Find me a streak o' excess fat anywhere on this rasher. Find me the telltale dash o' green that tells you the meat's gone bad. You see any o' that on there?"

Several men, enjoying the show, peered at the meat, shook their heads and looked up at Pete.

" 'Course you don't. And you never will! That's why they say Pete Kitchen's is the best ham in the land. 'For porker, rasher, loin or lard, you can't do better than Pete Kitchen's yard.' "

A round of applause greeted the jingle and Kitchen motioned the storekeeper indoors with a grand wave of the hand.

"Go on, Jim. Git yore shelves stocked. These men're hungry. And make sure you don't sell it to the poor beggars for a penny less than them fine hams're worth."

"You're the boss, Pete," replied Big Jim, turning toward the door with his load of rasher.

Satisfied with his day's advertising and promotion work, Pete Kitchen pushed back the enormous sombrero that sat atop his ruddy, almost bald head and leaned against the wall, his slate-blue eyes twinkling.

"I smelt Injuns all the way down here," Kitchen commented to no one in particular. One of the drifters that surrounded him—the hungriest-looking of the lot—quickly sensed Kitchen's request for gossip.

"That's right, Pete," he offered. "There's been warrin' Apaches all up and down this valley."

"What I figgered," replied Pete. "It's the reason I never make a habit o' taking the same road twice. I know a lot o' Injuns hanker for these porkers, same's white men."

Obviously anxious to please, the drifter continued eagerly.

"Oury and some o' the boys went up on the Aravaipa. Must've been over a hundred of 'em. They'll teach those Apaches a lesson."

The twinkle went out of Kitchen's eyes and he leaned forward.

"The devil, you say. Oury attacked 'em at Ft. Grant?"

"Sure did," replied the drifter, looking around him for support. Several of the men standing closest moved away and the others shuffled uneasily, turning their eyes toward the ground.

Pete Kitchen's red face got redder.

"God damn his hide!" he bellowed. "Them ain't warrin' Apaches! Those Aravaipas been settin' there mindin' their own business. The last thing we need is Bill Oury gettin' another hornet's nest riled up."

Feeling himself losing popular support, the drifter took on an apologetic tone. "Well, the way Oury figgered, the Aravaipas were the cause o' that raid on San Xavier."

"The hell they were. Those weren't Aravaipas. They were Chiricahuas. Any damn fool could've seen that by their paint an' arrows."

"Ah—what's the difference," muttered one of the bystanders.

"What's the difference?" roared Kitchen. "There's a league and a half of difference. You ever hear of the right hand and the left hand? Well, Bill Oury may've cut off the left hand, the one that stays quiet, but the right hand's gonna come visit Pete Kitchen and squeeze his nuts. Bill Oury is a fool and a nitwit, but it's Pete Kitchen, up there on the hill, bringin' you the best hams in the land I might add, who's gonna have to pay." Kitchen tore off his sombrero and hurled it down on the planks. Several of the men jumped back. "Git outta here! All o' you! I'm goddamn plum sick o' the whole pack an' lot o' you and your nitwit ways."

His impatience had an immediate effect. A minute later, the porch was cleared. A sullen Pete Kitchen, his sombrero recovered and replaced, leaned against the door jamb, staring at the distant hills. Big Jim lumbered back and forth silently from wagon to store and store to wagon, toting hams. The oxen remained motionless.

Louisa Wentworth waited until the men had cleared away before crossing the street. When Pete Kitchen heard her step on the porch, he lowered his eyes and gazed out malevolently from under the brim of the sombrero. But his expression changed to outright admiration at the sight of the dark-haired beauty in a new, white frock stepping up to the door of the store.

"Howdy, ma'am." He lifted the flashy, white sombrero that capped his dome.

"Howdy, ma'am," she mocked. To her amazement, the old, grizzled warrior, reddened and windburned and hardened, blushed at her sarcasm.

"I'm—er—sorry, ma'am. Didn't mean to be forward."

She smiled at him, realizing that if it hadn't been for his sombrero, she would have been taller than he.

"That's all right, Mr. Kitchen. I give all the fellers a hard time."

"I expect you do, ma'am." He recovered some of his ease—and his dignity.

"Say, Mr. Kitchen, you appear to know a great deal about this territory."

"I 'spect I do. As much as any man."

"Possibly a bit more."

"You might say that. You might also say, there's some men that don't know what they see even when they see it 'cause they don't have the capacity for interpretation. Which is to say, ma'am, beggin' your pardon, they don't have the brains of 'n ox."

"Yes," replied Louisa. "I believe you're right. That's why I'd like to ask a question of you, if you don't mind." He obviously didn't. "I hear a friend of mine is livin' out in these parts. An Englishman by the name of Conrad Carlington. I thought perhaps you might've heard of him."

"An Englishman, you say?"

Kitchen measured her closely and she felt her heart begin to pound with an almost uncontrollable excitement. It had been a long shot. She hadn't really expected anything to come of her question. But it was obvious, from Kitchen's response, that she'd touched the right chord.

"Do you know him?"

Kitchen didn't answer her directly. "You say he's a friend o' yours?"

"An acquaintance, certainly," she replied.

"Well, ma'am, that's a curious coincidence. Jest the night 'afore last, I had an Englishman show up at my place on the hill. He didn't seem to come from nowhere and he didn't seem to have nowhere in particular to go. I thought it might be a woman he was searchin'."

"Did he . . . carry anything?" Louisa could hardly control her impatience.

"Nope. Not a damn thing."

"Oh."

"You were 'spectin' him to?"

"Well—" She struggled to cover her curiosity. "He was always a fancy dresser."

Kitchen shook his head. "Ain't no more. And—beggin' your pardon, ma'am—you're too good for the likes of him."

"I didn't ask for your opinion, Mr. Kitchen."

"That's true. You didn't. Still. I put 'im up a night or two and had a chance to observe his habits."

"What habits?" She tried again to keep the curiosity out of her voice, and failed.

"The habit of sleep. He 'pears, ma'am, to be more fond o' sleep than anything in the world. Includin' my hams. Now—if you'll excuse me—I've got a transaction to complete . . ."

"Oh, Mr. Kitchen." The sweetness in her voice caught him halfway through the door and made him turn around.

"Yes, ma'am?"

"Where did the gentleman—Mr. Carlington—go?"

"Can't rightly say, ma'am. Last I saw, he was headed up the road toward Sentinel Peak."

"When was that, Mr. Kitchen?"

" 'Bout six o'clock this morning. I dropped him off on my way into town."

In spite of herself, Louisa Wentworth uttered a curse word that would have made a murderer's eyebrows wither. Pete Kitchen looked at her in stark amazement.

"Beg pardon, ma'am?"

"Nothing, Mr. Kitchen," she replied coldly. "Just a little expression I use when things aren't goin' so well."

Louisa Wentworth's skirts and petticoats made a hissing sound as she turned away from Pete Kitchen and made her way down the steps of Big Jim's General Store. The oxen looked up as she passed, but soon lost interest and lowered their heads again.

Brad Spear felt the cold, rigid weight lift from his chest. Resurrection? he wondered.

A wave of water hit him hard, smashing into his face like an icy fist. He rolled his head and groaned. He felt like a pop-up gopher at a penny arcade. Any way he moved, he was going to get brained.

"C'mon, Spear, get a move on." The voice that prodded him was distantly familiar and not unpleasant. In fact, given the circumstances, it came across a lot better than the singing of saints.

He opened his eyes and looked up into the face of Hal Quinn.

"Sweet mother of Jesus," Spear muttered, sitting up.

"Nope. Not by a long shot." The voice came from his left. Brushing the worst of the clouds and cobwebs out of his vision, Spear recognized Frank Emory.

"What happened?"

"Looks like you won this one," replied Quinn, nudging the cold Mexican that he'd just pulled off

Spear with the toe of his boot. "There's Mexicans and Papagos lying all over this trail. Far as I can see, you're the only one that lived through it."

"Where's Emma?" demanded Spear.

Frank Emory pointed down the valley, keeping his eyes turned away from Spear.

"Down there, goin' through the wreck."

Traces of smoke rose from the charred remains of the Indian village. Spear struggled to his feet, bracing himself against the wall of the crevasse. A few feet below him, the dead Papagos lay face down, an outstretched dagger clutched in his hand. Shot through the throat, he must have attempted to crawl up to Spear. A final revenge, unsuccessful.

"So Oury had his way," muttered Spear. "How many killed?"

"More 'n a hunnerd," replied Quinn. He spat in the dirt. "Most of 'em women and children. There wasn't more than a dozen braves or so in the whole lot."

"Nothin' but bows and arrows," Emory added.

"Shit."

Spear started down, holding onto the wall of the crevasse. He went past the Papagos, around the corner of the bluff and stood in the center of the trail. The sun was just starting to set over the San Pedro River Valley, its rays turning the last vestige of grey-black smoke into plumes of gaudy ostrich feathers, rising from the rubble below. Emory and Quinn were behind him, and they paused to untie their horses and mount up. Spear stumbled on down the trail, his eyes on the village. He didn't want to turn around. He didn't want the blacksmith and the kid to catch up with him.

And they didn't try to. They let him walk ahead, following on their horses, a few paces behind. Apparently they respected his unspoken request to walk the rest of that trail alone. Or maybe they could tell, from the set of his shoulders, that something in Brad Spear had melted down into a ball of hot steel. Whichever it was, they didn't try to see his face and he made sure not to turn and show them what was in it.

Pierre Dufond lay on his back, watching the ceiling swim in circles above him. A bemused smile spread across his face as he considered his position. He was half-asleep and slightly drunk, lying in a cheap hotel room in Tucson. A two-day ride from the nightmare of his past. He'd run so long and so far that he was stunned by his return. For no reason he could discern, Dufond had moved steadily south for weeks, sinking through Arizona toward Mexico and the province of Sonora. He hadn't intended it. But neither had he resisted the homecoming that his travels promised. It amused him. Was he crazy?

Dufond coughed. Something was eating his insides, consuming him. Even drunk, he felt it. He wondered if he was dying. He wondered if he cared. He coughed again. Sure felt like death.

Dufond chuckled at the thought. A coward, haunted by his own flight from danger, the defrocked priest had escaped everything that had been thrown at him. He was a practiced survivor. And, perfectly ruthless in his pursuit of his own preservation, he was even proud of the strange kind of courage a cowardly fugitive must constantly display. Like a second-rate boxer, Dufond could never put an opponent away, but he had the grit to stand in the ring and knew how to slip a punch. The image pleased him. The frail drunk liked thinking of himself as a battler, a boxer, a man who scrapped with the best of them. Not strong, but tough.

But coming to Tucson wasn't smart. The one man

he hated, and the only soul on earth who truly pursued Dufond, was almost certainly nearby. A powerful, vengeful enemy, the cuckolded governor of Mexico's northernmost province. Dufond feared him, yet moved ever closer to his territory. He *was* crazy, Dufond thought. He chuckled and his chest hurt.

The late afternoon quiet of the street below was suddenly shattered by a scream. Others' troubles were of no particular interest to Dufond, but this noise set his nerves on edge. It blared again and he wished it would stop.

Then the sound of the woman seeped into his reverie. It was Asha-yo-mo, the damned Indian girl.

"Aiiieeeee!" she screeched.

Pierre Dufond looked instantly around the room. She wasn't there. The rifle was gone.

"Damn," he croaked. She was stealing his possessions. Painfully and a bit awkwardly, the dirty little man rose from the bed and wobbled to the window. Below, Asha-yo-mo kicked at a Mexican, her hands pinned behind her by a second sombreroed assailant. A dozen or so other Mexicans sat on their horses watching. The troupe looked formidable. Cartridge belts crossed their chests and several wore two pistols. All were armed to the teeth and dusted with the dirt of a long ride.

The burro stood in their midst and Dufond's prized rifle gleamed from its back. They could have the girl, he thought, but the burro and rifle were valuable. Yet, looking down on the mustachioed faces of the group, he decided this was not the time to be rash. Dufond inhaled deeply, trying to flush the cobwebs from his skull.

As he groped for a course of action, they hoisted the girl onto the burro and one horseman led it down the street, out of his view from the window. Dufond wondered if they actually wanted her. It was incredible! Losing a magnificent rifle because some Mexicans wanted an Indian girl. Jesus!

Dufond looked for his boots. He couldn't find them and thought, briefly, she'd made off with his footwear, too. Then, struggling to focus, he saw the toe of one peeking from behind the rough blanket draped over the foot of the bed. Trying to balance on one foot as he pulled on a boot, Dufond fell to the floor. There, laughing to himself, he squeezed the rough, worn leather boots onto his feet and then ran to the street.

An ancient, impoverished, toothless Mexican farm worker leaned against the posts which supported the hotel's rickety porch roof. The man cackled. The worn yarn ornaments that fell from the brim of his sombrero danced as he laughed.

"What happened?" Dufond asked the old man.

He kept up his laughing, watching the dust settle down the street where the troupe of Mexicans had disappeared.

"What happened?"

"They take the Apache, comprende?"

"Yeah, I comprende all right. They took my burro with her."

The man nodded, his shrug of mild sympathy annoying Dufond.

"Why did they take her?" he asked.

"They kill Apaches," came the odd answer.

"What?"

"They kill them. It is their work. And they take her to celebrate."

"Where?"

"To the grand rancho, to the fandango."

"Where?"

The old man looked at Dufond as though he were an idiot. "Josefina's Dream," he replied.

"What?" Dufond recoiled at the name. A coincidence? It didn't seem possible that a piece of ground might have been named after his young lover so far to the north. "Josefina's Dream?"

"Si, señor."

"Who owns it, the ranch, I mean?"

"Delgado. Señor Enrique Delgado."

"Jesus . . ." It was him. The governor. In Tucson.

Anyone studying Dufond at that moment would certainly have been perplexed by his expression. The man grinned. Then shook his head as though recalling some joke that particularly tickled his fancy. Virtually everything Dufond possessed had just been stolen by a band of roughnecks and was headed for the home of his oldest enemy. The rich and powerful Delgado held Asha-yo-mo, the burro and his rifle. Dufond sat down on the stoop next to the old man and stared into the dirt.

"Delgado left Mexico?" It wasn't really a question, but an invitation to explain.

The old man looked at Dufond and said, "Si, years ago. He killed his wife and the government not happy. He ranch here. Very rich. Very angry. A man who kills for fun. Very angry."

Dufond's eyebrows climbed across his forehead as he rubbed the back of his neck. It was, he thought, time for a quick drink and a quicker exit. There was nothing to be gained from staying in Tucson. And plenty to be lost. Then the blurred ache rattled once again through his chest and he coughed, almost gagging on the phlegm that rose in him.

It was funny, all of a sudden. Really funny. He had no choice. There was nothing to be done about it. As reasonable and timid as he tried to be, the cards had been dealt in such a way that Dufond couldn't help but play those he held. He didn't want to be brave. He didn't care about the girl. He wasn't concerned with revenge or with expiating his sins. But the situation suddenly struck him as crystal clear, fated. It was much like the end of a long night of study, like the end of laborious concentration on arcane religious arguments. As a divinity student, Dufond had pondered obscure points for weeks on end, reading constantly, trying to decipher some bizarre twist of Catholic logic. And every once in a while, he would understand something. The flash, the epiphany of scholarly recognition always thrilled him, even when the point he'd finally mastered seemed trivial in the light of day.

And now, sitting dirty and lost on a stoop, he had the same feeling. It had come around. He should have known that it would, eventually. It was spread before him. How, the sick and exhausted little man thought, could he resist?

Chapter 12

After Pete Kitchen's meat wagon receded in the distance with the oxen emitting steady grunts and Pete singing an off-key version of "Clementine," Conrad Carlington stood for a while at the side of the road. Finally, with a sigh, he turned and trudged toward Sentinel Peak. He felt old and tired. Pete Kitchen had sold him a good-sized ham—about fifteen pounds' worth of what had been described to him as "the leanest piece o' porker you ever saw." These Americans were a strange bunch, thought Carlington, but they didn't come much stranger than Pete Kitchen and all his advertising slogans.

The ham was weighing him down. So was the gun at his belt. He hadn't wanted the gun. Carlington figured a gun brought a man more trouble than it kept away. If you wore a gun into town, that meant you had to be ready to use it. If he didn't wear a gun, he figured, no one would have a reason to draw on him.

But Pete Kitchen had strongly advised him to take one along. It wasn't just the gunfighters a man had to worry about, according to Pete. Up in the mountains, there were rattlers and coyotes and a parcel of other wild beasts that could do harm to a man. By rights, according to Kitchen, a man ought to carry a rifle. But that was more firearms than Conrad Carlington could contemplate. So he'd settled for the .44 at his waist, paying Pete Kitchen a fair price for the gun and holster and a belt filled with extra cartridges.

It hadn't taken Carlington long to figure out he couldn't stay at Pete Kitchen's forever. There were too many men coming and going, all sharing the news. Quite a few curious glances were cast in his direction and eventually one of the hands sidled over and asked what his business was, whether he planned to stay, how he aimed to keep alive in this country. It was a big territory, but the way men asked questions and kept an eye on your movements, it closed in pretty fast. Eventually the time came when everyone knew your business.

So when Pete had offered him a ride into town, Carlington had accepted readily. It was just impulse that made him step off the wagon right here. Impulse, and the call of that leather bag.

He had thought he could leave it behind forever. But it wasn't so easy to forget about a sack full of diamonds. Now it was calling him again, whispering him promises—the kinds of promises that he knew a sack of diamonds couldn't keep.

He would need those diamonds. He had a plan. Conrad Carlington was going to San Francisco. He was going to lose himself in the crowds. He would bank his wealth, carefully sell those uncut gems one by one. He would start a business of some sort—shipping or merchandising—that would be a front for him. It might take months, even years, but he had the patience now. He felt wise, secure, strong. When the time came for Conrad Carlington to board a ship for London, he wouldn't be sailing as an everyday passenger tucked away in steerage. No, it would be Conrad Carlington, owner, sailing first class on Conrad Carlington's own ship of the line, the best ship money could buy.

Carlington looked up in wonder. To his amazement, there was an emormous ship perched on the top of Sentinel Peak—just the kind of ship he'd been thinking of a moment before. The sun was high and hot now. He was hatless. His eyes were covered with a moist film of perspiration.

Carlington swept his hands across his eyes. The ship went away. He sat on a low, flat rock. What was the matter with him? he wondered.

He was tired, very tired.

He heard a skittering sound under the rock and instinctively pulled his hand away. A scorpion stared up at him, its tail poised. Carlington staggered to his feet and the animal skittered under the rock.

The diamonds.

When he'd come this way, two days before, he'd seen a ruined, adobe mission house halfway up the mountain. Carlington shaded his eyes. Off to the north, tucked into the flank of the mountain, there should be a narrow gulch. The house was in that gulch. Carlington squinted, tried to make out something familiar on the landscape. The ship was there again, poised on the top of the mountain. Nothing else looked familiar.

Carlington hoisted the ham to his shoulder and stumbled on. The sun burned down on his head. His clothing was soaked. Step by painful step, he worked his way up the mountain, plodding slowly. The ship hovered in front of him.

It was late afternoon when Carlington finally came over the ridge of the narrow gulch. Stumbling across the few stones and branches that obstructed his way, the Englishman started down the treacherous slope, fell and rolled to the bottom. Some dim corner of his consciousness instructed him to hold on to the only food he carried, and he was still clutching the ham when, dizzy and sick, he rolled to a stop at the foot of the slope. Minutes passed before he raised his head and looked at the naked adobe house.

The door was open, but the interior appeared dark and grim. Lifting himself from the dirt, Carlington crawled into the dim passage, rolled over and stretched out. In seconds, he was asleep.

He awoke, what seemed like hours later, to find that it was still light. He wondered whether days had passed, or weeks. With a sudden burst of energy, he staggered to his feet and, after a monumental struggle, managed to drag a piece of wood as far as the front door.

That was as far as he got. He left it there. Breaking up the wood, starting a fire—all seemed like too much effort. He couldn't seem to endure any more. Crawling on his knees, dragging himself with his hands, he crossed the floor and propped himself in a dim corner.

The enormous ham still traveled with him, a stone and a burden around his neck, but always a companion.

"Friend," he said, taking the ham in his lap. His hand probed his pocket, found a folding knife and he opened the blade. The last, fading light of the day lit the shaft of the knife and Carlington thought to himself, I am dying.

The thought struck him suddenly, like a revelation. And with its occurrence, there was the odd sensation of suddenly being at ease. The melancholy was almost overwhelming. And yet it was reassuring to know that his struggles were coming to an end—that, soon, all would be over.

Yet he wanted a fire. He wanted food. Carlington looked down at the pocketknife in his hand and smiled.

His father had given it to him before Conrad began Michaelmas term his second year at Eton. "Keep it honed," his father had told him. "Wi' a well-honed blade, a man mought keep himself alive in any circumstances."

The thick, Yorkshire accent came back to him, the kindly look on his father's whiskered face. Conrad looked up, half-expecting to see the old man. But there was no one there—only the arched opening of the adobe hut and the blackness beyond, twinkling with stars.

Through a thick torpor, Conrad Carlington managed to open his clasp knife and cut himself a thick slice of ham. He put the meat on his tongue, where its saltiness tingled. He chewed steadily, relishing the smoked flavor. "Best ham in the land," he murmured to himself, Pete Kitchen's famous motto drifting back to him. These Americans! What a knack they had for the sales gimmick. Such innocents, left to their own devices in a land too big for them by a factor of ten! Perhaps that was what made them such reckless daredevils.

Carlington stopped chewing. His head lolled to one side and he slept.

He awoke to feel a strange sensation of warmth that spread across his body and illumined his face. At first he thought he was feverish and as soon as he opened his eyes, he was convinced that he was in the throes of delirium. A beautiful woman was crouched in front of a small, crackling fire, tossing on sticks. She turned when he stirred and the fire lit up her smile.

"Who are you, my dear?" he asked, fully expecting her to vanish at the sound of his voice.

"Louisa."

Carlington tried to pull himself up to a sitting

posture, but the crook in his back prevented this. Seeing his effort, Louisa put an arm around his shoulder blade and helped him rise to a more comfortable position. For an instant he felt her soft breast press against his cheek.

"Is that better, Conrad?"

"Yes, my dear."

She rose to her feet and went outside. Through the open doorway, Carlington saw the profile of a horse. The woman took a roll from the horse's saddle, brought it into the hut and unwrapped a wool blanket. She spread the blanket over him, tucking it in around the edges of his body as if he were a child.

He turned his head to look at her again. The fire glow lit up the adobe walls. Her features were very fine, her skin smooth. He lifted his hand and touched her dark hair.

"How did you know my name?" he asked.

"I've been looking for you," she replied.

A smile cracked his lips. "You should have told me sooner. I'd have given you more than an even chance of finding me." He started to laugh, but his amusement ended in a hoarse, racking cough that shook his whole frame. "Afraid I'm—not good for much." He wheezed, struggling to catch his breath.

"That's all right." Her dark eyes examined him curiously. "I've come for the diamonds."

"Hee - hee - hee." His almost hysterical laughter dissolved in to a series of dry coughs again. "Won't find 'em here."

"No—I didn't think so. Where are they?"

"Sweet young lady like you—looking for diamonds!"

His head rolled from side to side against the wall as his hollow laugh filled the mission house. Louisa knelt, leaned forward and prodded the fire. Her expression didn't change.

"Now what would you be needing diamonds for?" he demanded. He didn't like the way she'd turned her back on him.

"You wouldn't be interested."

"I bloody well would," he wheezed. "They're my diamonds."

"I hear tell they ain't your diamonds."

"Did you come to torment me?"

"No." She stirred the fire again and looked at him with that same expression of objective curiosity. "I came with a man—the wrong man, Mr. Carlington."

"That's for sure." He winked at her.

She laughed and shook her head. "No, I wasn't made for your kind of life, either."

"What man might you be speaking of?"

"Horace Klonner." Then she repeated the name more slowly, as if to expel him from her life with an incantation. "Horace G. Klonner. I believed in him, Mr. Carlington. I thought he would bring me a fortune. And more than that. I believed he would give me the respect I deserve."

"Where might he be now?"

"In the Tucson jail."

"You followed him clear to Tucson?"

She nodded.

"Just to find me?"

Her nod confirmed his words.

"He must be a damn sight cleverer than you give him credit for, Louisa. A trail as thin as mine is hard to track."

She smiled and shook her head.

"But he didn't find you, Mr. Carlington. I did."

"That's so." Again, the thin, dry laugh filled the mission house. "It's a hard life, miss. A hard life."

"Would you like some water?"

"Thank you. I'd be most grateful."

She rose and returned a moment later with a canteen. Lifting him up, she pressed the mouth of the canteen to his dry lips. He took a long gulp, nodded and then she helped him lie down. Carlington closed his eyes and, for a long moment, there was no sound in the mission house except the crackling of the twigs in the fire. Then his thin, cultivated voice broke the silence.

"It always seemed odd that an old man like me should know when his time had come." He rolled his head to look at Louisa. "I didn't believe it would happen so. But it's true, miss. My time has come."

"Perhaps you'll feel better in the morning."

"No. That's a young person speaking. But me—" He coughed. "I've inhabited these skin and bones nigh on seventy years. Precious little I've learned in all that time. Only thing I've come to know is that when the machine wears down, the body turns cold."

"Where are the diamonds?" Her voice was gentle, soothing, persuasive.

"You will know." He smiled at her and his eyes glowed with a kind of ill-concealed youth. "Wealth! That's what you want. All the jewels in the world. You want to ride a fine carriage and see the riffraff turn their heads as you pass by. Ah, my dear." He reached out his hand. She took it. Her fingers were warm. "It is such a beautiful dream."

She returned his smile.

"All my life, I have searched for such wealth. Many times it has seemed almost within my grasp. I have lived like that and I can tell you with authority: you are right. It is wonderful. Never, for a single instant, have I regretted the pleasures that money can bring."

"Where are the diamonds?" The repetition of her question was like a lullaby. It made him smile.

"I won't keep them from you. I would never do such a thing. You shall have the diamonds and perhaps you'll manage to live like a queen. But listen." He struggled to sit up, his eyes gleaming with enthusiasm. "Help me." She lifted him and leaned his head against the adobe.

"Louisa, listen. You want this wealth and you will have it. But there's something that goes with it. You must be warned. You will be sitting in your fine carriage, with all the servants and riches you can possess, and suddenly a despair will grip your soul. There will be no prologue, no announcement. Simply the despair, as strong and desperate as the force of a hurricane wind. Louisa—" His eyes gleamed out of the dimness. His hand gripped her arm with desperate strength. "You must fight it. You must hold onto yourself. You will conquer. You will live to enjoy your wealth—your beauty—all . . ."

He fell back.

"Conrad." She seized his shoulders, shook him. His head lolled to one side against the dry adobe. "Where are the diamonds? You must tell me. Tell me!"

Panic-stricken, Louisa held him fiercely in her grasp. There was no response. She stopped suddenly and leaned close, listening. To her relief, she heard the sound of dry, rasping breaths, filtered through the narrow channel of his contracting lungs. Gently, she lowered him onto the blanket. She tried twice more to waken him, but there was no response.

She shivered and stood up. Walking to the door, she looked out across the sleeping valley. A single light still glimmered in Tucson. Otherwise the world was lifeless, motionless, completely at rest. She gathered a few twigs and, returning inside the hut, tossed them on the fire. Seating herself in front of its warmth, she pulled the coat around her shoulders, prepared to keep her vigil till morning.

A grey light was seeping across the floor of the mission house when Louisa awoke. She sat up quickly, terrified. The fire had burned down to ashes. There was no sound in the hut.

He's dead, she thought. As she turned to the prone figure, she was relieved to see his lips moving. The sound of a voice drifted toward her, a voice so vaguely whispered that it seemed to come from another world.

"I am not a duke," she heard as she bent toward his whispering lips. "I am not an earl." There was a pause. Then, with added force, "I am a gentleman, all the same. Do you hear—I am a gentleman!"

"Conrad. Conrad." She shook him gently. His eyes opened. He gazed up at her and his hand reached out to stroke her hair. He seemed transfixed by the sight of her. She shivered and grasped his hand.

"Last night—you were going to tell me—" Louisa urged. This was the final chance, she was certain. She tried to keep the urgency out of her voice and yet she could feel the tension in her whole body as she strained to catch some whispered clue.

"The diamonds?" he asked. His words were quite clear now.

"Yes, the diamonds." Relief swept over her.

"When I left the Apaches," he murmured, "I didn't know where to go. It seemed to me this was the ends of the earth. Where is an old man to go? Where?"

His eyes pleaded with her but she looked away, trying to hide her disappointment. He was wandering again. Too far gone, she thought. Now she would never know. She let his hand fall.

"Come—come—I will tell you."

She had to bend over again. The bony, gnarled fingers, held in her palm, shook with quivering strength.

"Long ago—some lost tribe—left its mark on the far mountain."

"Please, Conrad, please."

"There, on the far mountain, when the gold light fades, an arrow points . . ."

"What arrow? Conrad . . . what arrow?"

Suddenly, his eyes opened wide. He gazed at her with a look so intense she could not move. The expression in his face frightened her and at the same time fascinated her.

"What arrow, Conrad?" she urged, pressing his hand.

"My darling," he said. "You are . . . so . . . beautiful."

"Conrad—"

A tremor shook his body and his hand clutched at her so fiercely that she had the uncanny sensation that he might be able to drag her with him. He opened his eyes again and his face seemed to shine with that youthful enthusiasm she had seen before. A laugh started from his lips, was choked off. He shivered, relaxed and lay still, his eyes piercing her with their intensity.

Finger by cold finger, she relinquished her hand from his grip, never taking her gaze from the fixed eyes.

"An arrow . . .," she murmured, turning away.

She rose and stood for a moment staring into a valley that was chilled grey by the morning's suggestion of sunlight. As her vision blurred, she wondered, with a clear consciousness of her own doubt, whether she regretted more the passing of the old man or the loss of some tremendous knowledge that he might have given her.

But her conviction was firm. She would look for the arrow.

Chapter 13

The immense adobe home glowed in the night as Dufond peered at the scene before him. Lanterns, hung from the roughhewn timbers that protruded from the building, spread an eerie, dancing, uneven light across the courtyard. And candles, flickering in the night air, were set on barrels, tables and stairways all around. The scores of tiny flames conspired to give the building the look of a Christmas tree, bedecked with ornaments. And the small amount of light that each offered lent the open ground a strange glow, illumination coming from a hundred directions, highlighting thirty or forty drunken, dancing, caterwauling men and women.

The house itself had a bleached yellow sheen, the lights from inside mingling with those in the open air. The ranch house was huge, an imposing, if simple structure that stretched, one story high, for two hundred feet.

A very wealthy man, Dufond thought. He strained to see, squinting into the faces that gyred and gimbaled before him. But Enrique Delgado, master of the house, didn't seem to be around. Dufond slumped in the tall grass, watching. His heart pounded in his chest, terrified to be within a stone's throw of so many of Delgado's Mexican hands and thrilled to be observing them. He was hidden in the darkness, one of Dufond's favorite conditions. And he was sober, alarmingly so. It occurred to him that they were drunk, and getting drunker as they celebrated. If he was patient he could walk through the place unharmed in an hour or two.

A huge man, riding a wide-eyed palomino, galloped into the courtyard. A young woman, naked to the waist, but wearing a bright red shawl over her head and shoulders, sat sidesaddle in front of him. She laughed as the vaqueros at the party and on foot scattered, bumbling away from the horse's hooves. And as the animal reared, the rider waved his hat in the air, whooping. Naturally, he fell to the ground, pulling the girl with him. Dufond chuckled as she brushed the dust from her dress, her breasts bobbing. The horse disappeared into the darkness.

A boy, not more than twelve, chased a small black dog through the legs of the partying men. The youth swung a rope over his head and hurled the lasso at the dog now and then. Finally, he caught the mutt by one hind leg and pulled it yelping to the ground.

Six men stood in a circle, drinking and laughing as a spectacular young woman in an emerald dress danced in their midst. She grinned at each in turn, her thin blouse clinging to her body as she pranced. She was showing off, performing the *bamba*. A glass, clearly filled with beer, was balanced on her head and she high-stepped in and out of a wooden hoop. Now and then she'd raise the hoop to her knees and spin it there, her feet rising and falling in time to the guitar strumming near her ear. Probably drunk, she spilled the beer and it foamed down the front of her loose chemise. Soaked, the fabric clung to her and the audience rejoiced.

A man dressed in black dragged a frightened

woman through the front door. He held her roughly, tearing at her dress, and she thrashed away from him.

A terrified-looking vaquero wielded a knife near a horse trough. His arm was restrained by the bare hands of a pleading girlfriend. But he leaned away from her, struggling toward an angry man with a knife in each hand. Before the two could have at each other, though, a few amused Mexicans hauled one of them away.

A man in striped pants played a battered, old fiddle for two or three couples, who listened idly, drinking and smoking. The musician sat on a barrel, grinning. A filthy vaquero reached over the churning violinist's head and filled his hand with a companion's girlfriend's breast. He was quickly doused with her beer. For some reason, everyone found this hilarious.

In the shadows, but visible, a woman lay on the ground, her bilious petticoats hiked over her head so that her face couldn't be seen. And a bearded, balding man, his trousers rolled down to his spurs, plowed into her. He was kneeling, holding her like a strange, writhing wheelbarrow as his hips bucked against her. She lay, her arms spread, a glass of whiskey held calmly in one hand.

Finally, two men dragged Dufond's Indian companion, Asha-yo-mo, into the middle of the group. Her hands were tied behind her and a trickle of blood ran from above her hairline across her cheek. Helpless, she kicked at them and managed to catch one drinker, who was concentrating on his bottle, in the groin. The man doubled over and the taller of Asha-yo-mo's captors bashed her in the ribs with his elbow. She fell and they dragged her up the short main steps and into the house.

Dufond shook his head. She was crazy, this girl. She should spread her legs and keep quiet. They'd beat her to death if she wasn't careful. He looked for the burro at the fringes of the party, but it wasn't to be seen. He wished he had his rifle and then fingered his .44, a worn, old weapon that hung from his hip. Very tricky situation, he thought.

Dufond slowly retreated from the scene. He backed away from the open courtyard, watching to see if anyone noticed his movement. But the revelers were intent upon their party. And a playful wrestling match between two women had erupted in their midst, capturing everyone's attention.

Dufond ran along a hard-packed dirt road around the ranch. Circling, he came to a split-rail fence and slammed into it in the dark. Cursing, his shin aching from the blow, he crawled under the barrier and looked at the huge open windows at the back of Delgado's house. Light streamed from two of them and he could hear laughter and screams coming from within. But this exposure was dark, long shadows stretching away from the moon.

Dufond crawled into the black enclosure of these shadows and inched his way along the rough adobe walls of the building. He limped, his leg smarting with each stride. As he came to the first lit window, he dropped to his hands and knees and then crept below the opening, out of sight. Inside he heard the unmistakable sounds of raucous sex. Amid the universal language of grunts and groans, of moaning and sighs, he heard the voice of a Spanish-speaking woman. She cheered her lover on with a voice so loud it filled the night.

Dufond's sense of the absurd overcame him then. He laughed aloud, and bit his fist in order to remain silent. Ludicrously crouched, his wheezing chest heaving with stifled amusement, he listened. She cried out in the rough Spanish of a farm girl, her dialect a world apart from the Castilian teacher who had instructed

Dufond in school. Still, he could make it out. And her bawdy gusto was so enthusiastic, so blatantly intended to spur her lover on, that Dufond couldn't help but stop and listen.

"More, my giant, more," she cried. It was at once a plea and a challenge. She seemed to be defying him to fail her. Insisting that he succeed.

"Deeper, yes, deeper, God, God, more, don't stop, you bull, deeper, giant, animal, more," she bellowed on and on, her exhortations a constant wailing. Dufond wondered how the poor man could stand it. But perhaps, he thought, she was right. Distracted by her demands, the struggling vaquero might go on forever. He sniggered, listening to her words and the man's labored breathing. Dufond had to look.

His head poked above the windowsill, fear and delight in his eyes. In the middle of the dimly lit room, the two squeaked the springs of a huge bed. It, and the floor around it, were covered with pillows. Comforters stuffed with down were draped across the plush mattress, their rich and varied colors bright even in the half-light.

The man, on his back, lay buried in the soft debris of the bed. Dufond could see his upraised knees and the top of his head, but the rest of the man's body was immersed in the soft folds of the sagging bed. Astride him, sitting like a pierced queen, huge, black-haired and screaming, the woman leaned her back against her servant's knees. She rose and fell like the swells of an ocean, the round, heavy melons of her breasts bouncing with his every syncopated thrust. And she carped at him, each demand coming like a burst of desperation between the rise and fall of his efforts.

"Harder, damn, harder, yes, more, yes, more," she went on and on.

Her eyes were closed, her arms dangling at her

sides. The lush, plentiful, ponderous size of her surprised Dufond. She was, simply, immense. Lovely,
sweating and huge. The breadth of her shoulders
stunned him, the proportions of her waist, hips and
bobbing thighs overwhelmed him. The land of the
giants, Dufond thought. No wonder he was buried in
the bed; it was a miracle the man hadn't been crushed.

But from her constant bouncing, Dufond knew
the man labored on. Was it possible, he thought, to actually reach such a creature? To penetrate such a
vastness? But before the question formed in his mind,
the answer echoed through the room. Her cries turned
to wails. She abandoned language and took to a gut-
teral form of blared approval. She throbbed above him,
leaning forward. Her buttocks bounced, her head fell
and her back arched. And even in her ecstasy, her energy seemed endless. The man, apparently lifeless,
dropped his knees. He lay flattened, nearly invisible,
submerged in the bed. And she surged above him, gal-
loping relentlessly, crying out as her breasts swayed in
the air over his face.

Then, with the soft, slick sound of moist flesh
slapping flesh, she fell, exhausted, onto him. Only her
buttocks could then be seen and they still ground into
the motionless man with languid, circular movements.

"My pet," she cooed. "My loving pet." Her voice
now gentle, even tender, Dufond waited for him to respond. But there was nothing, not a word, only the
sound of her mouth smacking him with slow kisses.

Perhaps he's dead, Dufond thought. It was possible. He dropped to his hands and knees and crawled
away toward the next open window, the sounds from it
angry, clattering.

Dufond's spine quaked when he heard the hoarse
tones of Enrique Delgado's voice. It had been years
since he'd listened to the rasp of the man's orders, but

he recognized the sound instantly. Dufond froze. His head twitching uncontrollably from side to side, palms sweaty, the ragged little fugitive huddled like a field mouse in the shadows below the window. The words coming from the room above him were angry, irrational. Delgado was raging, his furor was insistent, petulant, like that of a child. But his explosions of anger filled the night not with the high-pitched scream of an infant, but with the ragged croak of the voice Dufond knew so well.

The sound stung Dufond. He had forgotten its power. Its raw force.

"Where does this Indian bitch come from?" Delgado demanded.

"From the street," a retiring voice answered.

"Not the village?"

"No, señor, no. She was on the street, with a burro. I swear."

"Then she escaped the village?"

"We do not know, señor," another man answered.

"Well, squaw? Are you from Aravaipa Creek?"

Dufond heard the sound of Asha-yo-mo spitting, her disdain for Delgado unbelievable. Then she screamed. One of the men inside that room had decided the girl should show Enrique Delgado a certain amount of respect. Her cries trailed off into a whine as the voice went on.

"Enough. Now, girl, are you from Aravaipa Creek?"

"No," she gasped between sobs.

"Liar."

"Years. Years since I left, they threw me out." Dufond could hear the pain in her voice, the desperation. He was familiar with that sound, too. She would collapse soon, he thought.

"Liar," Delgado bellowed.

Asha-yo-mo wept, her moans filled with resignation and indifference. The inquisition was smothering her with a heavy blanket of hopelessness and pain. Then Dufond heard someone strike her and she seemed to gag, a choked rumbling coming from her throat.

Dufond fingered his pistol butt. Whatever chill liquid ran through the man's veins heated at the sound of Delgado's senseless questioning. He heard the man's insistent anger, his repetitive, vicious probing go on. He asked if she were Apache. If she were from the Ft. Grant area. If she knew Eskaminzin. If she knew where he was. If she'd lived at Aravaipa Creek. He asked these questions over and over, never varying their order, never accepting her stuttered, halting answers.

Within minutes, the process began to wear on Dufond. The rough tone of the interrogation and the biting voice of the questioner unstrung him. Crouched in the dark, listening, he heard the man talking to Asha-yo-mo. But in his mind he listened to Josefina's moans, not the Apache's. The homely little Indian girl gradually lost the power of speech, slowly sinking into unintelligible grunts and denials. And as she did so, Dufond's dream of Josefina's torture took shape in the room above him. He forgot Asha-yo-mo, transfixed by the sound of Delgado's voice, and pictured the beautiful young woman he'd once loved being beaten only inches from his head.

Dufond's chest constricted, tightened like a fist. His head spun and his hands shook. He saw Josefina, ravaged with the knife, bleeding, helpless, tears running down her bloodied cheeks. And he imagined Delgado towering over the woman, his hands bruised from beating her, asking the same questions over and over. Until, delirious with suffering and near death, Josefina had told her husband it was Dufond. She had whispered the name. And he had exploded, tearing the skin from her in an orgy of hatred.

Dufond struggled to escape his vision, to shed it like a coat too large to wear. But Delgado's voice surrounded him. He couldn't escape it. Then, suddenly, it was years ago. The courage he'd lacked then and ever since was all about him. Suddenly, Dufond felt rage.

He stood and looked into the room. Asha-yo-mo was lying on her back in the center of a huge dining table. Goblets and plates lay all around her and overturned chairs were scattered across the room. Her hands were still tied behind her and she stared blankly at the ceiling. Delgado approached her, knife in hand, and cut the clothing from her body with quick, lashing tugs of the blade. As each bit of cloth tore from her, Asha-yo-mo flinched. And Dufond, watching, saw her eyes, bloodied head and crimson, bruised lips as those of his long-dead lover.

Holding his pistol in both hands, he raised the weapon. Just as one of the two men watching Delgado saw Dufond in the window, the ex-priest fired a round into his chest. The vaquero threw up his hands and staggered backward to the wall. But before he fell, an alarm frozen on his lips, Dufond killed the second Mexican, a slug opening a bright hole in his forehead.

Delgado turned and looked at Dufond. His stunned expression quickly turned to recognition. He knew the little man in the window. Delgado walked toward Dufond, marching into the muzzle of his gun.

"Stop!" Dufond shouted.

But Delgado came at him.

"Stop!" This a high-pitched scream.

Delgado's knuckles turned ivory-white as he clasped his knife, his jaw tense and eyes narrowed in hatred.

"I will kill you as I die, Dufond," Delgado roared, standing not five feet from the window.

"So be it," Dufond cocked the pistol and fired.

In an instant the ruby stain spread across the huge man's white shirt. He seemed to study it, looking down into his own blood, and then, incredibly, marched toward Dufond. A second shot rang out and blood streamed from the corner of Delgado's mouth. But still he came, staggering. Pierre Dufond's eyes turned to unblinking dishes, round, amazed. The madman wouldn't die. He fired again, at pointblank range and threw himself aside into the shadows.

For a moment Dufond wondered if he were dreaming. Had these last few instants really happened? But the smoking barrel below his nose told him they had. And the ashen, grinning face of Enrique Delgado that appeared in the window seemed to confirm his worse fears. But the man simply stared into the distance. He stood silently above Dufond's cringing form and looked into the night. Asha-yo-mo moaned inside the room. The fandango raged in the courtyard. And still Delgado stood. Then he fell through the window onto the ground at Dufond's feet, his eyes open, searching, his hand still clutching the knife. But he was dead, finally dead.

Dufond examined Delgado's blank expression as though he were considering a defective machine he didn't understand. The powerful man lay silent, his voice stilled. And Dufond couldn't believe it. A dreaded creature had been eliminated. A man too terrifying to consider lay before him, stiffening in the night air.

Dufond's only thought was to escape, to flee the bloody scene. He dropped his gun and scrambled on all fours along the wall of the house. His palms ground into the rough stones strewn everywhere and his knees smarted as he crawled away from Delgado. The panic which gripped him, the frenzied pumping of his heart and shallow gasping for air he heard from himself seemed to propel Dufond. It seemed to him that he had finally blundered, finally committed an impossible error. What had he done? Jesus. He'd killed him in Delgado's own home, surrounded by his hired guns. Jesus. He was crazy.

Dufond stood, wavering under the sheer weight of his own fear. And then, concentrating as best he could on being quiet, he retraced his steps, headed for the safety of the night.

Almost in a trance, Dufond walked slowly past the window through which he'd watched the two lovers only moments before. As he did so, he heard the groans of renewed efforts coming from the bed. Turning, he saw them.

The huge, pale woman who had so recently clammered atop her man now pointed her buttocks to the sky, her face buried in a pillow. And a tall, thin cowboy, wearing a dark, broad-brimmed hat, knelt behind her. He had a long, thin, drooping mustache and his ribs poked through the thin skin stretched across his chest. The man pounded into her from behind, holding onto the white expanse of flesh she presented him as though it might escape at any moment. She bucked, meeting him, but her lover didn't seem to notice. His eyes rolled and he whooped, exploding into her with frantic jarring lunges.

Dufond was paralyzed by the great white whale of a woman and the gaunt beanstalk of a man who labored so diligently with her. He slumped against the wall of the house, laughing. He felt the rough adobe clawing at his back as he slid to the ground and heard the woman urging her spent man on despite his obvious inability to continue. Mingled with the muffled tones of his own weird laughter he heard her crying, "More, please, more." Then everything went silent and black. Dufond had passed out.

Dufond heard the sound of a coughing fit somewhere in the distance. It rattled on and on, the sort of wheezing seizure that, like a swell in the ocean, never breaks into a wave. The noise bothered him. Then, growing steadily more conscious, he realized that the coughs were his own.

He instantly decided not to open his eyes. Recollections of the bloody scene at Delgado's swept over him and his mind's eye pictured the huge, dying man stumbling toward him. Dufond felt certain he'd been captured. Discovered by Delgado's men. They would kill him, of course, unless he could think of something, quick. And, to buy time, Dufond elected to follow the course that had always served him so well: hide. Apparently being unconscious had proved an excellent way of concealing himself. He'd go on with it. Dufond's cough subsided, gradually, and he clapped his eyelids tightly closed.

Wherever he was, it was quiet. Almost silent. There was a faint, muffled snore in the distance, but nothing else. A guard? And, he noticed, whatever they'd put him on was hard. His back hurt and his shoulders ached. He wasn't tied up, though. Dufond rolled a bit, trying to imitate a slightly restless sleeper. Lying on his side, he decided to open one eye and have a look around. Surely there were scores of grinning banditos circling him. Surely he was doomed. A simple enough job, Dufond thought to himself, a run-of-the-mill ambush, and he'd botched it. For a moment he considered the manner in which they would kill him. Undoubtedly it would be slow. Perhaps they'd let him have a drink first. Would pleading help?

Pierre Dufond opened his left eye. The sight which greeted him made no sense at all, so he closed it again. Through the thin veil of his eyelashes, Dufond glimpsed Hoby McVill, barkeep, polishing the gleaming, nickel-plated rifle. He opened the eye again. Incredibly, Dufond was in McVill's bar back in Tucson. He was lying on the pool table. What was going on?

"Sure is a nice piece," McVill remarked, rubbing the rifle.

"Yes," Asha-yo-mo answered.

"Too bad about him, though."

"He will survive. It is his sickness that weakens him."

"Sure," McVill's indifference sounded truly monumental, his offhand agreement barely a whisper. He had the rifle, for only one hundred dollars, and that was enough.

Asha-yo-mo counted the bills in her hand in the way she'd seen men count money. She had no idea if the amount she'd received for the rifle was correct, not being able to distinguish the denominations on the currency McVill had given her. Still, she felt she should put on a show.

As the woman fingered the worn bits of paper, she remembered the scene at Delgado's. Her lip, swollen and blue, ached. And the heavy man's coat she still wore over her slashed clothing smelled of whiskey. But she was alive. She'd rolled painfully from the dining room table and crawled to the window. Below, Enrique Delgado still clutched his knife, and his bodyguards, dead inside, lay on the floor. The sound of the celebration going on in the courtyard continued, the singing and laughing seemingly growing in volume.

Her hands tied behind her, Asha-yo-mo's mind fogged with pain. Nearly senseless, she'd stood for what seemed hours looking at the body on the ground below. She didn't know what had happened and couldn't decide what to do. But her terror told her she must get away. In any direction. Finally, she'd jumped to the ground through the window and rolled to the corpse's side. Laboriously, she'd pried Delgado's fingers from his knife, the death grip like a vise around the weapon. It was the most terrifying moment of her life, touching him in the darkness, groping with her hands tied behind her, hoping she could wrest the knife from him before being discovered. At last it had come free.

After cutting her bonds, Asha-yo-mo had inched along the wall of the building, headed for the corral which held the burro. Not twenty feet from Delgado, she'd stumbled over Dufond's unconscious form. Peering at him in the darkness, she thought he was dead. But his rattling chest convinced her he was somehow still alive. She wondered what he'd done. Saved her again and then run away? Leaving her behind? It didn't make sense.

Yet, he never did behave in a way she could understand. Why question this latest insanity?

Battered and weak, she'd dragged him into the darkness. Then, slowly, she'd led the reluctant burro to him, amazed the beautiful rifle was still on its back. It had taken quite a while for her to hoist him over the beast's back and the better part of the night to walk back to Tucson. During the trek, all she could think of was the money that would be required for them to escape. Her only source of cash was Hoby McVill's offer to buy Dufond's rifle, so she'd gone straight to the bar.

Now there was nothing to do but wait for Pierre Dufond, the West's most unlikely, even unwilling hero to wake up.

Kitten, the plump blonde whore snoring in a chair, grumbled awake. "Hey, it's morning," she said, surprised.

"Yep, sweetie, sure is," McVill didn't bother to look up at her.

"Shit, mighta rousted me outa this here chair 'fore this. Damn back's killin' me."

"Sorry 'bout that, sweetie. Thought you had a customer there for a while. And then I just couldn't bring myself to wake you up," McVill hated being courteous to the girl.

"Damn." She twisted her back, trying to work the kinks out of it. Her bountiful breasts stretched the tight fabric of her dress as she did so, but McVill didn't notice. "He drunk?" Kitten asked, pointing to Dufond on the pool table.

"Not yet," Dufond croaked, his eyes still shut. "But soon."

"Ah, you wake," Asha-yo-mo smiled.

"A drink, please." The little man needed bolstering.

Asha-yo-mo shook her head. He was amazing. His eyes hadn't opened and he was asking for whiskey. Amazing.

"Don't drink on the table," McVill ordered, pouring a shot of whiskey for Dufond. Asha-yo-mo took the short glass to Dufond, who sat up, swinging his legs over the felt-covered bumpers at the table's edge. He downed the liquid with a quick toss and grimaced.

"He's dead, isn't he?" Dufond asked the Indian girl.

"Yes, dead."

"What?" McVill looked at the motley pair standing in his bar. "Dead? Who?"

"And you got me out of there?"

"Yes," she answered him.

"What?" McVill shouted.

Dufond tossed the jigger across the room into Hoby's hands. "Fill it again, if you please," he ordered.

As the bartender poured, he queried the two of them once more, this time trying to be polite. McVill didn't like having people around who were involved with killing, but he thought it best to remain calm until the drunk and his Indian explained themselves. "You kill somebody?"

"Three, I think," Dufond answered. He turned to Asha-yo-mo and she nodded.

At that moment, Paddy and Garvey O'Rourke walked into the bar. The twins were agitated, hurrying. They ignored Dufond and went straight to Hoby.

"Golly," Paddy exclaimed.

"Jeezum, too," Garvey echoed.

"Didja hear about the killin', Hoby?" Paddy asked.

"Yep, but I still ain't sure who's dead."

"That Mexican guy," offered Paddy.

"Yeah, the Mex," his brother added.

"What Mexican guy? For Christ's sake, will somebody around here make some sense?" It was, thought Hoby, too early in the morning to tolerate this pair of idiots.

"Deader 'n a doornail," Paddy reported, apparently thrilled to be the bearer of such first-class news.

"Stiffer 'n a board," Garvey agreed.

"The Mex, I mean," explained Paddy. "That rich guy, Delgado."

Hoby glanced at Dufond, who responded by raising his second shot glass of whiskey in a mock toast.

"Oh, God," Hoby muttered. Terrific. The drunk had killed one of Tucson's most powerful men and was drinking in his bar. Smelled like trouble to Hoby.

Dufond had, over the years, developed a sixth sense which unerringly told him when he wasn't welcome. His life often depended on the whimsical shifts of attitude that overtook dangerous men and so he was a practiced observer of them. But, in spite of Hoby's obvious discomfort, Dufond was elated. Delgado was dead and he was alive. It was baffling, wonderful. Dufond felt like kicking up his heels. Hoby hadn't panicked yet, so there was no need for Dufond to run for it. As he sat sipping his whiskey, Hoby McVill turned and pulled his pistol from the beer glass on the bar. Then he reached into the empty mug and extracted his badge. He pinned the tarnished thing on his shirt.

"Well, my dear, it seems we'd best be going," Dufond stood and raised his elbow, offering it with comic formality to Asha-yo-mo. She looked down at it and furrowed her brow, handed Dufond the money and walked to the street. The little man, beaming with his good fortune, watched Hoby out of the corner of his eye. Dufond counted the bills and hobbled out the door. As he looked around for Asha-yo-mo, it occurred to Dufond that he was about to embark on a long and dangerous journey. He turned, then, on his heel, and walked back into the ramshackle building. He handed Hoby a ten-dollar bill and picked a pint bottle of whiskey from the shelf behind the bar. Fully equipped to take on the world, Dufond exited, walking into the early morning air.

By late afternoon, the burro had grown irritable. It nipped at Asha-yo-mo as she walked along and the woman whacked it on the muzzle with the back of her hand. The animal stopped instantly, braying. Drunk, Pierre Dufond dug his feet into the burro's flanks, trying to set it in motion again. But the animal held its ground.

"You must walk now," Asha-yo-mo said. "It is tired."

"Then we'll stop for a bit," Dufond responded,

slipping from the burro's back. They'd moved through a sea of vegetable and fruit farms as they'd fled Tucson. And along the way, Asha-yo-mo had stolen two ripe melons and some squash. As they sat by the side of the road, she cut into one of the fruits with Enrique Delgado's knife. Its handle was carved ivory and the blade was engraved with an elaborate hunting scene, riflemen pursuing a deer.

"A lovely weapon," Dufond observed.

"Yes." She didn't want to think about it.

The sweet juices of the melon dribbled down Dufond's chin as he bit into it and he wiped the liquid away with his sleeve.

"The man must have cherished the thing," he mused.

She nodded. Dufond took the knife from her.

"Do you know the history of this knife?" It was not a question, actually. "It comes from Spain, a nation famous for the way its steel holds a cutting edge. A demented people, I think, the Spanish. Lyrical, but demented." Dufond smiled, his the broad, sloppy grin of a drunk grown enamored of his own ramblings. He tossed the knife into the air and caught it. It was heavy.

"Imagine covering a knife like this with so much beauty. Just think of applying grace and charm, of engraving such loveliness into a thing meant for killing people."

Asha-yo-mo silently studied the man. His lips formed the wry, twisted shape that a bitter lemon might cause. The woman thought him foolish. Her people considered killing a terrible duty and so approached it with a kind of reverence. An Apache weapon was always ornamented, always lavished with feathers or carvings so that the importance of its purpose would never be forgotten by the man who wielded it. Battles were rituals to the Apaches. And so she thought the knife's decorations fitting, appropriate. She wondered why they offended Dufond.

"A thing like this ought to be ugly," he continued. "And it should grow uglier with use."

She shook her head, chewing on a bit of melon.

"For instance, given its history, this clean, white handle should be stained with the sweat from his nervous hand. There ought to be some sign of filth where he touched it. And this blade should be worn or marred or something. Some evidence of my Josefina's pain should show on this shining thing."

Asha-yo-mo started. She suddenly understood that Dufond held the very knife with which Delgado had tortured his wife, Dufond's lover. He was holding the thing that had unhinged a priest's life, that had sent him into the bottle, that had separated him from the normal comings and goings of men and women. She shuddered as she watched him finger it, almost lovingly.

"You see here, at the point, there's a nick, a tiny one, but still a nick." Dufond held the blade in the air. "From a bone, perhaps."

"Stop," she pleaded.

"And feel this edge," his finger ran along it. "Honed by a magician, I would say. Patiently sharpened for its work."

"Stop," she begged again. It was too terrible to hear.

"No, no, consider it, really, for all its uses and in spite of years of faithful service, this knife shows little wear. It is a beautiful thing, almost art. Look, look here where the deer carved in the blade is wide-eyed with fear. And see, here, the hunter's rifle even smokes. He has fired his shot. The animal is soon to be dead. But not yet. Imagine that, imagine how some gentle craftsman, an artist, had stopped the bullet in midair. Kind man. Gentle man. Really."

She couldn't speak. Asha-yo-mo stood and walked to the burro, took its reins in one hand and headed down the road. Pierre Dufond stood slowly, still holding the knife. He bent, slipped the blade under his boot and lifted, snapping the thing in two.

Dufond ran his fingers through the matted hair that hung from his head. It was an habitual gesture with him, one that he hoped might clear his mind at the same time it removed the strands of hair from his eyes. It didn't work, though. Having finished the pint of whiskey, he'd moved on to a bottle of wine Asha-yo-mo had somehow acquired. It was late and he was drunk. He looked down at the arcing stream of urine that rushed so furiously from his bladder. A new life, he thought, lay ahead. And this was a fitting christening.

Asha-yo-mo stirred the branches burning beside her, trying not to notice as her companion relieved himself. He seemed to ignore her completely most of the time. He could be cruel, bitter, a thoughtless runt of a man who used her. But she thought there was a hint of tenderness behind his sad eyes. It seemed to the Indian that no one could be so melancholy as Dufond without being somewhat sensitive as well. And there was her gratitude. Twice he'd saved her life. Even though he laughed at the suggestion, she owed him everything. Even though he swore she meant nothing, she doubted he meant it.

She turned the frying squash with a spoon, smelling the bacon grease. "Eat, Dufond."

Buttoning himself, Dufond plodded to her and sat, cross-legged and teetering near the fire. He blew on a slice of sauteed squash and bit into it.

"God, that's awful," he said, chewing.

"Yes, it is. We must buy food in the first town we come to."

Dufond chomped gingerly on the hot food. He had no comment. He didn't have any idea where he was going and wasn't at all sure the girl ought to be brought along. He drank the last of the wine and decided he wasn't hungry.

Through the blur of his intoxication, Dufond watched the girl eat. Her ability to consume absolutely anything amazed him, and turned his stomach. She must, he thought, have a belly lined with brick to endure such food. As tough inside as out, he thought to himself.

Dufond looked at her. The heavy coat had been shed and she now huddled under a coarse blanket. As Asha-yo-mo ate, the cloth parted in front of her and Dufond noticed that her clothing was tattered. Delgado's knife had shredded her shirt and opened three long tears in her buckskin britches. Tantalizingly half-concealed and refracted by his tipsy eye, the otherwise homely girl looked intriguing. Somehow sensual in the flickering light of the fire.

Dufond felt a stirring between his legs. Perhaps he'd keep her around. The ex-priest smiled to himself. He would become the reincarnation of Father Claude of Reims. Perfect, Dufond thought.

During his studies, Dufond had come upon a bizarre story of a berserk medieval scholar and priest. Father Claude, a brilliant writer and teacher, had studied the early church. The thirty-five years following Christ's death had been his specialty and he had inspired hundreds of students with his elegant, impassioned descriptions of the disciples' journeys and sufferings.

Father Claude's genius, however, overtook him.

Somewhere in the great libraries of Rome, he had drawn the conclusion that the "marriage" of nuns was intended to uplift priests, quite literally. Seized by the idea that celibacy was a mistake, a misinterpretation, he conducted a private pilgrimage throughout France. It was, Dufond knew, a tribute to the man's oratory that his journeys had proven so fruitful.

Literally scores of devout virgins had, after listening to him, thrown themselves at the man. He had fathered dozens of children, essentially raping religiously overwhelmed and sexually starved nuns with the sheer force of his argument and renowned good looks. Quite the salesman, Dufond thought.

Of course, the brilliant Claude of Reims had been excommunicated for his vision of salvation. Tried before an unsympathetic court, he had been burned at the stake. But, to the end, he had insisted his view was the correct one. "Better to have cast my knowledge to the people than to have spilled it on the ground," he announced just before his death. Dufond loved the biblical allusion to masturbation—it was perfect.

Wobbly, Dufond contemplated a life of ribald preaching among America's heathens. Perhaps he should begin with the Apache girl?

Asha-yo-mo was tired. All day they'd hurried away from Tucson. She'd run beside the burro for hours without pause, her thin moccasins barely shielding her from the ruts and stones of the long walk. A strong woman, accustomed to the hard work of running away, she'd held up. But only with difficulty. Now she longed for sleep. Nothing hurt, but there was a profound weakness to her. She had not slept in two days.

The plain Indian girl shook her head as she watched Dufond. When he thought seriously about anything, his mouth chewed on itself. And it did so now, his thin ears bobbing with the involuntary action of his jaws.

"Come here, girl," he indicated, patting the ground beside him. It was a surprising order. She stood, wrapping the blanket close to her and settled next to him.

"You improve with time," he muttered, the faintest trace of a smile on his lips. She shrugged.

"No, it's true." She shrugged again. "And I want you." Her eyes blinked, she couldn't believe the man. She was, essentially, his. He owned her. What game was this? He need only take her. Had she not been so tired, the prospect might even have been pleasant. Perhaps she would then discover the tenderness she suspected lay buried in him.

But Asha-yo-mo was worn, her mind unraveled like a tattered sleeve. In the most ardent plea she could muster, the woman let her chin drop to her chest. She was his, but not now. Not this night.

He parted the blanket at her neck and ran his thin, pale hand across her breast. It was a gentle touch, but unwelcome. There was, she thought, a halting sort of frenzy to him. He was out of control.

"No, please, stop," she whispered.

His hand climbed past her breasts to her neck and she heard the click of his pistol, its barrel soon rising to her nose. A fool, she thought.

"I would like you to undress, now." He was shaking.

"No, please," she wished in her heart that something, somewhere, sometime would offer her a chance worth caring about.

"Now." His bleary eyes seemed to bore into her.

Asha-yo-mo stood and let her blanket fall to the ground. She shivered as the faint night breeze tingled across her skin. An arm, rising in unconscious modesty, covered her breasts.

"And the rest," he ordered, pointing the gun at her. "Off. Now."

She rid herself of the shirt quickly. There was almost nothing left of it. Her dark, tight skin stretched over her frame like leather. She was small, her breasts tiny between broad shoulders, her nipples dark. A grumbling came from him.

"More." It was a simple demand.

"Please?" she asked.

"More."

Standing above him, staring into the barrel of the gun, she wondered if he would kill her if she walked away. A glint, ricocheting off his moist eye told her that he might. She bent, unclasping the belt at her waist, and let her torn britches fall from her thick hips. A shiver coursed through her. Never before had she been toyed with so coolly.

"A virgin?" he asked.

She shook her head.

"A slut, then?"

She shook her head again.

"Love, true love," he laughed. "Make a bed."

Asha-yo-mo spread the blanket on the ground and covered herself with a second, rough bit of bedding.

"Please, Dufond, no."

He grinned at her, fumbling with his clothes, finding the buttons difficult simply because he wouldn't put his pistol down. Soon, too, his bowed and hairy legs appeared, his wizened chest heaving over her. Asha-yo-mo thought he looked afraid, angry and afraid. His hands shook.

Dufond peeled off the blanket that covered her. She rolled to her side, trying somehow to deflect his leer. He knelt at her feet, the blanket now wrapped around his frail shoulders.

"It is me or this," he warned, sliding the barrel of her handgun between her clenched thighs. She gasped, truly terrified by him, and rolled onto her back. Ashayo-mo closed her eyes, lifted her knees and spread her legs. The cold metal of his gun barrel traced the curves of her thighs and probed between her buttocks. Tears ran down her cheeks, the mindless terror which consumed her now blotting away all thought.

First she felt his thighs on hers. Then she smelled the rancid exhalations which came from him. He pushed at her, his rampant, wretched member forcing its way into the girl. It hurt. Then hurt more. And she cried out, sound finally expressing the panic her tears revealed. Then she screamed, his organ ramming into her. Something tore, or stretched, and something delicate and valuable broke in her.

She bit her lip. His grunts and groans and rumblings a confused and ugly sound above her.

"No, please," she whispered, too late.

But he didn't answer her. He thrust into her with a kind of desperate, almost mechanical consistency. It seemed to her to go on and on. An exhausted, drunken man, forever in motion. Then as she grew numb, the pain blotting out pain, the fear turned to nausea. He moaned into her, spilling his release. Gagging, rasping, clammering against her body, he gurgled. The smell of him returned then, with a rush, an unwashed man.

Minutes later she covered Dufond's sleeping form with the blankets and walked into the night. The great heavy coat she'd taken from Delgado's couldn't still her quaking. But she'd be far from him by morning.

Chapter 14

The sun was already high in the sky when three, bedraggled-looking travelers rode into Tucson. Hal Quinn rode in front, his shirt unbuttoned, with trail dust clinging like a single, thick mat to his grizzled chest. He reined in by the sheriff's office, dismounted and wrapped his reins around the hitching rail.

"That horse o' yours looks mighty relieved to be rid o' you," said the black-bearded man behind him.

"Should be," replied Quinn, smacking the rump of the big palomino. "That's the hardest I ever rode him. Need a hand?"

Brad Spear shook his head, but his first movement out of the saddle was more an attempt than a recognizable action.

"Whooee," yelled Frank. "My gramma moves faster 'n you, Mr. Spear."

"Youngsters get uppity when they've had a taste of fightin'," observed Spear to Quinn. "You ever notice that?" Favoring his wounded leg, Spear swung from the saddle and heaved himself to the ground. Then the Pinkerton agent and Hal Quinn both watched while Emory more or less flowed out of the saddle. They were gratified to see his legs buckle.

The kid looked up from the dust, astonished to hear their hollers of satisfaction.

"My legs—!" he yelled.

"Don't worry," replied Spear. "Come next week, you're bound to get some feeling in 'em again."

He started up the steps of the jailhouse and was just about to push open the door when a voice stopped him.

"Hey, mister."

Spear turned around to witness the approach of the perfect parody of a government official. The man who came clattering up the walk had on a brown felt hat, brown suit and brown breeches. Somewhere, he'd managed to find a black tie that was subtly tinged with pink—a pink that almost matched the hue of his smooth cheeks. He grinned broadly and his hand was extended. Spear examined the hand somewhat skeptically and finally took it.

"You must be the sheriff!" exclaimed the man in the brown outfit.

"Maybe, maybe not," replied Spear, studying the trace of a quiver that made the man's eyelid move up and down like a butterfly's wing.

"Hah—you Westerners," exclaimed the man, continuing to grin. "Never can tell what you're up to."

"Who are you?" asked Spear.

"Oliver Jenkins. I'm the new Indian agent in this territory. I'll be stayin' at Ft. Grant. Thought I better get off on the right foot with folks around here, since I'll be in and out o' Tucson all the time, like as not. So I'm just stoppin' by to say howdy and as soon's I can get myself a new horse, I'll be on my way to see the— the—" He reached into his hip pocket and drew out an official-looking document which he unfolded elaborately. "The Aravaipa, they call themselves. An Injun tribe. You might's well know I'm here to straighten out these affairs, so there won't be no more warrin' with one tribe and t'other. Won't happen all at once, I figger. Might take a month or two to get things straightened out. But once I get goin', you're likely to see the most peaceable bunch o' Injuns you ever heard of out here."

"Mr. Jenkins," replied Spear, gradually lowering his gaze from the peak of a far-off hill. "I'm mighty glad to see you and so're the Aravaipa, I expect. The only trouble is, you're on the late side."

"Late? Whatta you mean?"

"I mean, Mr. Jenkins, most of the tribe you're supposed to be looking after is dead. Massacred, Mr. Jenkins. Shot down in cold blood."

"But—well—I'm sure there's an explanation."

"There's no explanation for murdering women and children in cold blood, Mr. Jenkins. However, I don't doubt your ability to find some explanation all the same. Just stay out of my way while you're doing it."

"Now, see here, Sheriff . . .," Jenkins spluttered.

"I'm not the sheriff. I'm not a general. I'm not a government official or anyone else you want to know. And if you don't get your mealy hide out of my way in about five seconds, I'm going to pull you apart and find out what makes you jitter."

One set of brown clothes filled with one set of worried bones stepped back one step and Spear pushed open the door of the sheriff's office. There was no one home but Charlie, and he was asleep.

"Hey, Charlie!" yelled Spear, clanging at the bars with the toe of his boot. Spear's encounter with Jenkins had added sour flavor to an already rotten morning, and he didn't really care who took the brunt of his bad temper. The world in general didn't look like a nice place. "Where's the sheriff?"

At the sound of Spear's voice, Charlie rolled from his bunk and landed on the floor with the impact of a dropped bushel of turnips.

"What the—?"

"I asked you a question!" Spear shouted. "Where's Pitkin?"

"He—he left!" complained Charlie, levering his thick body up from the floor.

"Where'd he go?"

"I dunno."

"You dunno," Spear mocked. "Maybe you were out taking your morning constitutional?"

"Uh-uh." Charlie shook his head. "It was last night."

"What was last night?"

"Mr. Butler came roarin' in here. He said Underwood had been killed by Injuns."

"So—?"

"So . . .," Charlie shrugged. "That was it."

The prisoner was a terrible liar and Spear was worn out by two days and nights of hard riding, plus other circumstances he hadn't been able to control. He pulled his .45 and implanted a bullet in the leading edge of Charlie's pine bunk bed. The noise that filled the small cell appeared to frighten the big man. Spear wasn't surprised.

"Charlie," he said, "you visited my hotel room when I wasn't home. You put a hole through my window. You've associated with men I don't like, and you've done things you shouldn't have done. I wouldn't mind putting a stop to you, seeing as how you're a walking disaster, but on the other hand, that wouldn't tell me what I want to know."

Charlie thought about that for three or four seconds. Then he figured it out and held up his hands as if to block the next assault.

"Okay, okay. Don't shoot. Butler came in here . . ."

"You told me already." Spear lifted the .45 about an inch.

"Okay, okay. Klonner spoke up. He said he knew a way they could all get a lot of money."

"I don't suppose he mentioned diamonds."

"Yeah, diamonds, that was it."

"Get on with it. I don't like suspense."

"Klonner asked Butler where the woman was."

"Louisa?"

"Yeah, that was her name. And Butler said she'd rode out of town last night, headed for Sentinel Peak."

"Rode?" Spear didn't like to show surprise, but this time it got away from him.

"Yeah." Sensing his hold on the listener, Charlie went on anxiously. "That made Klonner real nervous and he said, 'She's after him.' "

"After who?"

"That's what Pitkin asked, and Klonner said he'd tell him if the sheriff let him out of here and gave him his gun. Well, Pitkin didn't want to, but finally he let him out and then the three of them left."

There was a long pause.

"So?"

Charlie panicked. "That was all. I swear t'God, I jest told you everything I heard."

"Okay."

"I swear. I swear t'God."

"I said okay."

Spear turned to go. A case of rifles caught his eye. Breaking the glass panel with the barrel of his .45, he borrowed three Sharps and extra cartridges.

When Spear emerged from the jailhouse, Quinn was waiting for him. Spear handed him a rifle. Across the street and down a ways, Jenkins was standing in front of the Antelope. He pushed his way in through the bat wing doors as soon as he spotted the agent.

Frank Emory had picked himself up from the dust and was leaning against the rail, trying to act as if his legs worked. He took the third rifle when Spear offered it, but there was a question in his eyes.

"What's up?" asked Quinn.

"Butler, Pitkin and Klonner have gone after Carlington. Klonner's woman is ahead of them somewhere." During the long ride back to town, Spear had filled in Quinn and Emory on the details of his assignment. Now Quinn shook his head at Spear's words.

"Where they headed?"

"Sentinel Peak." Spear looked from Quinn to Emory and back to Quinn again. Then he grinned. "Anyone feel like going for a ride?"

There was a familiar trembling on the planks of the jailhouse. Then the windows started to shake, the door rattled and a bunch of grackles took off from the roof, alarmed by the tremendous laughter that shook the building beneath them. Hal Quinn's whole body shook.

It took a long time for Emory's dust-grimed face to crack, but finally Spear saw some teeth. The kid pushed against the rail, straightened up and let go his hold. Miraculously, he remained standing.

"Guess we better get some fresh horses," said the kid.

Gossip came with the fresh horses, free of charge. The liveryman seemed to consider it his bound duty to pass along names, identities, descriptions and any other scraps of information that had come his way during recent weeks. As he saddled up the horses and sized up his three new clients, Cranby gave details.

Evidently, William Oury had stayed only long

enough to borrow another horse, get provisions and head for parts unknown. There was a rumor going around town, probably started by Mr. Butler, that Oury had been well-paid for his services to the community. It was Mr. Cranby's opinion that the ex-mayor didn't want to explain his actions to Lt. Whitman. It was also Cranby's opinion that there would be a high-falutin investigation of the whole massacre, which was already being deplored by the second-guesser moralists residing in the Antelope Saloon.

"The way I figger, just between you an' me," confided Cranby, tugging a saddle blanket onto the back of an unwilling grey filly, "Mr. Oury's gonna take his wealth and comfort and set himself up for a while in San Francisco or some far-flung place sech as that. Way I see it, you won't detect him around here till the jackals settle down and stop lickin' their chops. Which leaves the rest of us'n folk, as you may've noticed, with a pack o' Injuns as mad as hornets."

Cranby knew other things, too. He'd heard about the shoot-out at the Mexican ranch the night before. "Some drunk," as he put it, had gone on a rampage, and he'd put a bullet or "mebbe half a dozen" into Delgado. And then that drunk had somehow or other got away. Cranby winked.

Spear was paying more attention now. The description of "some drunk" sounded familiar. It would be just like Dufond, he figured, to stray into these parts . . . if he was still alive.

Spear shook his head. Couldn't be. He'd left Dufond at the bottom of a mine shaft back there in Silver City. It would have taken a ton of miracles for that drunk to get out of there alive.

"Ever seen the fellow you spoke of—that drunk?" asked Spear, as he mounted the filly.

"Nope. But he got hisself some reputation damn

fast, shootin' Delgado like that—and then disappearin' in thin air."

"Delgado?" queried Spear. "Wouldn't be the same hombre that led the Mexicans in that raid?"

"One an' the same," replied Cranby, dragging three rifle holsters out of a dusty closet. "Now you take care o' that filly, you hear? She's one fine hoss and I'm fixin' to groom her up for racin' some day."

For Hal Quinn, the liveryman had somehow procured a Percheron that came close to suiting the ironmaster's frame. The horse was a big-boned, brown creature with the proportions of a draft horse, but Cranby swore it would pick up speed on a stretch.

"Don't worry," he confided. "That there Perch will run like a steam engine, once you git 'im movin'. In fact, you might consider the purchase of 'im, Mr. Quinn. It's my opinion that a seat the size o' yours needs a horse to suit, no insult intended."

"Thanks, Cranby, but I don't expect to be doin' much riding after this day's over."

There was something else on Quinn's mind besides horses. He signaled Cranby that he wanted to have a further word with him. When the liveryman came alongside, Quinn lowered his voice.

"Cranby, a fella in town here told me them raiders come back with a parcel of Injun babies."

"Yep, that's right. I counted 'round thirty myself. Couldn't miss 'em. Such wailin' and squallin' you never heard."

"What's to become of 'em?" asked Quinn.

Cranby shrugged.

"Hard t'say. I 'spect Pete Kitchen can use a dozen up on his farm, once they get growed. An' there's always plenty of swillin' an' muckin' to be done. God knows, I could use a couple of lads right here to give me a hand. I ain't gettin' any younger, you know."

"Or smarter," muttered Quinn, as he fixed himself in the saddle. His eyes took on a distant look as he examined Sentinel Peak.

"What's that you say?"

Quinn ignored the question.

"Put the word out, Mr. Cranby. If any harm comes to those Injun tots, I'll find the man that done it and introduce his head t'my anvil. I expect to be alive at nightfall, and I expect to be back before mornin'. So you don't got much time to spread the word around."

"Aw, Quinn, I got better things t'do than . . ."

"Nope." Quinn tossed Cranby a double eagle. "You ain't got nothin' better t'do."

Cranby examined the coin in his hand. "Guess you're right," he admitted.

"Spear!" called out Emory. He was riding a skinny, dun-colored horse, and the skittish creature had already carried the kid some distance away from the table. Emory's eyes were fixed on the distant mountain. Spear rode up beside him and reined in the filly.

"Look there," Emory pointed. "Got your glasses?"

"Nope." The binoculars were still in the saddle-bags on the back of the roan. And Emma had the roan.

"Hell."

"It's all right. I can see. Quinn!"

The blacksmith joined them.

"Over there, about halfway up the ridge." Spear pointed. It was only a second before Quinn's eyes picked out the three riders in the distance, creeping their way up the mountain like flies on a honeypot.

"Yep," responded Quinn. "Let's go."

The three riders broke into a canter.

It was already mid-afternoon by the time Louisa Wentworth broke the ridge and came around the west side of Sentinel Peak. She'd had to stop frequently and dismount, guiding her horse over rough places in the terrain. And every time she'd dismounted, it seemed, she'd skinned some part of her ankles or legs, or scratched her arms all to pieces on the thorny brush that surrounded the trail. Then her horse had picked up a pebble under its shoe and she'd had to stop and work at the stone with Carlington's pocketknife to pry it loose. Many times she had been tempted to leave the horse behind, shoulder her blanket and few belongings, and head out on foot for the bare range beyond. But she knew from the soreness in her feet and the sun beating down on her head that such an action would be a mistake. And she remembered those grave markers Klonner had pointed out along the trail—pitiful crosses made of two sticks lashed together.

Stumbling down from the ridge, she led her horse to a narrow strip of grass that was lightly shaded by a stand of mesquite. Louisa reached behind the saddle for the canteen and took a long swallow—then stopped so suddenly she almost choked. She shook the canteen, listening to the slight, faraway splash of the water that covered the bottom. Less than one-quarter left, and she had no idea how far she had to travel.

The remains of the ham were tied on to the pommel. She was hungry, so hungry there was a cramp in her stomach. But she didn't dare eat. The salty meat would only make her more thirsty.

Almost worse than the physical hunger and thirst were the doubts that plagued her. She hadn't intended to continue this maniacal search. If it hadn't been for her chance meeting with Pete Kitchen, her impulsive question and his ready answer, she might well have ridden out of town the very next morning in a comfortable coach bound for Ehrenberg. But she had asked . . . he had answered . . . and she had found the old man. Such fate was too much to resist. She was swept along, forced to do what she had to do as surely as if someone was holding a gun to her head.

Yet she was not. She could turn back any time. She could turn her horse north and ride alone to freedom.

Then she looked at the distant mountain and realized she could not give up. Not now. The search had taken her too far. And she had clues. What had he said? She struggled to recall the words of the dying man. "Some lost tribe left its mark . . . When the gold light fades, an arrow points . . ."

It seemed so cryptic. Those words might mean nothing. After all, the man was dying; he had been delirious. Even if he had known what he was saying, some diabolical impulse might have made him joke with her. He had lied!

Yet she was sure he had not. What was she to believe? "When the gold light . . ." Her head spun. She was dizzy from lack of food. She had scarcely slept the night before, keeping her vigil. She needed food.

The knife in her hand was worn with use, yet well-sharpened, carefully oiled. Carlington had taken good care of it.

Louisa Wentworth opened the blade carefully and came around to the horse's side. Holding the rope that was looped around the pommel to steady the ham, she cut herself a long, thin slice. Hungrily, she wolfed it down. The salty, smoked taste burned her tongue. Quickly, before she had time to think, she cut another slice, this one thicker. She gulped it down, licked her fingers. Then she lifted the canteen and drank the last of her water.

She felt better. Her head had stopped spinning.

She tried not to think about thirst or about the miles she might have to go before she could drink again. Now she was refreshed. Only the immediate present was important to her.

She looked at the far mountainside again and, suddenly, all consciousness of exhaustion disappeared. The sun had fallen lower in the sky. It lit up the brown side of the sheer mountain in stark relief. As if by magic, strange shapes began to appear on the mountain.

Louisa shook her head, closed her eyes. The wheezing, dying voice filled her ears: "Some lost tribe . . . left its mark." When she dared look again she half-expected to find the mountain inhabited by strange peoples, to see a whole civilization that had vanished in the mists of time. But no, there were only those marks, clearer now. Concentric circles like an enormous target. Zigzagged lines, crisscrossed in the swastika pattern she had seen in a Pueblo village.

No arrow was visible yet. But now she was sure. The excitement was almost unbearable. The old man had not been lying. She smiled. He meant for her to have those diamonds. She would have them.

She grabbed the reins of the horse and started down the slope, racing carelessly toward her goal. After a short treacherous distance of bad terrain, the trail leveled out and she could mount. She kept her eyes fixed on the distant mountain—hoping, praying that she would reach it in time.

It was the intensity of her concentration that made her miss first sight of the approaching riders. By the time she looked around—and it was only the chance flight of a quail from the brush that made her do so—they had already spotted her.

Terror seized her at once. She would have recognized Klonner anywhere. She knew him by the felt hat, by the way he sat in the saddle. She recognized, even at this distance, the ridiculous way his legs jutted out from the side of the horse as if he were a lame pigeon trying to take off.

But he was not lame. He carried a rifle and he was riding hard. Two men were with him—a skinny fellow she'd seen at Underwood's and a taller, fierce man who, she guessed, was the Tucson sheriff.

So Klonner had bought his way out. Once again, the weasel was on the run. And this time, it was Louisa Wentworth he was after.

He couldn't have her! She was determined. She was carrying more than a silly derringer this time. She had a rifle and a .44. She might die. But she would not go back to Klonner.

Louisa spurred her horse. Behind her, she heard a long, echoing shout.

"Louisa!"

No, she ordered herself. No, don't answer him. Again she touched her spurs to the horse, urging him on. A rifle shot rang out, blasting across the valley.

Don't look, she told herself.

She was within range of the marked mountain and, almost miraculously, the sun was turning gold. Please, she begged. Please, show me, she pleaded, as if it were a living mountain that held the secret. She looked over her shoulder. Two more shots rang out, too close to ignore. Now Klonner and the sheriff were both firing at her.

Her heart burned with rage at the men. She had given everything to Klonner, done everything for him. And now he wanted to kill her in cold blood.

She wheeled toward the mountain again and spurred her horse. Then she saw it. Gleaming in the gold light, an enormous arrow slashed its way down the side of the mountain, pointing to the right. The mountainside ended steeply, but there was a cluster of boulders at the base, near the tip of the arrow. Between Louisa and that gold arrow, there was no cover. If she could only reach the bottom of the slope and use the boulders as her fortress, she would have a stronghold she could defend.

She glanced over her shoulder again. To her relief, she saw that she had gained ground. The pursuers were reloading, and even though their horses were going at a full gallop, the distraction of the gunmen slowed the animals' pace. A few hundred feet, and she would be safely out of range. Exultation flooded through her as she saw that the trail was clear almost to the base of the mountain. If she could only reach that cluster of boulders!

A shot rang out. Then another.

Louisa felt her horse stagger, start to fall. Halted in mid-gallop, the animal plunged forward, its head dipping hard. Louisa jumped clear and reached for her rifle but the stock slid from her grasp, crushed under the falling animal. The horse sank to its side and Louisa ran.

She had no idea how far it was to the cluster of rocks. She didn't dare look ahead. She was only aware of the ground flying beneath her feet. She gasped for air, feeling herself weakening, hearing the thunder of horses' hooves as the riders approached behind her. In another moment, their rifles would be reloaded. They would fire again.

The shots came, flew past. She stumbled, recovered and fell behind the rocks.

The three men were so close she could hear them shouting to each other. She took one quick look over her shoulder to make sure of her position. There was the arrow, pointing down, the sunlight glimmering along the long, painted shaft. Above was the sheer wall of the mountain. High boulders surrounded her on all sides.

Louisa drew her pistol, stepped beyond the edge of the stone that concealed her, and fired three times in quick succession.

One long, melodic howl split the air. Louisa could not suppress a grin.

"She hit me! She hit me!" yelled Butler. "God damn her, that lady fired a gun at me."

"Butler, for Christ's sake, shut your yap," responded Pitkin. The complaints of Underwood's secretary subsided to a dull whining.

Louisa reloaded quickly. It had been a lucky shot, she knew. The three gunmen were just beyond the range of real accuracy. When they charged her stronghold, she would need all six bullets. Or more.

She leaned her back against the rock, trying to calm herself. Concealed by the boulders, she edged her way closer to the steep mountainside. Now she was at the very tip of the arrow. She looked around. Nothing.

Her heart sank. A new despair gripped her. She might die here, and all for nothing. The old man had lied after all.

A rifle shot spat against a boulder, ricocheted, stinging the rock behind her. She dove and her hand slid under the edge of the rock, touching leather. She stood up, fired quickly and crouched again.

Leather. Suddenly it struck her how odd it was. Slowly, almost dreading what she might find, she peered under the rock, moved a stone aside. The two handles of a leather valise, parted like an open welcome, looked out at her. A brass buckle shone.

With trembling hands, she dragged out the valise, opened it and reached inside. The heavy crystals flowed between her fingers, clattered into the darkness of the open, leather case. Stone against stone, the diamonds chattered against each other. Louisa's eyes clouded. The happiness, the sheer joy after such long anticipation, was almost more than she could endure.

Two more rifle shots echoing from the mountains, the lead flying past her head, brought her to her senses. She heard Klonner's voice.

"Louisa! Darling! I know you have the diamonds! We'll make a deal!"

"Go to hell, Horace!" she shouted.

"Listen, Louisa, it's just a four-way split this time. And then we'll work together as partners. I swear it."

She didn't reply.

"If you don't listen to reason, we'll have to come in for you. You don't want to die—do you?"

Suddenly she heard a pebble fall, up and to her left. Instinctively, she turned and fired. A head disappeared behind the boulder.

So that was it. Klonner was going to talk to her while Pitkin moved into position. He had deceived her again. She was pinned now. Klonner and Pitkin both had rifles. She might hold them off for minutes, even hours. But eventually they would get her. It was only a matter of time.

"It's useless, Louisa. We've got you surrounded. Butler's hardly scratched—ain't ya, Butler?"

"Yeah." The reply was weak.

"I don't want to kill you, Louisa. I'd never want to kill you. But I'm gettin' mad. You know how mad I can get."

Yes, she knew! She knew. The rage boiled up in her. She didn't care if they killed her. She didn't care what happened. She hated this man more than anyone on earth.

"Okay, Horace," she yelled. "I see it your way."

"I knew you would, Louisa." His triumphant voice revolted her, made her sick. "I knew . . ."

Klonner's words were cut short by his scream, as her first bullet found him. She stepped out, aimed and fired all in one motion. Her very first shot ripped into his side and he fell back, the rifle dropping from his hands. But even at the moment of firing, Louisa felt the futility of her desperate action. She should have waited. He was too far away, only wounded, and her next three shots only nicked the flanks of his horse. The horse whinnied, spun in terror and Louisa caught a glimpse of Klonner falling to the ground, rolling over and drawing his pistol.

Hating herself, cursing her wild action, she pulled back behind the rock. Then she looked up.

Pitkin. She had forgotten him. Her whole body went weak. Her mind simply recorded the diabolical grin of the lawman who peered down at her along the barrel of the rifle.

"Drop it, lady," he commanded.

No, she thought, and her mind was calm. No, I won't drop it, mister, she thought to herself, so clearly that she wondered if she had spoken the words aloud. With the smooth confidence of a newborn gunfighter, she raised the .44.

A rifle shot rang out. Too late, she thought. She waited for the pain to occur. To her surprise, there was none. Instead, she heard only a piercing scream. An enormous, red blotch appeared on Pitkin's forehead. He plunged from the boulder. Vertebrae crackled on the stones below. The shot from his rifle, like a final exclamation of dismay, ricocheted off a distant rock and spun into the dry, Arizona brushland.

Chapter 15

By the time Spear, Emory and Quinn crossed the ridge of Sentinel Peak, the three riders ahead of them were already riding hard in pursuit of Louisa. In a way, that was fortunate. With Klonner driving them at a full charge, Pitkin and Butler hadn't bothered to look back. If they had, they would have seen Spear bearing down at a fierce pace. The filly was a good one and she responded quickly. So when Louisa had altered her course, heading for the base of the mountain, Spear had gained ground by wheeling quickly and cutting toward the west. That had given him a slight advantage over the other riders, but only a hundred yards or so. He was still far behind when Klonner's shot caught Louisa's horse and Spear saw horse and rider thunder to the ground.

He had slowed then, with regrets. He knew what made that woman ride like hell and he felt partly responsible for it. Spear himself had torn her away from Klonner. Like it or not, he had started her on this wild ride that had ended so badly. When he saw her fall, he fully believed the chase had ended. He didn't think it was possible for the woman to escape from that tumbling horse. And even if she did, Spear calculated, one rifle shot would finish her off.

He was astonished, therefore, when he heard Louisa's pistol shots ring out, followed by Butler's manic screams.

"Goddamn, she made it," Spear muttered aloud. But he'd lost precious moments by slowing the filly. As he spurred the filly into motion and headed for the mountain where the three gunmen had staked their claim to the life of the lone lady, Spear suddenly realized what the old, painted Indian arrow on the side of the cliff was pointing to. Louisa had run to the diamonds after all!

Spear heard Klonner shouting to Louisa. He heard her reply echoing over the valley. Then he saw Pitkin climb up the boulder on the north side, getting Louisa in his sights.

Spear touched the filly with his heel. Quinn and Emory weren't far behind, but they had to put up with horses of lesser ability. Louisa was pinned between Klonner and Pitkin. She might still stand a chance, if she didn't show herself.

"Just hold on, lady. I'm almost there," Spear thought to himself.

Then it was too late. Louisa stepped out, fired, and Spear saw Klonner fall. At the same instant, Spear reined in the filly and he was glad once again that this horse knew how to keep her footing. When she stopped, she didn't budge and when Spear raised the Sharps rifle to his shoulder, she still didn't move. Spear saw Pitkin step up on top of the boulder and he got his sights in line as the sheriff aimed his rifle toward Louisa. Spear had only one shot, but he used it well. He was gratified to see the Sheriff of Tucson tilt forward and drop out of sight.

A strange silence followed the barrage of rapid gunfire, and for a long moment, Louisa was left alone behind the boulder with the crumpled body of the sheriff. She started to reload. She was certain that Klonner was only wounded, but was not sure how fast he could move.

But who had shot Pitkin? She looked across at the dead man as though he could give her an answer, but the body didn't stir.

Then, as if in a nightmare, Klonner's face appeared from behind the rock. Before Louisa could react, he was on her, his arm around her throat, the barrel of the pistol pressed against her temple.

"Ah, Louisa, my Louisa," he whispered. "My ticket outta here."

"Horace, it's no use. You can't do it, Horace."

His arm tightened on her windpipe.

"Please," she gasped.

"Louisa," he whispered in her ear. "Just do as I say, darling. You and I, together, darling, we can go anywhere."

"No—Horace—"

"Ah," he sighed. With his free hand he lifted the leather valise.

Still holding her tightly, Klonner shoved Louisa from behind the rock. She saw Butler, not far away, crouched behind a rock, blood oozing from a wound in his leg. But he wasn't looking at them. He was watching the man with the black beard who approached, riding a lean, sleek filly.

Brad Spear. As soon as she saw him, Louisa felt Klonner's arm tighten around her neck and for an instant she was sure he intended to strangle her. Spear raised his rifle, but Klonner's laugh rang out.

"Don't shoot, Spear!" he shouted. "You might hit the little lady."

Slowly, Spear lowered his rifle. Klonner's laugh sounded again.

"Too bad, Spear."

"Horace, please, help me," whined Butler. The wounded man, unarmed, cowered by the rock.

"Shut up," snapped Klonner. Then he called out, "Spear! You hear me?"

"Let her go, Klonner."

"No—this is my turn, Spear. I got what I came for," he yelled, lifting the leather bag. "Drop your guns, Spear. You hear me?" His grip on Louisa's throat tightened. Her feet lifted from the ground. Spear dropped his rifle.

"All of 'em, Spear. Nice and slow."

Spear slid his pistol from the holster and let it fall.

"Now get off your horse, Spear." The agent obeyed. "Turn around." Spear did so. "Start walking and keep walking."

The filly lifted her head as Spear turned away from her. Klonner grinned.

"Come on, Louisa," he urged. "Nice and slow. We're gonna ride out of here."

"Horace, what about me?" begged Butler.

"You—you ain't good for much," the gunman replied. "Why don't you just die here?"

"Look out, Horace," pleaded Butler. "There are two others. I swear. I saw 'em . . ."

Butler never had a chance to finish.

When Brad Spear, riding ahead, had fired on Pitkin, Quinn and Emory reined in. It took only a few words to decide their actions. Moving fast on foot, the two men divided, Emory going south to come up on the flank of the mountain. For all his bulk, Quinn could run, and he was well-hidden by the boulders along the north by the time Klonner stepped out with Louisa in his grip. While Spear dismounted and started walking, Quinn and Emory took advantage of their positions, moving in step by step. Neither could see the other, and they might have waited a lot longer if Butler hadn't spotted them.

It was Emory who stared straight into the eyes of the frightened clerk, who seemed astonished to see him. The first word that came to Frank's mind was a multisyllabic curse. But after that, he didn't think. He just moved.

"Klonner, you son of a bitch!" yelled Emory.

At Emory's shout Klonner whirled around, relinquishing his hold on Louisa for a fraction of a second. He dropped the leather bag and drew his pistol, firing three times toward Emory.

The kid didn't dare return Klonner's fire. Louisa was still too close to her captor. A stray shot could be fatal, and Emory wasn't all that sure of his aim.

Frank Emory suddenly realized the only thing he could do was jump back down and hide. But it took him a moment to come to that conclusion, and the moment was too long. By the time he'd realized his mistake, the kid had taken three bullets. He fell hard. He died believing that he'd failed.

Quinn was already halfway down the rock on the far side when the first bullet took Emory and, as the kid fell, the blacksmith's arms locked around Klonner's neck. Klonner turned his head sharply, trying to catch a glimpse of his assailant and his terrified eyes fixed pleadingly on the broad, kindly face of the blacksmith.

"No—" Klonner managed. Louisa slid from his arms. He raised his pistol and aimed it at the head of the giant who gripped him.

Then, quite mysteriously, all the strength went out of Klonner's body. It seeped from his finger tips first; then his toes; and, finally, oozed out of the muscles of his arms and legs.

The loss of control in his right index finger bothered Klonner the most. It meant he couldn't fire. He couldn't slip away. He was, finally, in the grip of something too big to wriggle from. He died choking, hearing his own pistol clatter on the rocks and wondering why the enormous man wanted to hug him so hard.

Chapter 16

Spear awoke to a cobweb feeling that wouldn't go away. He brushed a hand across his nose, then brushed again. Whatever was tickling him came back to torment him. Finally, much against his will, he was forced to open his eyes.

It wasn't cobwebs, after all. It was hair—a woman's hair. And when Spear opened his eyes, that woman took the liberty of lowering her face just a little farther and planting her lips on his.

He accepted. The sensation was far better than cobwebs, and from the moist wetness of her lips there emanated a tremendous after-effect of well-being that somehow lodged itself around his midsection, stiffening him perceptibly.

"How'd you get in?" he asked, when Louisa released him.

He reached up and pushed the abundant hair to her temples and stroked a hand over her cheek.

She smiled. "You left the door unlocked."

"Is that so?" He grinned. "Some agent, aren't I?"

"I think so."

To make this early morning trip from her room to his, she had wrapped herself in a hotel sheet. The sheet was easily pushed aside. The comforter that covered the better part of Spear's body was also removed without too much difficulty. And then there was only the blissful sensation of skin against skin.

Louisa lay on top of Spear with one leg between his thighs, her knee touching the bed and the soft mound at her pelvis pressed against a yielding part of his groin. A neat fit, Spear thought. From where he lay, he had a chance to run his hands down the contours of her body, from the gentle, hanging breasts to her belly, over her hips and around the soft globes of her buttocks. She pushed against him, kissed again, and this time they held their kiss while their tongues touched each other.

Then her hand reached down in that shared space between them, and suddenly Spear had the impression that someone had answered his dream. A small dream, really. Nothing on the order of religious conversion, fabulous wealth or extraordinary power. Just the total realization of a woman's soft finger tip playing lightly on a sensitive part of his body. He quivered.

Her hand reached farther. In the warm way her palm cradled him there was comfort. They rolled suddenly.

"Ouch." He'd forgotten about his leg.

"What's the matter?" she whispered, her finger tracing circles around his backside.

"Nothing important," he replied. The wound was down in the calf and out near the surface, a part of his body he didn't need to use right now.

"You saved my life," she said.

"Nope. Quinn did."

His lips fastened on hers, silencing hers. For the moment he had the image of Frank Emory falling, astonished, not even holding onto the holes that were bleeding. Then Spear forced the memory out of his head. But he conjured up the living kid, rewarded him.

This lady is yours, Frank, he thought, and his tongue fixed on the beautiful nipple that awaited him.

"Oh."

Spear sucked at Louisa's breast, and her hips rose, her belly undulated in response. His hand moved to the shimmering, almost imperceptible down that covered the softest part of her abdomen, and she flung her head aside on the pillow.

"Oh."

Now his hand found the curly, taut hairs and he roughed them, probing, seeking further. She parted her thighs, reached down, seized his hand and placed it where she wanted him. Using him, contributing her female awareness to the willing, male hand, she covered him with her moistness. Then her fingers sought another plaything that was harder but more sensitive and, as he eased down on her, she placed him at her moist entrance.

"Go in me," she whispered, but he had already penetrated her, and his tip was held by her responsive body. She reached out, her arms flung on either side and gripped the edge of the bed. Her body arched upward and he went deeper. Louisa sucked in her breath and her head turned away. Her eyes closed. The gentle, white face flushed and the flush crept around her neck, etching a beautiful lacework trail to her breast.

Spear penetrated her until he could go no deeper. She strained against him, arching, reaching for the root of his hardness with the awesomely hungry, anxious, searching tip of her own body, begging him with every undulation of her hips. And then she flung her legs out, opening wider still, opening so wide that Spear felt as if he were plunging straight down.

He drove into her again and again, the rhythm increasing. Now her neck held pearls of moisture. She moaned. There was no delicacy to her movement against him. Each of his thrusts was met with her hungry, passionate lust as she pulled him on, sucked him in and begged for the release that finally came.

It swept through her thighs first. She pinned him, released her hold on the bed and pressed his buttocks, forcing him in to stay. Beneath him he felt the opening grow wider, swell, as the panting in his ear became a single, long, drawn-out moan of pleasure and he released, pouring into her in a single, pulsing tide.

Her hips moved, and moved again. There was a slow series of subsiding undulations. Now he was sensitive to her skin but there was a warm sea all around him as she rocked herself into a kind of pleasurable reward of leisure. Her hands locked around his back. She pulled him down strongly and kissed his lips.

"Ouch."

Louisa looked at him reproachfully. "It hurts that much?"

"The lovin,' nope. The leg, yup."

"Poor cripple."

"Good nurse."

He left her and rolled on his back. She followed him with the motion of her body, leaning on her side, looking at him. There was some light coming in through the curtains. The leather bag was sitting on the nightstand where he'd left it. The brass buckle winked sunlight at him. Spear looked down at Louisa.

"You could've strolled in, taken that thing and strolled out again. I never would've known the difference."

"I didn't," she smiled.

He thought about that a minute. "What do you do now?" he asked.

"What *should* a lady do, in my circumstances?"

"Tell me."

"Mr. Spear," She rolled on her stomach and leaned on her elbows. "I've been thinkin'. Every time I dreamed of enormous wealth, you know what was in my mind?"

He shook his head.

"Clothes. More clothes than you could imagine. Somehow, and I'm just beginnin' to figure it out, my dreams always began and ended with the wardrobe. Oh, there were other things in-between, of course. Men and carriages and fine china and all the rest of it. But at the beginnin' and end, there was always the same thing waitin' for me—a new dress, a new pair o' shoes or the finest piece o' jewelry in the world."

"You figured that, huh?"

"Yup. Mr. Spear, I'm gonna open a store. The finest ladies' store you ever saw. I'm gonna buy everything I ever wanted to own and sell 'em just as fast too 'cause I figure if I want 'em, so does every other woman, from the finest lady right down to the cheapest whore."

"Well, I don't know about that. But I know it'd take you some money to start a store."

"Right."

"Well?"

"Mr. Spear, I never was overfond of Horace Klonner and I wouldn't defend his ways. Still, I threw my lot in with him for a time and I wouldn't mind getting my fair share."

"How do you expect to come by that?"

Louisa shifted her weight to take a position across Spear's chest. She smiled at him and stroked his eyebrow with her index finger.

"I seem to remember a pillow in Horace's room that kind o' crinkled when he moved. Since you arrested him, I figure you might have paid some kind of attention to that."

Spear regarded her thoughtfully while her finger continued to trace some kind of artwork across his eyebrow.

"Tell you what," he decided finally. "Over in that drawer, there's a pencil stub and a sheet of paper with the Pinkerton seal on it. You bring those items to me, and I'll do the rest."

She smiled, kissed him and got out of bed. When she returned, the items he requested were in her hand. He wrote quickly and handed her the sheet of paper.

"What's it say?" she asked.

"Says you get your pillow and the money that's in it. You hand that to the deputy this morning and I suspect he'll give you what you want."

Louisa kissed him again.

"Now, tell you what," continued Spear. "I'm going to turn over in this bed and go back to sleep for about three hours or so. That should give you time to pack your bags, collect your pillow and catch the morning stage."

She looked crestfallen.

"What's the matter?"

"Nothing." She looked away. "It's just that— Brad—I hoped . . ."

"Nope. Once you get your dress shop going, you advertise well and I'll find my way there some day."

She tried to smile and almost succeeded. Standing, she picked up the sheet she'd walked in with and wrapped it around herself.

"Good-bye, Brad."

"Good-bye, Louisa." She turned and headed for the door. "Oh, Louisa—one other thing." She paused, not looking at him. "If I ever hear of you in the thieving business again, I'll wrap a set of bars around you so fast it'll make your head spin. And all the cash pillows in the world won't do you a damn bit of good. Understand?"

She nodded, opened the door and left. When she had gone, Spear got out of bed, turned the key in the door, crawled under the sheets again, pulled the coverlet up to his chin and, for the next three hours, slept the sleep of the dead. Not even the rattle of the morning stage, leaving Tucson with Louisa Wentworth aboard, could wake him from his heavy slumber.

"Get my note?"

"Yep."

"She get her pillow?"

"Yep."

"No trouble opening the safe?"

"Nope. Combination was in the bottom drawer, right where you thought it'd be."

Hal Quinn, the self-deputized sheriff of Tucson, opened the drawer and handed Spear's note back to him. The Pinkerton agent took it and tore it up. After a hot bath and a change of clothes, he was feeling fine. The fact that it was two o'clock in the afternoon didn't disturb him. Morning was morning, no matter where you put it in the day.

"How's our secretary this morning?" Spear peered through the bars at the sleeping Butler.

"Not too bad," replied Quinn. "Doc looked at him. Said he'll be up and around in a couple of days if gangrenous hypochondria don't set in."

"Gangrenous *what*?"

"An overwhelmin' self-pity of the radial nerves is how the doc described it."

"I see. Hey, Butler!" yelled Spear.

Butler came awake instantly. His eyes opened wide with fear and his face blanched.

"Don't shoot! Please, don't kill me!"

"Sure. Anything you say," replied Spear. "Tell me something. Where did Underwood keep his money?"

"He—I don't know," said Butler, suddenly wide-eyed with ignorance. "He never showed me."

"Oh, that's too bad. And you never tried guessing."

"Oh, sure, Mr. Spear. I had my guesses, of course."

"Tell me one of them."

Butler's color was restored. His eyes shifted around. "I think it might be in the cold cellar somewhere."

"You think so, do you?"

"Yes."

"You could hang, Butler."

"Huh?"

"For annoying a Pinkerton agent. It's a capital offense, in my state of mind."

Butler thought about that a moment.

"Any more guesses, Butler?"

"Yes, sir."

"Try."

"In Underwood's office, there's a portrait. You might look behind . . ."

"Thanks. Now, the combination."

"I told you, it's just a guess," Butler whined. "I don't know the . . ."

"Tell me the combination!" roared Spear. His voice cut short the whine and made the thin figure, lying on the jail bed, jerk spasmodically.

"Thirteen, twenty-six, thirty-one."

"Thanks. If it doesn't work, I'll be back. Come on, Quinn."

Quinn locked the door of the jailhouse with the

key he'd retrieved from Pitkin's body. A pair of dead-beats recruited from the aisles of the Antelope were on their way to Sentinel Peak to pick up the less valuable remains of the sheriff and the thief. Among his self-prescribed tasks for the morning, Quinn had already worked out a budget for coffins, service and burial for the pair. He figured he could bury them both for something less than five dollars, including the undertaker's gratuity. The economy gratified him.

There was a third coffin that wouldn't cost anything. He was going to make it himself—solid oak, with forged steel handles along the sides. And a brass plaque on top. Quinn also planned to read the service himself and dig the hole for Frank Emory. He had some things he wanted these townfolks to hear at that service. Besides, the kid deserved it.

In front of Underwood & Sons, Merchandiser, a familiar roan wearing a pair of saddlebags was hitched to the rail.

"Well, Lil," greeted Spear, as he and Quinn came alongside the mare. At the sound of his voice, the horse swung her head around, fixed a big brown eye on him and yawned enormously.

" 'Parently she knows you," Quinn remarked.

"Yep. Many's the time I've bored her to death." Spear looked around quizzically. An Indian girl came out of the general store with a young boy balanced on one arm. A girl clung to her other hand, her eyes darting around curiously. The girl had to run to keep pace with her older sister.

"Emma!" Spear called out. She smiled when she saw him.

"I brought your horse!" She came up to him quickly, then stopped in front of him. There was an awkward silence. It was the boy who broke it.

Reaching out suddenly, he made a grab for Spear's beard.

"Yeeow!" The little fist had a lot of strength and the kid wouldn't let go. Emma laughed.

"Naiche, let the man go," she scolded, prying the fingers loose. Hearing a rumbling behind her, she glanced up at Quinn.

"Let's go find that safe," said Spear quickly. He was afraid that a bout of laughter from the blacksmith would scare the kids to death. "Bring them in," he spoke to Emma. She stared at the building as if it threatened her very existence. "It's all right," Spear reassured her.

"I killed him," said Emma. She reached down to her belt and pulled out the knife with the diamond in its hilt. She had found a sheath for it, a strip of leather with some beadwork on the surface. "This knife killed him," she added. Her eyes met Spear's. "It has served its purpose. I am returning it to you."

"No," Spear replied. "The knife is yours now. You don't need to worry about vengeance, Emma. There isn't a single man in this town that's going to hear what you just told me. As for the Underwoods, there are none left, thank God. He was the last of the rotten line."

Gratefully, Emma returned the knife to its sheath and tucked it into her waist.

Spear pushed open the door and led them inside. At once, the two children started exploring through the dry goods and odds and ends that cluttered the main office. Seeing the children were distracted, Spear touched Emma on the shoulder.

"Don't worry," he soothed. "We'll figure a way you can take care of them. I hear there's a whole bunch more."

She nodded.

"Naiche!" Her voice caught the boy with his hand halfway into a barrel of flour. He pulled it out and ran, spreading a thin layer of white stuff all over the floor.

"Better teach him to hide his tracks," Spear laughed.

The rumble that indicated an impending explosion started again in Quinn's throat, and Spear ushered the blacksmith quickly upstairs.

"See here, Quinn," Spear commented on the way up, "if you don't do something about that hee-haw of yours, you're going to scare every kid in the place clear to hell 'n back."

"Can't help it, Spear. Can't help it."

The door to Underwood's office was locked. Quinn nudged it with his shoulder and it wasn't locked anymore. Spear strode in first and looked around. The windmill on the roof was making a rattle as the spring breeze turned its sails, and the fan at the window whirled slowly.

"Coolin' system," explained Quinn. "Only one in town."

Spear nodded. His eye caught the glowering visage of Franklin Underwood. The portrait was so life-like, staring down from the gloomy wall, that Spear almost jumped.

"Hell," he muttered. Crossing the room to face the old Indian hunter, Spear lifted the portrait, turned the heavy frame around and placed it on the floor against the wall. The dial of the hidden safe stared at him like a cyclops. Spear spun it quickly and the weighty door swung open.

Spear looked inside the safe. Then he looked at Quinn. "You going to remember that combination?" he asked.

"Yep."

"Good."

The blacksmith shook his head wonderingly. "How the hell . . .?" he began.

"It's what you call ill-gotten gain," replied Spear, swinging the door closed. "The trouble with that stuff packed in there is that you can't undo the ill that got it. Shit!" Spear's voice was mean and he spun the dial furiously. Then he took a deep breath.

"Quinn, I've got a lady to meet and a train to catch, two days' hard ride from here. And I've got some diamonds to deliver to the Pinkerton office in 'Frisco. Besides me, only you and Butler know about that safe, and I figure Butler doesn't count. Now, I don't know what you plan to do. But I do know there's Emma and her two kids and about thirty Indian babes that need a home, and there's this building that could be made over into the right kind of place, if the name was changed over the door and a man had the money to do it with."

"Yep, I was thinkin' the same thing myself."

Spear held out his hand and, too late, realized his mistake. His knuckles, in the grip of the giant, experienced a crackling sensation he could feel all the way up his arm. Quinn started to laugh, then stifled it.

"Better cure that habit," cautioned Spear shaking his hand.

"Do my best," replied Quinn.

LOOK FOR . . .

The Frisco
LADY

Another powerful Western in the Brad Spear series—
bringing you the sights and sounds, the beautiful women
and the ruthless underworld of San Francisco. Here are
just a few of the unforgettable characters you'll meet in
this forthcoming novel:

ANNABELLE RIGG—Child of a Chinese father and a
San Francisco heiress, she was unbelievably beautiful and
utterly untamed. Who was she? Where did she come from?
And why did she want to murder Brad Spear?

DONALD SLADE—A shipping magnate worth millions,
he would sacrifice everything for money, even his own
lovely daughter. But his involvement with the opium trade
complicated his ambitions.

VALERIE SLADE—She defied her father, but fell into
the clutches of a man more ruthless than he. She gave her
love, riches and virtue to the sea captain Michael McGinty
and he beat her mercilessly for her trouble.

WAN HOO-SAI—He looked like a Chinese grocery-keeper, but he ruled the most vicious tong in Chinatown. And he sent out the order to kill Brad Spear.

LADY JANE—Readers of previous Brad Spear novels will never forget this Cockney woman with wheat-blonde hair and the courage of a gunfighter. Kidnapped by a ruthless millionaire, she is the unwilling victim of an episode of lust and violence.

CHANG—Lady Jane's Chinese cook returns, in *The Frisco Lady*, to carry Brad Spear a timely warning when he is at the brink of death.

And, of course, **BRAD SPEAR** himself . . .
Hard-hitting, yet as stealthy as a cat, he could lure a woman into his bed or a man into the grip of his iron fist. The women he loved would never forget him . . . and the men he hated would pray for his death.